The Reluctant Pawn

By

Michael P. Conlin

ISBN: 1-4107-5675-0 (e-book)
ISBN: 1-4107-5674-2 (Paperback)
ISBN: 1-4107-9390-7 (Dust Jacket)

This book is printed on acid free paper.

1stBooks – rev. 09/19/03

Index

Chapter 1

It's a good night for sleeping. It was fifty-seven degrees with a light breeze blowing through the window making the lace curtains dance seductively into the bedroom. There's a complete blackness in his head. Suddenly a faint glow and a flicker of an amber flame. Julie is in bed along side him, watching as he starts to perspire just like the previous six nights. Against the blackness there are more flames and the darkness is fading. Julie is waiting for him to wake from the dream just like previous nights.

The flames are dissipating as a carousel of faces comes spinning into view. It resembles a human pizza, with skin stretching from one face to the next. The faces are motionless and fixed in various stages of agony. The carousel is slowly rotating from right to left with many faces visible from top to bottom.

Suddenly the carousel stops rotating and an almost peaceful looking face is sitting in the middle of the anguished others. The eyes and mouth on this face are closed and looks almost recognizable to him. Although he knows what's coming, because he's had the same dream for six nights already, the anticipation of the upcoming events were welling inside his body as he could feel it becoming rigid. The eyes of this tranquil face have opened, followed shortly thereafter by the mouth and the familiar voice as it said what always woke him from this nightmare. "Michael."

He was sitting up in bed. Julie's hand was on his back. He slowly raised his hands to his face and slid them gently through his hair. He felt the perspiration that coated him from head to toe. He turned and looked at Julie. She was giving him that same smile that couldn't hide her underlying concern. Even though she already knew the answer, she asked if it was the same dream about his brother. "Yeah," he replied. She could hear the exhaustion in his voice.

He never told her all the details about the nightmare, but she knew it had to be far worse than what he was telling her. She let out a small sigh.

"Maybe you should see a psychiatrist."

"I don't need to see a fucking shrink," he snapped.

Julie rolled over on her side, facing her back to him. It wasn't so much what he said, as it was the way he said it. "I was just trying to help. I thought with you getting laid off from your job and your brother dying all within the last month...I thought the stress might be causing your nightmares. And nothing I'm doing is helping."

Michael was finally cooling down, but his mind was still going over the image of his brother's face surrounded by the grotesquely disfigured others. "I'm going to take a shower," he said as he got up and headed toward the bathroom. He didn't notice that Julie had started to cry. The stress was taking its toll on her too.

It was 5:30 a.m. when he finished showering. Julie had already fallen back to sleep. He went to the living room and laid on the couch. He adjusted his robe, and turned on the television. He began clicking through the channels trying to find something to distract his thoughts.

Julie woke to find herself alone in bed again. She wondered if last night really happened or was she thinking about the previous nights. She made her way through the house to the kitchen. Michael was waiting with breakfast. It had been a long time since he had done that.

"What's the occasion?"

"I'm sorry I was a jerk, and I'm sorry for what you've been put through lately."

"Well if this is the kind of service I'm gonna get, I think I can deal with it." She smiled. Now he was smiling too.

He approached her and loosened her robe, revealing a small portion of her naked body underneath. He slipped his arms underneath the robe and around her waist, pulling her towards him. "This is a full service kinda place and I expect a big tip," he said with a sly looking grin.

"Doesn't the tip come after the meal?"

"Okay, okay, the foods getting cold anyway."

He brushed her long brown hair over her shoulder and proceeded to kiss her on the side of the neck right below her ear. He kissed his way steadily from there to her lips.

"We'll pick this up later."

They sat down to a breakfast of scrambled eggs with cheese and onions. (Her favorite). They didn't say much during breakfast, probably due to the toast with a 1/2" layer of peanut butter on it. (Just the way she liked it).

After breakfast, they went to the bedroom and crawled back into bed. They just laid there gazing into each other's eyes and exploring each other's bodies. The foreplay was longer than normal, probably just due to the fact it had been a month since they last made love. They laid there in bed just holding each other. It felt so comfortable, as if they had melted into one body.

A lot had happened in that month. Michael's brother had died of cancer, and then he was laid off from his job as a product designer after twelve years. Michael laid there silently while Julie laid with her head on his chest. He started thinking about what Julie had said earlier.

"I think I know why I've been dreaming about my brother Mark."

Julie pulled herself back and bent her arm under her head so she could see his face.

"The last day that I was in the hospital with him, I promised that I would take his ashes up to the cabin and spread them around the property that my parents left us. I don't have an excuse for not doing it, there's no commitments keeping me from it."

"What about me?" she asked.

He pulled her close. "I'll always be committed to you."

They began to melt together again.

They showered together, as they had a tendency to do on the weekends. Not so much for the intimacy as it was the fact that the water heater seemed to run out of hot water if they showered separately.

After the shower Michael started packing for the trip to his parents land. Julie asked him if he was going to call his sister and let her know he was coming out that way.

"You know Margaret doesn't like surprises."

"She doesn't go up there unless it's a holiday weekend so I probably won't even see her."

"What is it with you two? After what you guys went through, you'd think it would make you closer as a family."

"I don't know. There's always been some kind of tension between us," he said as he was loading the last of his stuff into the Jeep Grand Cherokee.

What Michael didn't know is that Margaret was always jealous of his and Mark's relationship, and especially their relationship with their father. She always wanted to be one of the boys. She never got to go on the fishing or camping trips they used to take together.

Julie handed Michael the cooler of sandwiches and sodas she had put together for him. "Are you sure you can handle the ten hour trip without any sleep?"

"Yes," he replied while giving her a look telling her without words not to mother him.

"Got everything?" she said grinning.

"Ok, what did I forget?"

She held up the wooden urn that held his brother's ashes.

"Christ! I'd forget my head if you weren't here!"

She laughed. "I know."

She leaned her head inside the window. He put his hand on the back of her head and gave her a nice long kiss. "Hurry home," she said as she pulled away.

"I should be home in a couple of days," he said as he started down the driveway and waved as he watched her waving in the rearview mirror.

He wasn't even three blocks away and he was already missing her. They had been together just over three years. He knew this was the woman he wanted to marry, but yet he hadn't asked her. To Julie's credit, she never pressured or even asked him about marriage, not that the thought hadn't crossed her mind. It was as if Michael was waiting for something, what though she didn't know.

———

He was halfway on his way to his parents land. It was funny how he still considered it his parents land. His parents had passed away about 10 years ago in an auto accident. It had been awhile since he had thought about that time in his life. His parents had both just retired, and a week later were killed by a drunk driver on their way home from the retirement party his sister Margaret had thrown for them.

They had never drawn up a will, which had caused some tension amongst the siblings. The main sticking point was the land where the cabin was. Actually, there never was a cabin there until his sister and her husband built it after a long squabble over the land. She only wanted it because she felt it was her right to enjoy what she had missed growing up, and the boys had their time up there with their father.

Michael did not take this battle as well as his brother Mark had. It sort of left a permanent rift between brother and sister.

They did go up to the land as a family, but by then Margaret was a young teenager and the resentment was already firmly entrenched. She was always offered to go out on the lake with them when she was up there. She would just quietly decline and say she had other things to do. By now she had learned to hide her pain.

Michael's favorite song came on the radio. He turned it up and started signing along to "You're All I've Got Tonight," by The Cars when he realized he was going by the exit to his sister's house. Actually, that was his parent's old house.

She had given up her portion of the life insurance money so she could keep the house and the land in Eagle River. Michael and his brother both received a fair amount of money from the life insurance. Now that his brother had passed away and left the remainder of his portion of the life insurance money to both Michael and Margaret, he was pretty financially secure. He couldn't quite retire at age 36, but he certainly could live comfortably without the worry of any financial collapse.

The last time he talked to his sister was at their brother's funeral. They were actually very civil, but then again a funeral is not really the place to settle differences.

He arrived at the land at 12:30 a.m. He drove past the cabin and headed for the hill that his father used to take him camping on. He got out of the Jeep and went around to the back. He grabbed his tent and immediately began setting up, using the headlights to illuminate his surroundings. Surprisingly the bugs weren't too bad for early June. A few moths began dancing in front of the headlights causing the light to dim and brighten again as their large soft shadows were cast around the campsite.

Satisfied his campsite was complete, he stepped just inside the woods to gather firewood. The insistent buzzing of a mosquito around his ear made it difficult to hold the wood he had gathered as he flailed in a futile attempt to keep the miniature vampire from achieving its quest.

As he was piling the wood in the firepit to start the fire, he flashed back to how his father had taught the boys to build a fire. A little paper twisted up, some kindling, stand the wood up like a teepee, light the paper, gently blow and wait as it begins to burn.

Michael threw the match on the pile of wood and WOOSH, instantly the flames were three feet high. He smiled as he held the can of lighter fluid in his hand. His father surely would not have approved of this!

Michael sat on a small folding camping chair right next to the fire. It was the type with no back and just enough room to place your butt. He looked to his left and grabbed his brother's urn off of the large cooler. He slowly rotated it around in his hands. It looked much more beautiful in the soft amber glow of the fire. The etchings in the wood disappeared into the shadow created by the firelight as the urn rotated.

He undid the clasp that held the top of the urn open and poured a handful of his brother's remains into his left hand. With his right hand he placed the urn on his right knee and closed the lid and snapped the clasp closed.

As he held his brother's remains in his hand, he started thinking about all the times he had spent around a fire just like this one. He could almost see his brother and father's faces standing out from the surrounding darkness, illuminated by the warm glow of the fire.

The moment of reflection was broken by a sound that was bringing him back to reality. At first he didn't realize what the sound was until he turned his attention totally to the sound. It was the howl of a wolf. The lonely cry, although off in the distance, cut right through the symphony of crickets and frogs that had been chirping in the background. The howl quit as suddenly as it had started.

The fire crackled as one of the bigger logs on the fire split in two, revealing a hot bed of coals underneath. The fire was still going pretty good, but was beginning to dwindle.

Michael opened his hand with his brother's remains and gently tossed them on the fire. Suddenly the flames roared to life as if someone had replaced his brother's remains with gunpowder. Michael was barely aware that he had started to fall backward over his chair as he threw his arm up to protect himself. He was now lying on his back squinting at the intense light. He stared at the flames as they swirled and started to form into a familiar shape.

He wondered if he was dreaming; it was just after 2:00 a.m. Then he realized what shape he was looking at. It was a human shape. "Michael," his name emanated from the human flames. His face went blank. He had to be dreaming. Yet he knew he was experiencing reality that seemed like a dream, not a dream that seemed like reality.

"You have been chosen."

Michael's throat was dry. He swallowed hard, unable to speak. He just kept staring at the figure as if he couldn't believe what he was seeing.

"Keep your promise to me and questions will find answers."

The flames suddenly seemed to be sucked straight down into the pit and the figure was gone.

The fire was out, not even a burning ember was left in the fire pit. It was if the fire had been out for hours. Michael's eyes had not yet adjusted to the darkness. It was just then he realized he was still on his back. He rolled onto his left side, reaching out with his right hand surveying the ground behind the cooler where he had left the flashlight.

Having found the object he was seeking, he clicked it on. He spun himself off the ground, coming to a sitting position on the cooler. He waved the flashlight frantically in all directions. He wasn't sure what he was looking for, but one thing was for sure, the flashlight wasn't giving off enough light to ease his uncertainty.

He shined the light up to a tree branch that was about 3 feet to his left and about 5 feet off the ground. His kerosene lantern was still in the tree. He rose quickly and scrambled to the lantern, pumping the primer valve furiously as he reached into his pocket and pulled out a book of matches. Holding the flashlight under his armpit, he struck the match. He let the flashlight fall to the ground as he stuck the match into the lantern and proceeded to turn up the gas.

Instantly the campsite lit up. Michael spun to face the fire pit. It took a few seconds for his eyes to adjust to the surroundings as he had been looking directly at the lantern. He glanced in all directions. Nothing seemed out of the ordinary, other than the fact that the chair he had been sitting on earlier was now laying on its side.

He approached the fire pit with the caution of a snake charmer. He grabbed the stick he had been using to poke the logs around to keep the fire going. He stuck the end of it in the pit, swirling it around half expecting something to rise from the ashes. To his surprise, there were no burning embers to be found.

Had he been knocked unconscious and the passage of time had only seemed like several minutes? That had to be the explanation. He looked at his watch. It was now 2:15 a.m. The time just ruled that out as a possibility. The fire could have only been burning just over an hour tops. There definitely would still be embers left.

He walked over by the cooler and picked up the can of charcoal fluid. It was still almost full and the cap was secure.

He set it down next to the cooler and lifted the lid to the cooler. He pulled out a can of Mello Yello. Closing the lid, he sat on the cooler and opened the can. Without even taking a breath, he drank the whole can. Although it quenched his thirst, he regretted not bringing something stronger.

He looked to his right and saw his brother's urn laying on the ground a couple of feet behind the camping chair he had been sitting on. He walked over and picked it up. He set the chair back up and sat down. He looked the urn over. It was still closed.

As he held it in his hands, he started thinking about what he had been told by the flaming figure that had appeared in the flames. "You have been chosen." Chosen for what? A question that needed an answer. "Keep your promise to me and questions will find answers."

He knew of the promise. When his brother was in the hospital, Michael sat in the hospital room alone with his brother exchanging stories of their childhood and each other's perspectives on who caught the most fish, or who managed to hook their father's shirt the most times. It was then that his brother confessed he didn't have long to live. Michael and Margaret had just found out about Mark's condition the previous week.

Mark asked Michael not to tell Margaret how grave his condition was. He didn't want her worrying and fawning all over her big brother. He also made Michael promise to spread his ashes at their parents land. Not just anywhere, but four places in particular. In the fire pit where they used to camp, in the lake at Horseshoe Bay, at the spot where he had shot his first deer, and at their parent's house where they had built a huge treehouse.

Michael headed for the tent. He left the kerosene lamp burning at half its capacity outside the tent. He didn't feel comfortable trying to sleep in the complete darkness, not that he was going to get much sleep anyway.

He tossed and turned, only sleeping about 15 minutes at a time. The nightmare that had plagued him the previous week did not take place this night. He figured it was probably due to the fact he wasn't even slipping into a state of unconsciousness.

Chapter 2

He woke the next morning feeling terrible, it was 6:00 a.m. and he knew there was no use in trying to go back to sleep. He needed some coffee bad. He got up and proceeded to pull the camp stove out of the back of the Jeep. He got some water boiling and added some instant coffee. It wasn't the best tasting coffee, but then again he wasn't drinking it for the flavor.

The sun had already risen over the horizon, but there was still a chill in the air. He sat in his chair for a while drinking cup after cup of coffee. He was staring down at the lake, which was as tranquil as it had ever been. It resembled a mirror more than a lake. A perfect reflection was cast onto it by every tree at its edges and by every cloud in the sky. He noticed how sunlight seemed to be captured in the dew that had formed on the grass overnight, bright little bulbs of dew twinkling here and there.

His thoughts suddenly changed from the serene surroundings to the events of last night. He stood up and with coffee in hand walked over to the fire pit. He dreaded thinking about what could happen at Horseshoe Bay, but he wanted to keep the promise to his brother. Although his curiosity was peeked, he had no intention of staying another night. He just wanted to get it over with and try to get his life back to normal.

He took his time packing up. Before he knew it, it was 11:30 in the morning.

He made his way over to where the boat was at the edge of the lake. He pushed the boat into the water, which now had only the occasional small ripple of wind blown waves streaking across its surface.

He rowed his way, all the while thinking about the times he and his father and brother had shared on the lake. He remembered the first time his father had paddled the boys out to Horseshoe Bay in a canoe. Their father would only let them use cane poles for fishing, which only allowed them to fish 4 feet on either side of the boat. With worms on their lines, the boys plunked their lines in the water. The first hour went by and not even a nibble. Nothing could have been worse for kids the ages of 12 and 8.

10

Suddenly Mark's pole was just about yanked out of his hands. "Holy shit!" Mark cried. The front end of the canoe was starting to swing around in the other direction. It was obviously a very large fish. As their father fumbled for the net, Michael lifted his line out of the water, not knowingly placing his hook (worm still attached) on his father's back. As his father leaned back from grabbing the net, he felt a sharp pain in his right shoulder. "Son of a bitch," he said while gritting his teeth. He grabbed the pole out of Michael's hand and proceeded to snap the line.

Meanwhile, Mark was still struggling with the fish, which was still pulling the canoe around pretty good. All this activity in the canoe was like being in an earthquake that registered 8.5 on the Richter scale. Mark was obviously having trouble holding the pole. "Give me the pole," said their father.

As Mark started to lean past Michael to hand him the fishing pole, their father also leaned to that side of the canoe to take the fishing pole. Michael moved all the way to the right side of the canoe and sat on the edge. With the two larger males leaning to the other side, the canoe tipped slightly more to the left. Just as his brother was about to hand the pole off Mark went rolling out of the canoe. It was like slow motion to Michael as he watched his brother's eyes widen at the realization he was going overboard. Mark had started to scream, but the sound of his voice quickly ended as he completely submerged below the water.

Almost simultaneously their father was reaching for Mark as he went into the water. He too was now going head first into the water. (Not exactly by choice.) Both boys had lifejackets on and Mark was sure to pop back up to the surface in a few seconds, but instinct had taken over. Their father just reacted in that split second without having time to think about the consequence of his actions.

Having seen his father now enter the water almost completely, Michael could feel a smile coming to his face. The smile was quickly replaced by a slight grimace. He realized shortly after seeing his father enter the water that the canoe had begun to pitch the other way, due to the weight loss on the other side of the canoe.

Before he could even think of how to regain his balance, he felt his head entering the water on the other side of the canoe. He could see his feet pointing skyward. Suddenly everything was black. His eyes had involuntarily closed upon entry. He couldn't really hear anything other than the sound of air bubbles rushing past him on their way to the surface.

Suddenly he could hear again. When he opened his eyes again, his lifejacket had already brought him to the surface. He was still right next to the canoe. He grabbed the side and pulled himself up just far enough to hang one elbow over the side. There he saw his father already attempting to put his brother back into the canoe. As Mark rolled into the canoe, he ended up on his back. He still looked a little startled by the whole thing.

Michael began to smile as he looked at his father on the other side of the canoe. His hair was pasted flat against his forehead. His glasses were amazingly still on his face but they had slid to the edge of his nose. There were beads of water all over the lenses. His father always had rugged good looks, but right now he looked like the biggest geek in the world. Michael started laughing. Soon they were all laughing, imaging how comical this all must have looked from the outside. Thankfully there was no one else around to see this embarrassing comedy of events.

They dared not try to get back in the canoe because it was already loaded with about 6" of water from stem to stern. They collected what they could find of their belongings and threw it in the canoe with Mark. Michael and his father, each on one side of the canoe, began paddling their way to shore. It was only 50 yards, but it took twice as long due to the laughing and giggling that still continued.

Michael had now reached the bay where the event had taken place. He realized he was smiling. He looked to the south and saw storm clouds approaching. He noticed the wind was picking up when he was rowing across the lake but with his back to the south he didn't see them right away.

The bay looked pretty much the same. He could see a couple of houses on the far side of the bay. When he was growing up on the lake there were no houses or cabins. He was actually quite surprised there wasn't more development on the lake.

He reached into his backpack and pulled out his brother's urn. He gently poured a handful of his brother's remains into his hand. He put the urn between his knees and fastened the lid back on with his left hand. He put the urn back into his backpack and then leaned over to the right side and glanced into the water. He could see the bottom about 10 feet down. It was a very weedy area on the lake.

He opened his hand and let the ashes fall into the lake. He watched as the fine grains began to sink slowly toward the bottom. He watched as they seemed to be drifting under the boat. The wind was blowing the boat over the spot he had dropped the remains.

As he put his left hand on the other side of the boat and got ready to look over the edge, he saw a splash well up from the water right next to the boat. He tried to pull himself backwards, but he hardly moved at all. He felt something cold and wet on his left wrist. It didn't take him long to realize what had a hold of him. It was a clump of dark green weeds. He reached down with his right hand to free himself from the death grip of the weeds. Another splash erupted from the water. Now the gripping weeds had a hold of his right wrist too. He tried to pull himself back. His face was grimacing in effort.

Suddenly he lurched forward as his hands slipped from the edge. His chest crashed onto the edge of the boat where his hands had been. Along with his breath, it knocked the fight right out of him. He was now looking over the edge of the boat. His face was growing redder as he struggled to draw a breath. He felt as if his whole body was going numb. He could feel tiny pinpricks all over his body.

What Michael didn't realize was that it had started to rain and the pinpricks were actually raindrops landing on his body. Still staring at the water, he drew as much oxygen in the first gasp as he could. It was a relief to finally get some oxygen to his nearly unconscious body. He took a deep breath, but this one was painful. He winced at the pain in his chest. His face was still very red and his eyes began to water. The weeds were still pulling him hard against the boat. His body was still starved of oxygen, as he could only draw short breathes due to the pressure on his sternum.

He watched as a large clump of the mossy bottom weeds floated to the top. He thought about pulling away, but his body didn't react. He was still in the grip of the weeds and incapacitated by the lack of oxygen. The moss was now only inches from his face. He now realized that it was raining. With his peripheral vision he could see the rain pounding the lake. He also noticed that the weeds that had taken a hold of his wrist had morphed into hands and arms. A voice started emanating from the clump of weeds that had risen inches from his face. "There are those that will try to stop you from achieving your mission. You must be wary. Lives are at stake, including your own."

Michael saw a flash of light. It was intensely bright, he closed his eyes for a split second. His ear drums almost burst when it was followed by a deafening boom. He saw the weedy creature release it's grip and slip beneath the waters surface. Apparently the lightning had struck rather close and ended the bizarre event. He pushed himself away from the edge of the boat. He collapsed onto his back. He lay there writhing in pain. The rain was still coming down relentlessly. He felt as though he was going to throw up. That was the last thing he remembered just before he passed out.

Chapter 3

John Reilly was tossing in his sleep. He had laid down just like everyday to take his afternoon nap. He was getting up in years and at 71 years old; the days just seemed to go by so fast. His mind and body just couldn't keep up with the pace of everyday life now. The naps didn't help the feeling that the days seemed to have shortened, always stealing a couple of precious hours of the day, but they did help him re-energize and fully enjoy the hours he was awake.

Lately though, the naps were needed more than ever. He had not been sleeping so well at night. He kept having strange dreams about people he didn't know. There was one person in particular who was committing gruesome murders. The part that disturbed him the most was some of his dreams seemed to be coming true.

Today was different though. In all his years, he'd never had a religious experience, he just simply believed in higher powers beyond those of man. He was a true man of faith. He was experiencing an intensely bright light filling his vision. Still napping he raised his hand to shield his eyes. Consciously he realized his hand was in front of his face, yet he was still dreaming and his hand was not in front of his face. He felt odd being consciously aware he was dreaming and yet he couldn't wake up. He put his hand down, as it was doing no use against the light.

He noticed the light began to fluctuate, dimming then brightening, dimming then brightening. His heart rate began to quicken. "Am I dying?" he thought.

"You're not going to die yet, John. Relax." The voice was so soft and reassuring that his breathing and heart rate instantly returned to normal.

"Why have you come to me?"

"You have been selected to give guidance to someone who will need your wisdom."

"Who needs my guidance?"

"They will seek you," replied the light.

He began to hear a ringing in his ears. The light was now fading quickly. He had so many more questions, but it was apparent that there wasn't time. He opened his eyes. The phone on the nightstand next to his bed was ringing. That's what must have interrupted the vision he was having. He rolled over onto his side and grabbed the phone. "Hello." His voice was quite raspy. Even he was surprised at how hoarse he sounded. He coughed in an attempt to clear his throat.

"I didn't wake you again?" said the voice on the line.

"Of course you did. You always interrupt me when I'm at my best."

It was Father Davis on the line.

They had a long history together. John Reilly had thought for awhile about becoming a priest. He had even gone to a seminary, which is where he met Father Davis. They formed an instant bond to one another that was evident to both of them as a life long friendship. John Reilly left the seminary, but the two remained very close. He had decided early on that his own beliefs were not exactly going to allow him to continue in the Catholic Church.

He decided instead to study many religions, and how they related to man. It was always an area of interest to him. He even taught some courses on the subject at several colleges in the surrounding area. He and Father Davis would get together and have many a heated debate about such things as religion or politics, but they never let it ruin their friendship.

Because John Reilly had retired so much earlier than his friend, he decided to move closer. Father Davis offered to let him live at his house, he had the room, but John had insisted he have his own place.

He was always at the church helping Father Davis out. One of the very first days he was at the church one of the church busy bodies came up to Father Davis and asked him who his friend was. Just as John was about to introduce himself, Father Davis took over the introductions. "Sally Gilbright this is Father John Reilly and he would love to help you with the social events for this week."

Before John could even get a word in edge wise, she had him by the arm dragging him around talking about the upcoming events and introducing him as Father Reilly to other parishioners. John would try to start explaining that he wasn't a priest, but he was always interrupted by Sally yelling for other people to come over and get introduced. Before he knew it a dozen people had been pulled into Father Davis' little joke. He decided he better set the record straight. He told them all he was just a friend and that Father Davis was joking.

They all seemed rather disappointed, but remained sincere in their happiness to meet him.

He felt a little relieved to have that behind him. Unfortunately, he didn't notice an elderly couple that had overheard Father Davis introduce him as Father Reilly. They were on their way out as Sally had dragged him in the other direction.

The more people he met from the church, the more annoyed he became. They were always coming up saying "Nice to finally meet you Father Reilly." He was getting tired of explaining that he wasn't a priest over and over. Father Davis, sensing his friend's frustration, addressed his congregation and explained the story. John was quite relieved to finally get that over with.

A lot of people still referred to him as Father Reilly as a running joke. Eventually the name stuck. At first it was hard to get used to, but it was just a nickname, and even he got used to it. Now almost everyone he knew called him Father Reilly.

Father Davis was ten years younger than Father Reilly and had only been retired from the church for a few years. John Reilly had been retired for twelve years already and was living in a studio apartment. It wasn't that he couldn't afford a better place, he just felt more comfortable in the older part of town.

He never was one to collect too many belongings, and at this point in his life he didn't believe in possessing things you couldn't take with you when you left this life. It was glaringly apparent in the apartment – not a single picture on the walls, just a bed and nightstand in the bedroom. The only true luxuries he had were an alarm clock with a radio and a 13" TV. He never used the alarm on the clock. He was retired and didn't need to live his life by timelines or deadlines. Besides, Father Davis was always willing to remind him it was time for their weekly chess match.

"You up for it old man?" queried Father Davis.

"Well if I don't show up, you'll probably consider it some kind of moral victory."

"See you in an hour."

He hung up the phone and sat up in bed. He was excited for the chess match today. It wasn't really the match, but rather the fact he couldn't wait to tell Father Davis about the vision he had. He knew it wasn't a dream because he'd been having them for sometime now.

He was just too aware of what was going on for it to have been a dream.

He was already dressed to go outside. He just took some time to brush his teeth and straighten his hair. As he walked down the hallway of his apartment complex, he was greeted by one of the buildings other occupants. A young mother of two was just coming back from doing laundry.

"Hello Father Reilly," she said.

"Hello Mary, how are the children?"

"They're doing fine. Off to your chess match?"

"Every Sunday at 3:00 p.m. You can set your watch by it," he said with a grin.

"Good luck," she said as she passed by him, trying not to catch him with her laundry basket. He thanked her for the well wishes just before he arrived at the door to the stairs.

He always took the stairs even though there was an elevator available. For a 71-year-old man, he was still quite agile and looked good for his age. Even still, his legs were aching a little by the time he had reached the ground floor.

He greeted Mrs. Kalnacheck as he was leaving the complex. She was a kind old woman who had been living on her own for the last couple of years. Her husband had passed away, but she seemed to be doing fine on her own. She was a medium. She read taro cards and held séances in her apartment. She even had a sign in her window inviting people to come in at all hours.

He was surprised at how much business she actually did. She had offered to do readings for him, but he always declined, partly because he was skeptical that any human could foretell the future by reading cards, and partly because he feared that if she could tell things about the future, where would the mystery be in life.

He stepped outside. It was a glorious day, 75 degrees and a light breeze. He made his way down the large concrete stairs that led to the apartment complex and headed for the park.

Chapter 4

Michael felt a pounding on his forehead. His mind still not conscious did not know how to interpret what his body was feeling. Another blow to his forehead, he thought he could feel blood beginning to trickle down the side of his head. He opened his eyes. Suddenly there was another blow to his forehead. His eyes blinked with the impact. He opened his eyes again. This time it was like slow motion as he watched a drop of water drip from the leaf and plunge toward his head.

He could barely move, he turned just enough so that the water glanced off the side of his head. He sat up and rubbed his face. It was only water that was running down his face. He started squinting because the sun started to shine through an opening in the clouds.

The boat was resting against the shoreline. The wind had blown the boat right under a large birch tree. His chest was still sore. Other than a small bump on the back of his head, he was all right. He stood up and grabbed an oar. He pushed the boat away from the shore. As he began to row, he winced a little as his chest muscles felt very tight.

He made his way back to his Jeep. He was exhausted. He decided to drive over to the spot where his brother had gotten his first deer.

Michael never did get a deer in all the years he hunted with his father and brother. Every year he would just tell them he hadn't seen any or purposely fire off target. He just didn't like the thought of taking another creatures life just for the sport of it. He knew he could never eat all the meat that the deer would provide. Besides his brother and father were always willing to share whatever they had.

His father and brother never could figure it out. He was a great shot on the rifle range. They both knew shooting on the rifle range and trying to hit a moving target was totally different, but they just figured he must have gotten the jitters every time he saw one. The only part Michael regretted was all the flack he took every year after not getting one. His brother used to call him the Susan Lucci of deer hunting. Michael took the ribbing in stride. He was there for the camaraderie more than the hunting.

He was now at the gate that led to the back forty acres of property. His sister had fenced off the last forty acres with barbed wire. At one point she had wanted to get some horses and keep them up here, but she still hadn't found the time to get that hobby going. She knew she didn't have the time to care for them, or afford to pay someone else to do it. She only came up to the land on holiday weekends and even then spent most of her time in the cabin. Her husband Bill and her two children, Penny and Josh, loved it up there, but even they did not spend as much time there as they wanted to.

Michael only had to walk about 20 yards from the gate. Although the storm had passed, the sky was still overcast and there was still a pretty good breeze blowing. Michael watched the tall and varied tan colored prairie grasses waving in the wind.

He did not know the exact spot where his brother had actually shot the deer, but he did remember the rock his brother sat on to pose for a picture. He remembered how his brother Mark was beaming with pride as he held the eight point buck's head up by the antlers.

His brother had continued to hunt on the land after their parent's death. He even got Margaret's husband Bill interested in hunting. For Michael it just wasn't the same without their father around, and with everything that had happened between him and Margaret he had decided that this was the time to quit the charade as a hunter.

He arrived at the rock. It was only visible about two to three feet above the ground; depending on which side you were looking at it. The diameter of the rock was about ten feet, which implied the majority of it was hidden underground. It was very flat on top with a gradually ascending slope to the backside. The dark gray color stood out from the surrounding tan prairie grasses.

Michael unclasped the top to his brother's urn and poured a handful into his left hand. He looked into the urn. He had just enough left to spread at the tree house. At first he had no intention of doing so. He hadn't figured out how to do it without his sister Margaret catching him. He knew she would object to him doing such a thing without her involvement. But now with everything that happened each time he spread the ashes, he felt like he had to find a way to do it; with or without his sister's approval.

He took the handful of remains and tossed them toward the rock. The wind blew most of it over the rock. What remained on the rock was now tumbling up and over the edge as a gust of wind carried the last of the remains to the other side. Michael stepped back expecting the rock to come to life or something. When it didn't, he stepped forward.

He could see some movement just over the edge of the rock. What he did not know is there was a large fire ant mound on the other side of the rock. He stared in amazement as the insects quickly gathered into a lumpy mass. It looked like someone who had been coated with a layer of fire ants. He was pretty sure it consisted entirely of fire ants because no one else was around at the time, and it seemed to be having a hard time holding together as the figure was swaying slightly trying to keep it's balance.

This time Michael was prepared for something bizarre, and felt he had an opportunity to try to get some questions answered. "Who are you and what do you want from me!" The fire ant figure either didn't hear the question, or just chose to ignore it. "There isn't much time for you to complete your mission." Michael somewhat frustrated replied, "What mission?" The fire ant figure swayed forward. Michael stepped back another step.

Even though the rock was between them he still didn't trust it wasn't going to grab him or something like the weed figure had. It apparently had just lost its balance again and swayed back to an upright position. "You have been chosen to help save the human race from evil." Michael wasn't sure if was answering his question or if it was only able to convey messages. So he asked another question hoping for a response. "Why me?" The lack of an immediate response pretty much gave him the answer, but the reply erased all doubt. "You must make your way to 1580 Summit…"

The mass of fire ants was still speaking but Michael's ears were now tuning in on an odd sound coming from behind him. He turned just in time to catch a glimpse of what was making the sound. He had just enough time to throw his arm up as the wolf plowed into him.

The force of the wolf's momentum caused him to stumble backward. He felt himself falling over backward. He was concentrating so hard on keeping his balance he didn't even feel the rock stop his progress. It had caught him behind both knees. At first he went into almost a perfect sitting position but the wolf's momentum carried him all the way onto his back. He was now laying back staring skyward directly at the wolf's face. Luckily he had managed to get a hand around the wolf's throat as he had fallen onto the rock.

The wolf started growling and lunging forward snapping its jaws just inches from his face. He was straining in an effort to widen the distance. He turned his head from side to side with each attempt the wolf made. He could feel it's hot breath and saliva landing on the sides of his face. It was growling so loudly Michael couldn't hear anything else going on around him.

He was already worn out from his experience on the lake and knew he couldn't hold the wolf off much longer. He looked directly into the eyes of the wolf, as it was about to make another lunge at him. He had never seen anything look so angry. The wrinkles in its forehead and bared teeth only added to the menacing look of those yellow eyes that were locked into a gaze with his.

As the wolf lunged forward in another attempt to bite him, he raised his knee directly into the wolf's stomach. It let out a painful yelp as it was raised about six inches above him. Almost simultaneously he kicked his left leg in the air sending the wolf flying over his head. He rolled onto his side and watched as the wolf careened off the rock right into the mass of fire ants. The mass of fire ants was still speaking just before the wolf plowed into it. It was as if the fire ant figure was oblivious to what was going on. The figure had fallen along with the wolf below the edge of the rock.

As Michael pushed himself off the rock and began to stand up, he could hear the wolf howling in pain. When he walked to the edge of the rock he expected to see the wolf lying on the ground with a broken leg or something as the high pitched yelping continued.

The wolf was twisting its head as far around as it could and was biting up and down the length of its right side. It let out another yelp and twisted to the left toward Michael. It was obvious this strategy was going to take a while to succeed because he could see there was still a large number of fire ants crawling on the wolf. The wolf noticed Michael watching him. For a brief moment it ignored the pain of the biting ants to look directly back at him. Michael was a little worried it was going to make another attempt to take his face off, but with a final sneer and growl it took off under the barbed wire fence.

He watched the wolf darting through the prairie grasses and finally disappear into the woods. Michael continued to stare into the woods well after the wolf was gone from sight. He could almost feel the adrenaline leaving his body as new aches and pains became apparent to him. He was still breathing heavily when he jumped down from the rock.

He noticed it was starting to get late as he was looking for his brothers urn. He had no idea where it went when the wolf attacked him. He found it on the other side of the rock just a few feet from the fire ant mound. The ants were still milling around looking for something to take their aggression out on. He walked over and picked it up, brushing off several fire ants before they found their way to his flesh. The entire contents had been emptied during the attack. He didn't realize he had lost it from his grasp as he was flung backward against the rock. He closed the lid on the urn.

The only thing he could remember hearing from the fire ant figure was the address 1580 Summit. The only Summit he knew of was in the old part of town where he grew up. It was a couple hours drive from here. He knew he was in no condition to make it all the way home, and then drive almost the whole way back.

As he crawled into the front of the jeep he caught a glimpse of himself in the rearview mirror. He turned the mirror so he could see his face completely. He saw two long red marks running down the right side of his face. He wasn't sure if it was from the claws or teeth of the wolf. Either way the skin was swollen and pink, but at least the skin was not broken. It was as if the visual appearance of the wound made his brain even more aware of the other aches and pains on his body.

He had already made up his mind to stay and find out what all this meant. He thought briefly about stopping at his sister Margaret's house and trying to stay there, but there would have been too much explaining to do. Besides he just wanted to shower and go to bed.

He pulled into a hotel parking lot just at the edge of town. As he entered the hotel room he flung his duffle bag on the bed. He turned and saw himself in the mirror above the dresser. A smirk came to his face as he realized why he had gotten a few wide-eyed looks in the lobby. He looked so disheveled. The scratches on his face were almost gone, but still visible. His clothes were dirty and wrinkled. His shirt had been torn slightly and he had a little bit of grass in his hair.

He immediately went over to the phone and began dialing. Julie answered the phone. It was good to hear her voice again. "Hey Honey," he said. She could tell right away from the tone of his voice something was wrong. "Are you okay?"

"I'm fine. There was a big storm and I didn't get much sleep, so I'm kind of tired. I'm actually at a hotel outside my hometown right now."

"So are you going to be home tomorrow then?"

He hesitated a moment. "Actually I was thinking of staying in town for one more day."

He heard her sigh on the other end of the line but continued talking before she could start trying to talk him out of it. "It's been a long time since I've been home, I thought I'd hang out for an extra day."

She wanted to tell him to be home tomorrow but she knew he needed some time to himself. "Don't be too long. I'm starting to get lonely already."

"I'll be home by Tuesday at the latest."

He was glad she didn't ask him any questions about the weekend. He wouldn't have been able to tell her the truth. She already thought he needed the help of a psychiatrist. If he told her the truth, even she would've thought he snapped. They exchanged their usual loving goodbyes.

Michael thought briefly about skipping the shower and going right to bed, but the need to feel clean was winning out. He started to remove his clothes. He noticed himself in the mirror again. He was surprised at the extent of bruising already starting to appear on his chest. There were also scratches that even extended to his arms. Most of them were like the ones on his face. They were already fading and probably would be gone by morning.

He turned the nozzle on in the shower before entering. He reached in and turned the showerhead directly against the wall. He stepped into the shower and adjusted the water temperature. He grabbed the showerhead and turned it toward his body. He immediately turned to the side and pushed the showerhead back to the wall. The pulsing sensation of the water against his chest was far more painful than he expected. The scratches felt as though they were on fire. He turned the adjustment on the showerhead to a fine, gentle spray. He stuck his head underneath the showerhead and leaned forward. He put his arms out bracing himself with his palms stretched flat against the wall.

His body was gradually becoming accustomed to the water, but he stayed in the same position for a couple of minutes. He wondered who or what was at 1580 Summit that was going to help explain what was happening to him. With his brothers ashes completely gone now he had no choice but to follow the instructions as best he could. The warm water relaxed him almost too much. He reached down and turned the water off. He could have stayed underneath the water all night, but he knew he had to get some sleep.

Chapter 5

Father Reilly lived about a half mile from the park and rarely arrived on time as he insisted on walking rather than being picked up or taking the bus. He had given up driving just over a year ago. He knew he could've continued to drive if he wanted to but he just didn't like the stress of paying so much more attention now that he was getting on in years. Besides he had Father Davis to chauffer him around.

Father Reilly arrived at the park first. He had been waiting ten minutes already for Father Davis to show up. Father Davis approached with the chessboard under his arm.

"What's the occasion?"

"I have something I need to talk to you about."

Father Davis set the chessboard on the concrete table.

"Well it must be something big because you haven't beat me here in two years. Can we talk while we play or is it serious?"

Father Reilly motioned for him to sit down. "Go ahead and set them up."

Father Davis sat down and opened the chessboard and began setting the pieces up.

He always set the white pieces in front of himself. Father Davis' hands disappeared briefly under the table. He held out his arms with his fist clenched. Father Reilly studied them less than a second. "I'll take that one," he said pointing to Father Davis' left hand. Father Davis' opened his left hand revealing a white pawn. Nine times out of ten Father Reilly was able to pick which hand held the white pawn. Father Davis slapped the white pawn into Father Reilly's out stretched hand.

"Are you ever going to tell me how you do it?"

Father Reilly smiled. "Let's just say you don't have a poker face."

"This isn't poker!"

Father Davis begrudgingly turned the board so the white pieces were in front of Father Reilly.

As the game started Father Reilly described the vision he had and asked his life long friend what he made of it.

"Well, do you think it's connected to the nightmares you've been having?"

Father Reilly nodded. "Definitely."

Father Davis made a move. "I remember some of your theories on religion. They almost got you thrown out of the seminary. Maybe that's the wisdom that's being referred to."

Father Reilly leaned forward and made a move. "If that's the case why send me a vision now and not back then?"

"Maybe you weren't ready then, or maybe whoever you're supposed to share your knowledge with wasn't ready. Hell even I wasn't ready to hear your theories back then."

Father Reilly had always shared his ideas with Father Davis. It sometimes led to some heated debates, but they never let it get in the way of their friendship. They had discussed Father Reilly's nightmares previously, and at first neither of them knew how to interpret them. That is until some of the things he had dreamt about seemed to be coming true.

Father Reilly watched Father Davis make his move on the board.

"You like playing devil's advocate to my ideas; how about this one. What if I'm the only one receiving these messages? Does that confirm I'm closer to the truth about religion than anyone else?" Father Reilly made a move and Father Davis responded quickly, both to the move and the question.

"Maybe, but it could also mean you're just losing your mind."

Father Reilly ignored the comment as if it wasn't even made, and just kept asking questions. "What if this is supposed to be kept low key for some reason?"

"Now you might be on to something!"

Father Reilly made another move. "I mean why wouldn't the visions be sent to the Pope or someone like that?"

Father Davis shrugged his shoulders indicating he didn't know.

"Maybe this person who is seeking you out will have some answers to your questions."

Father Reilly nodded in agreement. "I guess I'll have to wait to for this person to show up, or wait for another vision."

Father Davis wasn't prepared to tell his friend he too had a vision. He saw the same pulsing light Father Reilly had described. He was still struggling internally with how to interpret what happened. All it had to say to him was that his friend was going to need his help and he should do what he could to help.

"Why wait, I think we should go back to your place and start going over some of your theories right now."

Father Reilly gave him a curios look. "What about the game?"

A sly grin began to appear on Father Davis' face as he made his final move.

"Oh yeah, checkmate."

Father Reilly studied the board for about 10 seconds. It was obvious his mind was elsewhere during the match. "I was distracted and you know it!"

Father Reilly hadn't lost a match in two weeks. Father Reilly looked up from the board to see Father Davis' grin turn into a full-blown smile.

"Don't be a sore loser John, just be a loser!"

Father Reilly's lack of response only gave his friend more time to keep jabbing the loss at him. "C'mon, I'll give you a ride home and you can make me dinner."

Father Reilly still didn't say anything. He was just trying to keep himself from saying something he would regret later. He realized it was his own fault for not paying closer attention to the game. He just started collecting the pieces and putting them away.

Father Davis had never seen him look so serious before. He didn't say anything else. He just started helping put the pieces away. For the first time he was a little concerned about his friend. It was obvious what was happening to Father Reilly was starting to affect him; even if it was just the fact he was being a little more reserved in his protest to the loss.

As they turned to leave a young gentleman approached them.

"Hi fellas. I'm Detective Sean Richards with the Eagle River police department. You guys play here often?"

Father Davis smiled. "As often as we can, weather permitting," he said as he noticed some light gray clouds moving in.

"Is there something wrong?" asked Father Reilly.

The detective turned his attention to Father Reilly. "I was just wondering if you guys have seen any one unusual hanging around the park lately, or seen anything out of the ordinary?"

Father Davis was the first to respond. "Not that I can recall."

Father Reilly was shaking his head no in agreement.

"I don't want to alarm you guys but there was a murder on the other side of the park last night."

Father Davis' mouth fell open slightly at the news. "Oh! That's terrible! Is it someone we know?"

The detective shook his head. "We haven't positively identified the body yet so I couldn't tell you. I just want you guys to be careful and keep your eyes open."

The detective reached into his coat pocket and then extended his hand with a business card pinched between a couple of fingers. "Give me a call if you remember anything or see anything that you think I'd be interested in." Father Davis took the card and glanced at it briefly before putting it in his pocket. The detective turned to walk away. "Have a good day fellas."

As the detective continued down the sidewalk that encircled the entire park Father Davis looked at Father Reilly. "Let's get going." As they drove by, the young detective turned and waved to them. He was wearing the typical Columbo tan trench coat that was flowing gently in the breeze. The sun was now completely obscured by thin gray and ever darkening clouds coming in from the southwest. It didn't take a detective to tell rain was imminent. He glanced up to the sky and decided he had better start heading toward his car on the other side of the park.

Just as he was getting to his car a few drops started coming down here and there. He opened the door but paused to look over the roof of his car. He saw an investigator beginning to take down the police line tape from around the crime scene. He pushed the door open a bit further and got in.

As he started the car he looked down the block. He watched, as a line of hard rain was moving down the block in his direction. Now he couldn't hear the hum of the engine anymore as the rain continued on past the vehicle and was pounding on it. It was coming down so hard it sounded like static from a television. He looked out the passenger window and saw the investigator running from tree to tree, trying to get the tape down.

Sean was glad to be in the car. He glanced down at the passenger seat. On it was a yellow manila folder. Inside the folder were files on similar murders that had taken place in the last few months. He was

29

pretty sure this one was connected to the others but he had to make a visit to the coroner's office to be sure. Three murders in the last two and a half months were more than they've had in the last ten years.

He had made detective just two years ago. Even now some in the department considered him too young to have made detective. There were several officers in the force who were older and had been there longer. That caused him to have to deal with resentment over the two years but gradually the resentment faded.

He was tenacious. In his short career as a detective there wasn't a case he couldn't solve. He was born for this line of work. The only problem was, along with the town, the problems were growing. The current case he was on was not providing too many clues. The two previous murders had a very obvious connection, and as he was about to find out, so did the third.

The rain was still coming down as the coroner invited him in. "Sorry, but the power went out about twenty minutes ago. There's just some emergency lighting, but there are some battery operated lights in the lab."

As they entered the lab, the coroner flipped on the battery operated light. "It's just like the other two," he said as he pulled the sheet down that was covering the body.

"The victim was attacked from behind, with a stun gun. The slice across the throat was the first wound inflicted. Judging by the slice pattern, the assailant is right handed. And just like the other two victims, he was gutted while he was still alive. Also, the heart is the only organ missing, just like the other two." The coroner looked up from the body. "Are you alright?"

A look of pure disgust had come over the detectives face. "Yeah, I'm alright."

In his mind he was envisioning what the coroner had described. He was glad the coroner had handed him a mask to hold over his mouth and nose.

The detective left the lab. As he exited he threw out the surgical mask he had held up to his face. He leaned up against the wall and gently tilted his head back so it was against the wall. The coroner came out of the lab. "I'm sorry, but there aren't anymore clues with this one than there were with the other two. This guy is going to screw up sooner or later and we'll find something."

"Yeah, well the problem is I've got three dead people on my hands already. How many more is it going to take before this guy screws up?"

The coroner tried to reassure him. "It's only a matter of time, you'll get this guy."

The detective shook his head. "I just can't believe it, a serial killer in this town?"

The coroner looked out the window. "I don't think you'll be able to keep this out of the news too much longer."

"Why's that?"

As he was finishing the question, he noticed the coroner beginning to point toward the window at the front of the office. The detective turned his head and saw a Channel 6 news van parked out front. "Damn it," he cursed.

"Hey, you've done a hell of a job keeping her off this story already," the coroner said as he put his hand on the detectives shoulder. There was a thumping sound at the front door. The coroner put his hands up next to his head making those little quotation symbols with his fingers. "I know, no comment, this is part of an official police investigation."

"Don't worry, I'll take care of this. Just lock the door behind me."

As they headed for the door, the coroner wished him good luck.

"Thanks Jimmy, give me a call if you find anything else."

He pulled the door open and squeezed his way through, pulling the door shut behind him. It was still raining, although not as hard as before but still coming down pretty good. He heard the coroner latch the deadbolt.

Almost immediately the young reporter jumped in front of him, shielding him from the rain with her umbrella. He didn't even have to ask her if the camera was going to be rolling. He could tell just by the way she looked as soon as she approached him. The cameraman turned on the light and started filming.

"Detective Richards, we'd like to get a statement on this recent murder. Is it connected to the other murders in the last few months?"

She put the microphone right up to his face. He scowled at her and put his hand on her arm and pulled down to get the microphone out of his face.

"You know I can't comment on that."

He brushed past her and continued down the sidewalk toward his car. The rain was still coming down. He pulled his collar up and hunched over as he passed the cameraman. He couldn't feel the rain anymore and he knew why. She was right behind him with the umbrella trying to catch up to him. She grabbed his right coat sleeve to slow him down. "Come on. Give me something."

He came to an abrupt stop and spun around. She almost ran into him.

"Look, you're going to get the same story everybody else does. The Chief is going to make a statement tomorrow at 9:00 a.m. If you want more than that, you're going to have to sleep with someone else!"

He knew that statement was going to hurt her, but he didn't even wait to see her reaction. He turned away, hunched over and headed for his car.

She was still holding the microphone where his face had been. She swung the microphone down to her side, and let out a small sigh. A frown was on her face as she watched him get in the car and pull away. She was sorry for what she had done to him. She had tried to reconcile, but he was still so angry. She knew he had every right to feel that way.

A month had already gone by since they had split. They had only been dating for a few months but they had a great time together. That is until he had discussed an internal police investigation he assumed was off the record. The next night she led the news off with her report on the internal investigation. Although she said her source was unidentified, everyone in the police department already had a pretty good idea who the unnamed source was.

The worst part for him was that he had no idea why he was being called into the chief's office the next morning. He hadn't watched the news the night before because he was out late playing poker with some of the guys from the force.

He knew the minute the chief asked him to close the door it wasn't good. A few of the other officer's outside the chief's office tuned their attention that way as the chief's voice, although muffled, was raised above the normal commotion in the area. His tone quickly mellowed as he realized by the look on the young detectives face he had no clue about the news story. "Goddamn it Sean! I don't need the department's dirty laundry out there in the public eye. Part of my job is to get these things taken care of quietly before the fucking media comes along and blows the whole thing out of proportion!"

Sean just sat there without saying a word. He knew the chief needed to vent.

"You gotta get yourself a new girlfriend because this ones gonna ruin a pretty promising career! If any more of your pillow talk gets my ass in a sling…"

Sean cut him off before he could finish making his threat.

"It won't happen again."

The chief's face was still a little red but the interruption had allowed a little of the natural color to come back. "Good! Now get the hell out of my office!"

Sean knew it wasn't just this that prompted the chief to erupt. There were lots of factors, including the murders. This just happened to be the latest.

As he left the office he noticed a couple of people turning and trying to pretend they were busy doing something. A few of them couldn't even fight their own macabre desire to see his reaction to the ass chewing and just stared at him as he walked out of the office. He still felt as though everyone in the area was watching him. His anxiety quickly turned to anger as he walked by his cubicle and grabbed his jacket off the chair. Even as he left the building he could feel the eyes that followed him all the way to the door.

On his way to Pam's house he was becoming more and more angry. He realized he was gripping the steering wheel so hard his knuckles were turning white. He turned the radio on and punched the easy listening station. He didn't recognize the song but it was soothing enough to calm him slightly before he confronted her.

When she answered the door she was still in her pajamas. "Sean," she said somewhat surprised to see him. He pushed his way through the door as he spoke. "We need to talk." She just stepped aside as he entered and then closed the door behind him. She spun around and leaned against the door. She knew why he was here.

"Look I didn't have time to warn you. You were out late last night and you don't have an answering machine so I couldn't tell you."

"So what, the story couldn't wait until today?"

She knew she had better do a good job of explaining to keep him from flying off the handle. "Listen, we got a tip that channel four had gotten wind of the story and were going to do a piece on it. I did not want to get scooped on a story I had all the facts on."

"Did you even think about the trouble this was going to cause me?"

"Channel four had a different informant. We thought that would allow us to keep our informant confidential."

"So you consider me more of an informant than a boyfriend?"

She got an irritated look on her face. "Sean, you know that's not true. We were scrambling to get the story ready. We had no idea they were going to scrap the story at the last minute until they got some facts straight. We didn't know how much information they had. You know we only have two news channels in this town and competition is fierce for a story like this!"

He took a step toward her. She slid into the corner away from the door. The look on his face made her think he was going to take a swing at her or something. He was just reaching for the door handle. As he was pulling the door open he paused.

"You don't know me very well."

He knew by her reaction to his advance what she was thinking. "I've got a case I'm going to be very busy with. So don't call me, I'll call you! The informant has left the building!" He slammed the door shut as he left.

She was still staring where he had been standing. She felt foolish for her reaction to his advance toward the door. It quickly gave way to the sorrow over the emotional exchange. She slowly slid down the wall coming to a fetal position with her back against the wall. She put her head on her knees and wrapped her arms around her legs. She was a strong willed woman and even in the presence of no one, she didn't want anyone to see her cry.

Now a month later in the rain she wished she could have done things differently. What he had said about the case was true. It had taken up a large chunk of his time since that day. For him it was a good thing. It allowed him to concentrate strictly on the case. He was consumed with filling the void that their separation had left in his life.

She noticed the streetlights starting to come on down the block. Every second that passed the lights came on advancing in her direction. The lights in the office had come back on and the coroner was standing in the window. He had watched the whole exchange from the safety of the darkened office. She knew she wasn't going to get any information out of him so she just turned and gave him the finger. He in turn put his left hand up to the side of his head and fanned his fingers out while waving his hand back and forth, and then sticking his tongue out. He used his right hand to pull the drapes shut to be sure he had the last word.

Although she didn't like it, this story was going to have to wait for the news conference tomorrow. They crawled back into the news van and headed down the now well-lit street.

Chapter 6

Michael pulled the hotel room door shut behind him as he left. He reached inside his jacket pocket and pulled out a pair of sunglasses. Although it was only 8:45 a.m. the sun was blinding, causing him to squint until he put the sunglasses on. He got into his jeep and headed into town.

He noticed a large gathering of television and newspaper reporters outside the police station. He had no idea what was going on, but for a town this size it had to be something big.

The chief of police was about to address the media and warn the citizens of Eagle River that there was a serial killer committing murders in their town. He didn't plan on giving any details about the murders, just that they were all related. He was going to urge them not to go out alone after dark.

Michael just kept on driving by. He was more interested in who or what was waiting for him at 1580 Summit. He drove past Crestwood Park. It looked a lot different now. The trees were so much bigger and fuller than he remembered. It looked like they had put a nice circular path all around the park. It even had paths intersecting through the middle. He was a little awe struck by the changes that had been made to the park.

He was so busy looking around he almost missed his turn. He hit the brakes kind of hard to keep from going past Summit. He was glad no one was coming the other way down Summit. He could feel the effects of the sharp right turn forcing him against the driver side door. He quickly got the car back into the proper lane.

He was looking at the street addresses as he continued down the block. He intentionally passed 1580 Summit. He tried to notice anything special about the building. It was a nice but older looking apartment building. It was in the old part of town and was probably constructed in the 1960's. He didn't know why, but he didn't feel like parking in the lot for the apartment complex. He drove down to a gas station at the end of the block and parked there.

Mrs. Kalnacheck was trying to get in touch with the spirit of Roy Shannon's recently departed brother. His brother had passed away several months ago and left Roy his estate on the outskirts of town. At the age of 69, Roy figured he didn't have much time left either.

His brother had told him several times that he never put any of his money in the bank. He didn't trust them to give it back whenever he wanted it. So he buried his money in mason jars somewhere out on his ten-acre estate. He never told his brother where, or how much money he had buried. Roy tried a few spots on the property he thought might be an obvious choice, but it turned up nothing. He was getting too old to go around digging up the countryside. He was also too greedy to allow anyone else to get involved. He certainly didn't want the government finding out and trying to get its share of the buried treasure.

There was just one giant problem he wasn't aware of. His brother had spent almost all his money in the last five years of his life. That was one detail his brother kept to himself before he died. He knew Roy would look for it anyway, even if he had told him the truth. He thought it would be fun to let Roy torture himself looking for it. He never did have a good sense of humor.

Seated around the table from right to left as you entered the room was Roy's sister-in-law Darby, Mrs. Kalnecheck, Roy and his wife Betty. They were all holding hands.

Betty was closest to the door and farthest away from Mrs. Kalnacheck for a reason. She hated having to be there. She always had a fear of things supernatural in nature. She never had anything happen in her life that seemed supernatural; she just had a tremendous fear of the unknown. Roy was extremely persistent and finally got his way after two weeks of convincing her nothing bad would happen. The only way she would agree to do it is if her sister Darby was allowed to participate.

They all had their heads down and eyes closed. Betty couldn't fight her impulse to peek over at Mrs. Kalnacheck. The room was pretty dark. Only the light from several candles at the center of the table illuminated the surrounding area. The soft light seemed to accent every wrinkle on Mrs. Kalnachek's face as she slowly raised her head.

She had a Middle East skin tone and the wrinkles were very deep. They reminded Betty of the time they were at the Grand Canyon during sunset as a similar shadow hid the deepest part of the canyon. Betty thought the old woman looked kind of creepy and the faint glow of candlelight upon her face didn't help her perception.

Mrs. Kalnacheck began speaking. Betty squeezed her eyelids tightly shut as if she thought everyone knew she was peeking. After two minutes of silence her voice pierced through the calm in the room. "I can feel a spirit in the room!" She had a strong accent that Betty couldn't identify, but was able to make out what she was saying for the most part. Betty opened her eyes and started glancing around expecting to see something floating around in the room. She looked over at Mrs. Kalnachek. Her head was now beginning to lean back. She was now beginning to pull Roy and Darby's hands toward her as her entire body was now leaning back into her chair.

They too now had their eyes open and were looking at Mrs. Kalnacheck. She began squeezing their hands very hard. Almost simultaneously, Darby let out a painful "OW!" Roy shook his hand and said, "HEY!" They couldn't get loose from her grip. She was now digging her nails into their flesh on the back of their hands. She leaned forward. They were both now flailing frantically trying to get loose.

Betty just sat there with a terrified look on her face. She began slowly sliding her chair further and further as the events were unfolding. She noticed blood dripping from Roy's hand. There was no need to look at Darby's hand. Just by the sound of her painful moans she was probably bleeding too.

With a very angry look on her face, Mrs. Kalnacheck said, "You must go now!" She released her death grip on them. Betty was already at the door before Roy or Darby even had a chance to flee the table. Darby almost knocked Roy over as they tried to get through the doorway. He wasn't moving fast enough for her liking.

When they exited the main doors of the apartment complex Betty was waiting for them. Roy could see Betty was crying as he came down the stairs. He could hear Darby was doing the same behind him as he approached his wife. "I'm sorry, I don't know what the hell happened!" She didn't say anything; she just began to whale on him with her purse. He barely had time to raise his arm to defend himself. He headed down the street hunched over with his head down as Darby joined in on the purse beating. They stayed right behind Roy reaching him whenever they could.

Michael noticed the commotion up the block. He had no idea why the old man was being clubbed senseless by the two purse slinging old ladies, but he must have deserved it. It was a nice distraction because he was beginning to feel uneasy as he approached the building.

He began walking up the large concrete stairs that led to the entrance of the apartment complex. He paused to glance around when he noticed some movement in a window to his left. There was an old lady in the window waving her arm toward herself obviously encouraging him to continue coming up the stairs. He noticed a sign in the window that said, palm reading, tarot cards and more.

He entered through the main doors of the apartment. Mrs. Kalnacheck was already waiting for him. "Come in," she said, again motioning him into the apartment. He stepped forward and then paused when she turned her back to head into the apartment herself. He saw her take a seat at a table with several candles at its center. He finally entered and closed the door behind him. "Sit down," she said pointing to the chair next to her. He walked over and pulled the chair out.

As he sat down she said, "You are looking for something?"

He nodded. "Yes, I was told to come here for answers."

She took hold of his right hand. "Every answer needs a question."

He looked down at his hand to see what she was doing.

"Why is this happening to me?"

She turned his hand so his palm was facing up and began to rub her thumb over the palm of his hand. "You are being tested."

He looked up at her. "Tested? For what?"

She looked directly into his eyes as she listed each item, pausing a second in between each word. "Fear, anger, hate, faith, strength, and some others."

"Why am I being tested?"

She let go of his hand. "You have been chosen to protect a child yet to be born."

Michael was starting to wonder if he wasn't losing his mind. "Protect it from what?"

Michael P. Conlin

She leaned forward looking even deeper into his eyes. "From those who wish to stop the child from carrying out it's purpose!"

He was beginning to feel uneasy about how close she was getting as there was only about a foot separating their faces. "What is the child's purpose?"

Fortunately she backed away as she responded. "To change the path of mankind."

He was still feeling uneasy because she was still staring into his eyes.

"What is the path of mankind?"

Again she answered pausing as she listed each thing. "Destruction, decay, death."

He stood up and began pacing back and forth across the length of the table as he spoke. "Okay, and I'm supposed to believe this? I mean why the hell would I be chosen? There's nothing special about me! There has to be someone more qualified than me to handle something like this!"

She waited for him to turn in her direction before she answered.

"Oh, there are, but you are sort of a surprise element. Who would expect a man who doesn't believe in God to protect his child?"

He was a little surprised by what she said. His reply came out barely above a whisper. "What?"

"You think all that has happened to you is coincidence? You don't need to believe anything if that is what you wish, but denial will only leave you with more questions than answers."

He shook his head in disbelief. "And how exactly am I supposed to find this child?"

She reached over and grabbed a piece of paper off the counter.

"It is not the child that you seek!"

She took a candle from the center of the table and began pouring wax onto the paper in a circular motion. She then set the candle down on the table next to the sheet of paper and took another candle from the center of the table. She began making the same circular motion over the paper. She set that candle right next to the other and lifted the sheet of paper from the table and held it about an inch over the flames.

He could see the paper starting to turn brown as she was making the same circular motion over the flames. She set the piece of paper

40

back onto the table and began gently blowing on the paper. After a few seconds she wiped the now hardened wax from the paper with her hand.

She extended her arm holding the piece of paper so he could see it. He could see a face had burned into the paper but couldn't make out much detail because the two candles next to her were giving just a soft glow from behind. He took it from her and turned toward the center of the table where there were more candles and better light. He studied the figure. It was definitely the face of a young woman. He could tell by the way the hair seemed to curve around the face. Other than that there were no discernable features. No skin, hair or eye color could be determined from it.

"This could be anybody! How am I supposed to find this woman?"

She stood up. "You must go now."

He just looked at her blankly. "Yeah but I…"

She grabbed him by the arm and was practically pushing him out the door.

"You go now!"

He turned around after going out the door. She had almost closed the door completely but it was still open just a sliver. He couldn't tell if she was there watching him or not.

He folded the piece of paper she had given him and put it in his pocket. He heard a door open across the hall. It was a young black woman. She sort of looked him up and down. "Is there something I can help you with?"

He glanced back at Mrs. Kalnacheck's apartment. "No, I was just leaving."

He turned and headed out the main doors of the apartment complex. As he was walking down the stairs he turned and began walking backward down the stairs. Mrs. Kalnacheck was in the window watching him go down the stairs. He felt like he was being watched.

He was just about to turn around as he stepped off the last stair but he felt something slam into his side. It wasn't moving very fast whatever it was, but the contact made him instinctively close his eyes. Before his eyes even had a chance to re-open he heard a crunching sound and the breaking of glass.

He opened his eyes and turned his attention forward. There on the ground was a young and very pregnant woman. She had hair curved around her face just like the figure on the paper. Next to her on the ground was a bag of groceries. That is what obviously made the crunching sound. A jar of pickles had fallen out of the bag and broken open on the sidewalk.

She was struggling to get up, but in her current condition it wasn't going to happen on her own. "Oh, I am so sorry," he said extending his hand to help her up. She sort of smiled. "It's okay. I should have been watching where I was going." She knew it was partly her fault as she was looking in the bag trying to dig out a candy bar.

He pulled her to her feet and then leaned down to pick up the grocery bag. When he tried to lift it, the bag just gave way because part of it had been soaked with the pickle juice. "It looks like I owe you a jar of pickles."

He began handing her some of the groceries. He had to wipe pickle juice from a couple of the items with his shirt before handing them to her. She smiled at him as he looked up while handing her a couple of items. "That's really not necessary, I won't be needing them soon anyway."

He was glad she was smiling, but he still felt terrible about knocking her down.

"Well I wasn't looking where I was going either. The least I can do is help you get this stuff home."

Her arms were already full and she still had several items on the ground.

"I live just down the block."

"Great!"

Michael bent down and picked up a box of laundry detergent, a chocolate bar, and a loaf of bread off the pavement. He began brushing the glass and pickles off the sidewalk and into the street with his hand. A small piece of glass cut into the skin on his index finger. It wasn't a bad cut but the injection of pickle juice into the wound caused a great stinging sensation. "Aaah," he said as he raised his hand to his face. He quickly inspected it to make sure the glass wasn't stuck in the wound. He saw blood start to trickle out. He stuck it up to his mouth and sucked on it. That seemed to help get rid of the stinging sensation but it did little to stop the bleeding.

"Is it bad?" she asked.

He stood up and began brushing the reminder of the broken glass into the street with his shoe. "Nah. It's just a little cut."

He sucked on his finger one more time. "You ready?"

She smiled. "Let's go."

As they began to walk he looked up at the window. He could tell Mrs. Kalnacheck had just drawn the curtains to close because they were still swaying back and forth. They continued down the block with the pickled groceries.

———

Inside the apartment Mrs. Kalnacheck began trembling. She could feel the spirit leaving her body. She grabbed onto a chair and put her other hand on her forehead. She felt like she was going to be ill. Her intention was to sit in the chair but as she got along side it she could tell she was losing her equilibrium. She took her hand from her forehead and reached for the table in front of her. She grossly misjudged the distance and began to fall forward. She caught her chin on the edge of the table. It snapped her head to the side with such force you could hear her neck break over the resulting thump of her chin making contact. Her body continued its descent to the floor with a slight twisting motion and another thump as it came to rest.

Chapter 7

Father Davis woke up. He could hear Father Reilly talking. He let out a slight groan as he sat up and stretched on the couch. He rose to his feet and walked over to the kitchen table. There was paper everywhere. They spent quite a while last night looking over Father Reilly's theories, and some other literature. He could hear Father Reilly talking again. He walked over to his bedroom door. "John," he said as he opened the door. Father Reilly was talking in his sleep. He began breathing heavily, and then started shouting. "No! No! No!"

Father Davis knelt beside him and began trying to shake him awake. "John, John!" he said a little louder as he shook him back and forth. Father Reilly opened his eyes and began looking around like he was a little confused.

"Are you alright John?"

Father Reilly sat up. "I'm fine, it just took me a second to realize where I was."

Father Davis pushed himself up from the kneeling position and walked to the end of the bed. "You were talking in your sleep."

Father Reilly rubbed his eyes. "I was having a vision again."

Father Davis sat down on the end of the bed. "What was it about?"

Father Reilly spun his legs over the edge of the bed and was now sitting upright. "There was a voice and it was showing me images. I think I saw who was supposed to come see me."

"Who was it?"

Father Reilly raised his hand to scratch his head. "I don't know."

"Well what did he look like?"

"He was a young man maybe in his early thirties. He had dark hair. Other than that I don't know how to describe him."

Father Davis stood up. "How do you know he's the one?"

"The voice that was showing me the images said he was being distracted, so evil could serve its purpose."

"What are you supposed to do about it?"

"It said I must find him and show him the truth."

"Why were you yelling no, when I woke you?"

"It showed me what would happen if I fail to find him."

There was a pause. Father Davis wanted more detail. "Well?"

Father Reilly started staring off as if he could see the vision again. "I witnessed the birth of evil."

Father Davis still didn't like the level of detail. "Well, what does that mean?"

"There is a child soon to be in this world. Evil intends to manifest itself in the soul of this child and wreak damnation upon all that it can."

"What does the mystery man have to do with the child?"

"He has nothing to do with this child. It's another that he is supposed to protect, but he is being mislead by the forces of darkness."

"So you are saying there's another child."

"Yes. One that will embody the power of all that is good."

"How are you going to find him?"

"It showed me where he will be next. I must go there and wait for him."

Chapter 8

Michael tried to get some of the items from the woman's arms as she was trying to unlock the apartment door. A box of laundry soap fell to the floor as she pushed the door open. "I'll get it," he said. He shoved it with his foot sending it tumbling through the doorway. She laughed. "I could have done that." They entered and set what remaining groceries they had in their arms onto the kitchen counter.

"I'm Michael by the way the way." He extended his hand for her to shake it.

"I'm Jenny," she said smiling. Her smile quickly turned to a slight grimace as she pulled her hand away. "Oh! You're still bleeding." He turned his hand so he could see the wound. There was still some blood trickling out. She headed down the hallway. "I'll get you a band-aid."

He began to glance around the apartment. There wasn't much to it. There was a small loveseat with coffee table in front of it on one side of the living room. He took another step so he could see what was on the other side. There was a little television on a cart and a picture hanging just above it. He didn't get a good look at the picture because he heard her coming back up the hallway. He didn't want to seem like he was snooping so he stepped back before she appeared.

She re-appeared and handed him the band-aid. "Here ya go."

He smiled as he took it from her. "Thanks. So do you live here alone?"

She didn't answer right away and he sensed her hesitation immediately.

"I just noticed you don't have a lot of furniture or anything and considering your condition…you don't have a boyfriend or husband that can run these errands for you?" He finished putting the band-aid on.

"Don't even get me started on that guy. I haven't seen my boyfriend in over a month. He used to check in on me once in a while just to see how I was doing with the pregnancy, but now all I get is an occasional phone call. He claims he has to travel a lot for his work, but I don't believe it. I guess that's what you get when you meet your boyfriend at a bar."

He shrugged his shoulders. "I wouldn't know."

She laughed. "I used to have a roommate but she moved out last week. Most of the stuff here is hers. She left me what she didn't want to take with her."

He turned to throw the wrapper from the band-aid into the garbage. He turned back around and saw she had a surprised look on her face. "What is it?"

She was almost too embarrassed to tell him. "Ahhh, my water just broke."

He didn't know what to say he just stood there with his mouth half open. She now looked more embarrassed than surprised. She clenched her thighs together and headed down the hallway. "Oh my God, how embarrassing!" He heard her say.

He still didn't know what to say. He took the piece of paper out of his pocket. He stared at the image on the paper. She did bare a great resemblance to the image. He started remembering what the old woman had told him. He didn't think he was here at this specific moment just by coincidence. "Can I give you a ride to the hospital?"

"You really don't have to. I think you've done enough already. I'll just call for an ambulance or something."

He folded the piece of paper and put it back into his pocket. "It's really not a big deal. It's on my way anyway." She started coming back down the hallway. She had changed clothes. "If you insist," she said as she handed him a towel. He headed for the door. "I'll meet you out front," he said as he headed out the door to get his car. She stayed inside preparing to go.

He pulled up to the front of the apartment complex just as she was exiting. He didn't even get a chance to get out and help her in.

"You really don't have to do this," she said as she shut the door.

He just smiled. "It's alright."

He turned the jeep around and headed back toward Summit. He noticed there was an ambulance sitting with its lights on at the entrance of the apartment complex where they had bumped into each other. "Looks like it's a good thing you didn't call for the ambulance. It looks like they're busy." They both were looking at it as they passed but there wasn't much going on outside. He looked in the rearview mirror as long as he could but there was still nothing happening. There was no one in or around the ambulance. He finally had to make a turn and put it out of view.

"How are you doing?"

"The contractions are coming pretty close together." She let out a long, slow breath.

"Whoa! Not in my car you don't," he said smiling.

"Don't make me laugh. It might force this kid out sooner than either of us want."

Now she was smiling, and he wasn't.

———

Back at 1580 Summit, Detective Richards was just arriving. He wasn't involved with the case yet, but he happened to hear the call over the police radio and decided to stop by the scene. Just as he was pulling in front of the building he saw them wheeling the body out on a gurney. He continued on inside the apartment complex.

He pulled the main door to the complex open and saw investigator Chuck Adams standing inside the doorway of the first apartment. He was the only black man on the force. He and Sean had worked closely over the last year and a half. Along with their professional relationship, their personal relationship was also growing. They had started to hang around together outside of work a lot too. That was until Sean got involved with Pam. Chuck was secretly glad to be getting his friend back even if it was going to be temporary.

"Hey Chuck, what do we got?"

"Looks like she broke her neck. She must have caught it on the table. There was a big gash under her chin."

"Anything unusual?"

"Well we won't know for sure until the autopsy. It could've have been a heart attack or something. The lady across the hall says she saw a man acting kind of suspicious outside the apartment. She said he was just standing there peering through a crack in the door. She noticed when she came back from checking on her load of laundry that the door was still cracked open. She didn't think anything of it until she went to check her laundry for the second time about twenty minutes later and the door was still cracked open. She walked over and knocked on the door. She didn't get any response so she pushed the door open a little further and observed Mrs. Kalnacheck lying on the floor with a small pool of blood around her head."

"Did she try to revive her or anything?"

"No. She figured with all the blood, she was already dead, and the guy in the hallway may have had something to do with it. So she ran back to her apartment and called the police."

"Did we get a description on this guy?"

"Yeah. She's on her way down to the station right now to look at some photo's and give a description."

"Well I'm on my way in now, it's my turn to buy the donuts."

"I'll be done here in a little bit so save one for me."

"See you at the station." Sean slipped sideways through the door.

As he finished going through the door he heard voices coming from someone coming down the stairs. It was the two old men he met in the park the other day.

"Hey fellas, we meet again."

They were quite surprised to see him there. "Detective Richards," Father Davis said as they finished coming down the stairs. The detective extended his hand.

"I didn't catch your names at the park yesterday."

"Father Davis," he said shaking his hand.

"John Reilly, A.K.A. Father Reilly," he said smiling and shaking the detectives hand.

The detective gave him a curious look.

"It's a long story," said Father Reilly still smiling.

The detective just let it go assuming he wasn't going to be dealing with them for very long anyway. He motioned with his thumb pointing over his left shoulder.

"Did either of you guys know Mrs. Kalnacheck?"

Father Reilly looked over the detectives shoulder as he spoke. "She's lived here for almost twenty years. Why is there a problem?"

"She passed away this morning."

Father Davis and Father Reilly looked at each other.

"Is it connected with the murders you're investigating?" asked Father Davis.

"I don't think so. So far you two guys are my only leads in that investigation."

Father Davis turned his head toward Father Reilly as he spoke. "How so?"

The detective didn't mean it seriously. "That was just a joke," he said smiling.

They apparently didn't find it funny because their expressions hadn't changed.

"Well I'm heading back to the station. Do you guys still have my card?"

Father Davis reached into his coat pocket and pulled the detectives card out.

"Good, don't forget to call me if you see anything unusual."

The detective turned and headed out the door.

Father Reilly and Father Davis headed for the main doors also but paused to see if they could see anything through Mrs. Kalnacheck's partially open apartment door. After about twenty seconds they decided there wasn't much to see and just continued on their way.

Chapter 9

At the hospital Jenny had just gotten settled into her room. Michael entered just to see how she was doing. There was nurse in the room. "Are you the father?" The nurse asked.

"No, I'm just a friend," he said smiling.

"Oh! I didn't mean to assume," she said sort of blushing.

"It's okay," Michael said as he approached the bed and turned his attention to Jenny.

"How are you?"

"As good as to be expected."

The nurse tapped Michael on the shoulder. "It won't be long now."

The nurse began to leave the room. "Someone else will be back to check on you in a minute."

Michael looked back to Jenny. "So do you think your boyfriend will show up?"

"I doubt it. I'm not even sure how to get a hold of him. So unless he has ESP or something I'm not planning on it."

He put his hand on hers. "Are you going to be alright by yourself?"

"I don't really have a choice do I?"

He was glad she smiled when she said it. He was beginning to feel quite guilty for intending to leave soon. "I guess not. I still owe you a jar of pickles. I promise I will have them for you by the time you get back here."

"I already told you that you really don't have to."

He squeezed her hand slightly and then let go. "I insist."

She smiled. He could tell she appreciated the thought.

He noticed her gaze go beyond him to the doorway. He turned to see what she was looking at. There was a guy standing in the doorway like he was unsure he should enter.

"Jeremy," he heard her say over his shoulder. He didn't have to look at her face. Just by the tone of her voice he could tell she was surprised.

He entered the room. He was dressed all in black from head to toe. He was even wearing a pair of black Rayban sunglasses. He went to

51

the opposite side of the bed. He grabbed a hold of her hand and held it in his. "How are you doing?"

She still had a slightly surprised look on her face.

"Umm, I'm fine. What are you doing here? I mean, how did you know?"

"I got back into town and when you weren't home, I just called the hospital to check and here you are."

Michael felt kind of out of place. He wished he could just disappear.

A nurse entered the room. Michael stepped back to allow her room to maneuver. The nurse started asking Jenny some questions but Michael didn't even hear what they were. He was a little distracted because he noticed that while Jenny and the nurse were busy, her boyfriend was staring at him the whole time. It was hard to tell for sure because he still had the black Raybans on. Michael just stared right back.

He found it a little odd that this guy was about to have a baby and he was showing the emotion of a snail. They continued to stare at each other until the nurse stepped away and Jenny noticed them. "Oh God, I'm sorry! Michael this is Jeremy."

Michael stuck out his hand. Jeremy was slow to react, but eventually extended his hand across the bed. They shook hands but the whole time Jeremy kept his eyes toward Michael. It was sort of unnerving for Michael but he in turn kept his eyes fixed on Jeremy.

Just as Michael was beginning to wonder how long this staring contest was going to last the nurse pulled the curtains open to the room. The walls were all white and with the sunlight upon them everyone squinted slightly. Even with the sunglasses on Jeremy threw his hand up along side his head and turned slightly toward the nurse.

"Can you close those please?"

She had already begun to walk away from the window. She let out a sigh as she returned to the window and pulled the curtains shut again. Jeremy put his hand down.

"Sorry my eyes are sensitive to bright light."

Apparently he was not paying attention to the conversation she just had with Jenny. Jenny had requested that the curtains be opened. The nurse didn't seem to care what his reason was and just left the room without a word.

Jeremy turned his attention back to Jenny. "So what's this guys story?"

Michael was glad Jenny started speaking before he said something he might regret.

"He was kind enough to give me a ride to the hospital," she said smiling at Michael.

He smiled back. "It was the least I could do."

The room was now eerily silent. Michael wanted to disappear again but this time it was due to the fact he was beginning to feel angry. Not even a thank you from this clown. She seemed so sweet. He wondered how she could have even hooked up with this guy.

"Well I should be going. It looks like you're in good hands."

He didn't know why he bothered but he extended his hand across the bed to Jeremy. "Congratulations."

This time Jeremy was quick to shake his hand, like he couldn't wait to get rid of him. Still he said nothing to Michael. As he let go of Jeremy's hand he felt Jenny grab hold of his hand. "Thank you so much Michael." She smiled so sweetly at him it made him briefly forget about the jerk on the other side of the bed. "Good luck," he said as he let go of her hand. He purposely turned to his right, avoiding having to look at Jeremy before he left.

As he was passing the nurses station he started shaking his head from side to side and puffed out his cheeks as he exhaled. He felt like something wasn't quite right, but he didn't know what. It just felt good to get away from the tension that had been created back in the room.

He headed down the hall to the elevator and took it down to the sub-level where he had parked his car. He wanted to keep his promise to her about replacing the jar of pickles, but he didn't feel like dealing with her jerk of a boyfriend.

As he was leaving the parking ramp he began thinking about everything that had happened to him up until this point. He heard the old woman's voice in his head as he thought. "You must protect the child from those who wish to stop it from carrying out its purpose." He was still thinking to himself as he headed down the street. "Why would God put a life of such importance into the hands of people like that?" Something wasn't right.

Julie didn't expect him home until late tonight, so he decided he would at least go get the jar of pickles he promised to replace. If everything was fine when he returned to the hospital then he would head for home and leave it at that. What more could be expected of him? He had his own life, and even though lately it hadn't been the greatest, he was beginning to appreciate his own little corner of the world. He was already looking forward to getting back home and spending time with Julie.

He pulled into the supermarket parking lot. It wasn't very busy in the store. He began walking down the end of the aisles looking up at the signs trying to find the one with pickles in it. He walked down the aisle and began surveying his choices. They all kind of looked alike. He realized he didn't know exactly what brand of pickles she had. He finally reached up and grabbed what he thought looked the closest.

He began walking back down the aisle toward the registers. He noticed an older gentleman watching him coming down the aisle. He thought the old man was going to ask him for directions to the aisle with the prune juice or something.

"I've been waiting for you."

That wasn't what Michael expected. "Excuse me?"

"I know why you're here."

"Yeah, to get a jar of pickles," he said pointing to the jar in his left hand.

Father Reilly smiled at the joke, and extended his right hand. "John Reilly."

Michael shook his hand as he spoke. "Michael Foster."

The old man had a good grip and pulled Michael toward the end of the aisle.

He let go of Michael's hand and put his hand on Michael's back as they left the aisle.

"I know you've been looking for answers. Some of what you've been told is the truth...and some half-truths. That's why you still have more questions than answers."

Michael stopped just before they got to the register.

"So you're here to give me answers?"

Father Reilly smiled. "As many as I can."

Michael walked up to the register and set the pickles down. A young woman was working the register. She ran the pickles over the scanner and then looked up as she gave the price. He noticed her look away from him. "Father Reilly, how are you?"

He smiled. "I'm good Lisa, thank you."

Michael felt like he wasn't even there as he received his change, but at least he got some confirmation that this guy was who he said he was.

They walked out of the store together. Father Reilly directed him to a car with a man in the drivers seat. "That's my friend Father Davis." Michael turned his head toward Father Reilly. "You guys are both priests?"

"He is, but mine's kind of a long story. It's a nickname from my friend here."

Father Reilly opened the back door of the car. "Please, get in."

Michael ducked into the back seat and sat down. Father Davis introduced himself as Father Reilly was getting in. Father Reilly turned his head as much as he could while he was talking to Michael.

"I know you're not a religious man, so you may be wondering how you got involved in this whole mess."

Michael nodded. "That would be a good place to start."

Father Reilly continued. "Have you ever looked at the words God and Devil? Did you ever notice how they look like the words good and evil?"

Michael thought a moment and then nodded his head yes, even though he hadn't noticed until he mentioned it. Father Reilly continued with the explanation.

"What is happening to you is not about religion. It is however about good and evil. Throughout history man has put his imprint on religion, giving it as many human aspects as possible. No single religion has all the answers, and I'm not going to pretend like I have them all either, because I don't. I will try to answer as many of your questions as I can, but some you will have to discover for yourself."

Michael sat quietly for about ten seconds. "Is there a God?"

Father Reilly was already nodding his head before he spoke.

"Yes, but the more important question is, what is God?"

There was a long pause like he was waiting for Michael to ask the obvious question, but just as he was about to ask it Father Reilly continued.

"God is an embodiment of all that is good in the world. It's not something you can see, feel or touch, but it's there."

Michael looked over at Father Davis and then back to Father Reilly. "And the Devil?" Father Reilly leaned forward and turned back even further.

"Just as there is an embodiment of good, there is an embodiment of all that is evil."

Father Davis began speaking for the first time.

"They gain strength through us, through our love and compassion, our hate and fear…"

He looked over to Father Reilly who had picked up where Father Davis had left off.

"The power is usually quite low and has very little influence in our daily lives. We are pretty much left to make our own way."

Father Davis took the lead again. "It's that energy that helps create some of the miracles and tragedies we see in the world to this day."

Michael tried to absorb all that he was being told but now came the big question.

"What does all this have to do with me?"

Father Reilly looked at Father Davis and then back to Michael.

"We'll get to that in a minute. Did you know that the difference between good and evil could be as little as intent?"

Michael tried to figure out what he meant, but didn't get what he was trying to say. Father Davis picked up on the puzzled look right away. "For example, if John here asked me if this sweater made him look fat and I said no, I'd be lying." He started to get a big grin on his face. "My intent was not to lie to my friend but rather to spare him the humiliation of realizing he looks fat in this sweater."

Father Reilly looked over to Father Davis. "I look fat in this sweater?"

"Oh no John, it was just an example."

Father Davis turned his head toward Michael and winked.

Michael smiled and asked the question again. "So what does this have to do with me?" Father Reilly paused a moment rubbing his hand across his mouth. From the look on his face it seemed the conversation was about to get a bit more serious.

"Every once in a while there is so much energy built up that it must be released. The energy was at a fever pitch just a short time ago and had to be released."

Michael looked back and forth between them. "So how does it get released?"

Father Reilly paused before responding to the question. "I think we should explain a little more before we get to that."

Father Davis looked at Michael in the rearview mirror. "Sometimes the energy can control simple things like the wind, water, even animals...and sometimes human beings."

Michael looked over to Father Reilly. "So you're saying it can control a human being?"

Father Reilly was already shaking his head from side to side. "No. I think he meant influence and not control."

Father Davis was nodding his head in agreement.

Michael looked at both of them. "I still don't see how I fit in".

Father Reilly looked at him. "It takes a lot of energy to influence a human adult. They already have pre-conceived ideas about life and reality. A child on the other hand..."

Michael looked quickly back and forth between them like he was watching a ping-pong match. "You mean the child I was told to protect?"

Father Reilly waited for Michael to look at him before he responded. "Well sort of, but you've been mislead a little bit."

Michael's forehead wrinkled as he got sort of a scowling look on his face.

"What do you mean mislead?"

Father Davis twisted around so he could see Michael more directly. "The child you think you're supposed to be protecting is not the one you're looking for."

Father Reilly twisted himself around just a bit more too. "You were supposed to meet me at my apartment this morning but you didn't make it."

Michael leaned forward just a little. "No, I was there, but some old woman called me into her apartment and that's who I thought I was supposed to see."

Father Davis and Father Reilly looked at each other.

"What did she tell you?" Father Davis asked.

Michael reached into his pocket and unfolded the piece of paper she had given him.

"She told me I had to find this woman and protect her child from people who wish to stop it."

"Mrs. Kalnacheck," Father Reilly said as he turned his attention back to Michael.

"Did you find her?"

Michael started folding the piece of paper back up. "Yes, she's at the hospital giving birth. I was about to go back there because I owe her a jar of pickles." He held the jar of pickles up, showing it to them.

"That won't be necessary," Father Reilly said.

Michael was a little confused. "Why not?"

Father Reilly got a sad expression on his face. "Unfortunately she's already dead."

Michael was scowling again. "What do you mean? I just left her thirty minutes ago."

Father Davis let out a small sigh. "If only we had known sooner we may have been able to stop it."

Father Reilly began speaking before Michael could ask any more questions.

"The bond between a mother and child is one of the strongest of all. That is why it is necessary for them to get rid of her."

"How could you possibly know all this already?"

"I've been having visions. They're always when I sleep. I thought at first they were dreams, but a lot of the information in the visions has come true. I don't know for sure where they are coming from. I think it's easier for them, or whatever it is, to communicate when I'm in a sub-conscious state."

Michael thought briefly about telling them about his ordeals, but then decided against it. He wasn't positive he wasn't losing his mind at this point, plus he didn't trust giving the information to someone he had just met.

"Well, can't we stop them now. I mean the child can still be saved. We can go to the police or something."

Father Davis was shaking his head from side to side. "Do you think they would believe even half of your story? Before they discovered the truth, it would be too late."

Michael looked at Father Reilly. "Then let's go to the hospital and get the child. It's better than sitting here doing nothing."

Father Reilly smiled at Michael. "Your thoughts are noble, but that is not the child you are supposed to protect."

Father Davis spun back around in his seat; his back was killing him trying to keep direct eye contact with Michael. The mirror was going to have to do for now. Father Reilly continued to explain. "You have been deceived into believing that is the child, but your child is not even born yet."

"What do you mean, my child?"

There was nothing but silence for about five seconds.

"I know this is going to be the hardest part for you to hear, but please bear with me. The energy I've been talking about can from time to time be implanted in the soul of a child at conception. As time goes on, the child will learn to use this energy, and as the child grows, so does its power. Your child has this power."

Michael shook his head in disbelief. "So you're telling me that Julie is pregnant? C'mon, I think I would have noticed."

Father Reilly was smiling again. "It's not like she's ready to give birth tomorrow." Michael put his hand on the front seat and leaned forward. "Okay, say this is true. Why me and not some devout God fearing Christian?"

Father Davis spun halfway around again, "Haven't you been listening? This is not about religion. It is simply about good and evil."

Father Reilly quickly injected his piece of the puzzle. "That is why you were chosen. A Catholic, a Jew, a Muslim…they all might think others will not be worthy of this child's power. Only you are being entrusted to teach and protect this child."

"What if I don't want this responsibility?"

"Your responsibilities will be the same as any parent – to love, protect and nurture your child…but there is something you must know."

There was a long pause. Michael could tell he was gathering his thoughts, trying to figure out exactly how he should put it. "This is a critical time for your child. His power is very weak right now, and even years from now he will need your protection."

Father Davis reached over and touched Father Reilly on the shoulder. "Damn it John, just tell him."

Michael had been distracted by the move Father Davis had made, but he was now looking Father Reilly right in the eye. "Tell me what?"

"Your child is not the only one with this power. Fortunately right now they will be consumed with protecting the other child, but eventually when the child's power is sufficient enough that it can protect itself, they will look to stop you, and your child."

Michael leaned forward from the back seat. "Who are they?"

Father Davis turned his head to the side. "Just like we were chosen to protect the power of good, they were chosen to protect the power of evil."

Michael whispered a word, but Father Reilly couldn't tell what he said. "What?"

Michael said it louder. "Jeremy...but the question is, who else is involved?"

Father Davis looked over his shoulder again. "Who's Jeremy?"

Michael leaned back in his seat again. "He's this creepy guy that was at the hospital. He's the father of that child."

Father Reilly began to smile again. "I think you're starting to get the picture."

"Yeah, but that still doesn't mean I'm willing to accept it. Why would they want me to believe that was the child I was supposed to protect? What would be the purpose of that?"

Father Davis rolled down his window just a little. "Maybe to confuse you, or buy time, maybe to let us know they know who you are. I can't say for sure."

Michael reached for the car door. "Well, there's one way to find out." He pushed the door open. Father Reilly reached out and grabbed Michael's jacket. "Where are you going?"

Michael sat back down in the seat. "Sometimes you have to find the truth yourself. Nothing against you guys, but just because you tell me to believe it, doesn't mean I'm buying into it." He stepped out of the car and shut the door. Father Reilly rolled down his window. "When you've found the truth you're looking for, please come to me. Everyday you waste is an advantage for evil." Michael nodded his head and gave them a quick wave as he headed for his car.

Father Davis pulled at Father Reilly's coat as he was still watching Michael get in his car. "Do you think it's wise to let him go?"

"Well, we can't exactly make him stay. He'll be back," Father Reilly said as he watched Michael pulling out of the parking lot.

Chapter 10

Michael headed back to the hospital. If what they were saying were true, Jenny would already be dead when he got there. He made his way to the floor she was on, and headed toward the nurse's station. There were a couple of nurses there.

"Excuse me, can you tell me where I can find the young woman that was in 306?"

The nurse turned and looked at the other nurse, then back to Michael.

"She died while giving birth."

Michael could feel his face go numb. "What happened?"

The nurse again turned and looked at the other nurse. She took over the conversation. "Sir, are you a family member?"

"No, I'm just a friend."

"Well, I'm afraid we can't give you any details. The family has asked us not to discuss it outside the family."

"Did the baby make it?"

"Yes Sir, the baby's fine."

"Where's the father?"

"He went home. He said he wanted to get ready to bring the child home."

"Can I see the baby?"

He didn't know why he asked, maybe somehow the child would look different or something. The nurse was already shaking her head no. "I'm sorry but the family has asked for no visitors. Can I take your name? I'll tell them you stopped."

"No, that's alright."

Michael set the jar of pickles on the counter and walked away.

The nurse looked at the pickle jar. "Sir."

Michael just kept walking. "You can have them."

As he went past the nurse's station, he noticed some movement just around the corner. There was an elderly nurse, a little on the heavy side. She seemed sort of startled by the fact that Michael had walked past the corner so soon. He wondered if she was eavesdropping on the conversation at the nurse's station. He just shook his head and apologized for startling her. She never said a word, she just watched him walk past.

He felt as though he was just being too suspicious of everyone and just needed to loosen up. What Father Reilly had said was true, but it still didn't prove anything. He needed to get back to reality for a little bit. He needed to get home. He had a long drive ahead of him and he was already thinking about Julie.

Father Reilly watched Michael pull away from the hospital. He wasn't there to watch Michael, he was there waiting for Jeremy. He figured he was the one that he'd been having nightmares about, and now that he could put a name to his face it might give them an advantage.

After Michael had left, Father Davis and Father Reilly had a discussion. Father Davis wasn't very happy about having to go along with Father Reilly's plan, but he needed his assistance and he knew it was too dangerous for his friend to do alone. Father Davis stayed in the car while Father Reilly made his way through the hospital to the nurse's station.

A young nurse was behind the counter. "Can I help you?" she asked.

Father Reilly smiled. "Yes you can my dear. I'm here to give the last rights to the young woman who died just this morning."

The young nurse looked sort of flustered. "Oh, you're a priest. Did the family send you?"

"Yes, Jeremy asked me to come down."

The young nurse grabbed a clipboard from the station right next to hers. She looked down at the sheet of paper. There she saw the name Jeremy Evans listed as the emergency contact and as the father of the child.

"I would like to speak to Jeremy. Is he here?"

She looked up at him and handed him a sign in log. "No, he went home almost immediately after the death."

Father Reilly let out a small sigh. "I was really looking forward to talking to him today. Such a tragic thing, I hope he's not thinking of suicide."

The young nurse got a shocked look on her face. "Suicide?"

"Oh yes, he's told me on many occasions he didn't know what he would do without her. I wish I knew his home address so I could check on him."

He handed back the sign in log. She looked at it. He had signed it Father John Reilly. "Can I see some I.D. please?" she asked with a smile.

"Of course my dear."

He handed her a license that had expired almost two years ago.

"Do you have a more current I.D.?"

"Sorry, but I quit driving a while ago, but I can still get around," he said smiling back. She handed the expired license back to him. Everything seemed okay and he seemed like a sweet old man. "I have to make a phone call before you can see the body."

She handed him a piece of paper while she was talking to someone on the phone. It had Jeremy's name and address. That was all he really came for, but he knew it would look suspicious if he suddenly disappeared. She hung up the phone.

"It'll just be a minute."

"Thank you," he said smiling as he began tapping his fingers on the countertop, trying to hide his anxiety.

Father Davis was sitting in the car looking at his watch. Although it had only been twenty minutes, it felt like forever sitting there by himself. He looked over at the hospital. He saw a side door swing open. He watched as what looked like a nurse cautiously come out the door. She was looking around and then began walking down the sidewalk to the parking lot.

The closer she got to his car, the more detail he could see. She was overweight and elderly. He could tell by the color of her hair. It was gray like a dark overcast day. She was now close enough to the car that he could almost make out facial features. Suddenly she paused. He realized she noticed him watching her walking toward him. They maintained eye contact for a few seconds, but then she continued on to her car which was just a couple over from his.

He couldn't see her anymore as there were several cars between them, but he still continued to stare in her direction. He watched as she pulled out of her spot and continued on out of the parking lot. Although the behavior was odd, he was already trying to justify it in his own mind. "Maybe she was fired or something," he thought.

Back inside the hospital there were now two nurses sitting at the station again. The phone rang at the nurse's station. "I'll get it," said the young nurse who had been helping Father Reilly. Although Father Reilly could only hear half the conversation he knew something wasn't right.

The young nurse got a very concerned look on her face. "What? Did you call security?" She reached over and tapped the other nurse on the arm. She pointed to a nearby pad of paper and motioned for the other nurse to hand it to her. She began writing something down. Father Reilly was trying to get a look at what she was writing but the counter top was obstructing his ability to see anything. He stopped just short of completely leaning over the counter. He didn't want to be that obvious.

She tore the note off the pad and handed it to the other nurse. She read it, and then ran to a phone at the back of the station. The young nurse held up her finger asking Father Reilly to wait, while she finished talking to whoever she was on the phone with.

"Okay, okay," she said and then hung up the phone. "I'm sorry Father, but you won't be able to administer the last rights today."

"Is there something wrong?"

As he asked the question the other nurse came over. "They're on their way."

The young nurse turned her attention back to Father Reilly. "You had better go. The police are going to be here in about five minutes. I will call security and let them know you are on your way out."

Father Reilly still wanted to try to get some answers. "What happened?"

The nurse lowered her voice to a loud whisper. "They think that murderer was in the building." She quit whispering and continued. "I don't want you to be stuck here for half the day answering questions you know nothing about. Just stop at the guard's desk and they'll let you out."

"Thank you," he said smiling as he turned to head down the hall to the elevator.

At the guard's desk they checked his I.D. and padded him down. Father Davis was relieved to finally see Father Reilly come out of the hospital. He was walking briskly all the way to the car.

As Father Reilly opened the door, Father Davis started talking right away.

"What's going on?"

Father Reilly was a little surprised he had any idea something was happening.

"How do you know something's going on?"

Father Davis pointed out a security guard that had just made his way around the corner and was checking in the shrubs and bushes. "They've been walking around the building the last few minutes."

"We'll talk on the way back to my place."

Father Davis started the car and backed out of the parking space.

As they pulled out of the parking lot they could hear sirens. They had only managed to make it about ten yards up the block before a couple of police cars came barreling around the corner. Father Davis pulled over to the shoulder as they went by.

He was just about to start going again when another car came flying around the corner. It was an unmarked police car with just a single flashing light on top. They watched as the car went by. It was Detective Richards. He must have been pretty intent on getting to the hospital because he didn't even notice them as he flew by. Father Davis continued on his way but watched in the mirror as the detective turned into the hospital parking lot.

The detective jumped out of his car and walked at a very fast pace into the hospital. There were already a couple of officers inside. Immediately upon entering the hospital the detective began barking out orders. "I need you two to start walking the halls and look for anybody that looks like they don't belong. If you find anybody, bring them back to the guard's desk to be checked out. Do we have anybody on the outside right now?"

One of the officers turned around in the hallway. "Johnson and Tate are patrolling around the outside." The voice was echoing in the confined hallway, so it took a second for the detective to understand what he said. He gave the officer the thumbs up, and the officer continued on his way.

There were two security guards at a desk. "We've got two of our men out there too." Judging by the age of the guard that started talking the detective assumed he was in charge but still had to ask. "Are you in charge of security?"

"Yes sir."

The detective reached out his hand. "Detective Sean Richards."

The guard did the same. "Frank Vonnigan."

"Alright Frank this is what I need. I need to know who's been in and out of here in the last half hour. I need to know what visitors this woman may have had. That means family members, friends, and even the doctor's or nurses that could've gotten access. Can you do that for me?"

Frank realized they still had to keep an eye on the front door and right now his best security people were out patrolling around the hospital. He couldn't just come out and say he was afraid to leave the responsibility to the younger security guard sitting with him. "Sure, but some of it will be faster if you get it yourself. I'll have Billy here take you up to the third floor nurses station. You can get the access logs directly from there."

Billy was already on his feet ready to lead the way. "Follow me," he said as he waved his arm forward for the detective to follow. Sean smiled when he saw Frank's reaction to the gung-ho attitude. He knew how to read between the lines.

As he turned to follow Billy he thought back to his early days on the force. He hoped his senior officers didn't react the same way when he was this kids age. He must have been a little over-zealous too. In the kids defense this was probably the most excitement he ever had as a hospital security guard.

When they arrived at the nurse's station he noticed Billy begin to stand more erect, and puffing out his chest. "Hey Carol, I need to see the guest log for room 306."

She smiled. "Sure Billy. Who's your friend?"

Billy turned and faced the detective. "Aaah...damn it. I forgot your name already."

"Detective Sean Richards." The detective just smiled and reached over the counter to hand the nurse his business card.

The nurse handed the log over the counter to Billy. The nurse stood up from her chair and pointed to the corner of the page. "There's 306 right there."

The detective slid over to get a look at the names signed in. There were two names on the list. Jeremy Evans and John Hancock. There was also a column for relation next to the name column. Under

Jeremy's name it said boyfriend, and under John Hancock's it just said friend.

The detective turned to Billy. "How many guys do you know named John Hancock?" Billy smiled. He knew what the detective was thinking. The detective turned his attention to the nurse. "Did anyone get a look at this guy?"

She nodded. "Yes, I was here when he checked in. Sorry, but I really didn't bother to look at his signature."

"That's okay. Can you give me a quick description of this guy?"

"Sure."

As she was giving the description it sounded vaguely familiar to him. He began to realize he had heard the same description early that morning. "These two guys on the list are the only ones who were here to see her?" The nurse thought a moment. "Well there was this priest who came in. He said he was here to give the last rights, but that's when we discovered what happened. We had him sign in on a different log."

The detective leaned against the counter and handed the visitors log back to the nurse. "Why did you have him sign in on a different log?"

Before the nurse could even answer Billy was already chiming in. "Standard procedure. He wasn't really here to visit the victim. He was up here on official business just like you, or if we have to have some outside maintenance guy come up here to do some work or something like that."

"Well I guess I'd better sign in then."

The detective saw the nurse nodding her head in agreement.

The nurse handed the log over to the detective. He paused as he was signing his name. He noticed the name of the priest that had signed in. Father John Reilly.

"Wow that's weird," he said as he finished signing his name.

"What's weird?" asked Billy.

The detective tapped his finger on the page. "I just met this guy a couple of days ago." Billy leaned forward so he could see the name. "Small world huh?"

The detective handed the log back over to the nurse. "Is he still here?"

Again Billy interrupted. "Nope, we checked him out just before you got here."

"Alright, well I think I have everything I need here. I'm going to have someone bring a sketch by of a man fitting the description of the man you just gave me. Are you going to be here a while?"

"I work until five o'clock," the nurse said she sat back down.

The detective looked at his watch. "Great, thanks for your help."

She smiled. "You're welcome." She watched as they turned around to leave.

"Bye Billy."

They both paused and turned slightly to see her waving her hand back and forth. Billy sort of half waved back and gave her a nervous smile. "See ya later Carol."

He could see the detective smiling at his awkwardness out of the corner of his eye. He now knew why Billy was so sure to present himself with his chest puffed out when they arrived.

A little farther down the hall they ran into Chuck Adams.

"Hey Sean, they said I'd find you up here."

The detective waited until the gap between them narrowed to respond.

"Yeah, I was up here just checking on a couple of things. Did you see the body?"

"Oh yeah, it's definitely your guy!"

"Well I think I finally got a break on this one. Do you remember the description of the guy we got this morning?" Chuck nodded his head in agreement. "Yeah."

The detective pointed down the hallway. "Well I just got that same description from a nurse down there. He was here apparently visiting the victim." Billy noticed an immediate jump in Chuck's excitement. "Did you get a name on the guy or something?"

Billy injected his two cents into the conversation. "Yeah, John Hancock," he said with a snort of laughter.

Neither of the other two men seemed to find the humor in it that he did. "I'm just gonna head back to the lobby now." As he turned his back to walk away he rolled his eyes and cocked his head a bit to the right, and then mouthed the word "Whatever."

The detective turned his attention back to Chuck. "I need to get a sketch of this guy over here so I can get a positive match. Do you

Michael P. Conlin

have time if I get a copy of it sent over to get it checked out?" Chuck pulled his coat back and put his hand on his hip. "The bodies already on it's way down to the morgue, so I should only be here about another hour." The detective looked at his watch. "That should work."

They were just about to part when Chuck started speaking again. "How am I supposed to know which...?" The detective raised his hand and cut him off because he knew what he was going to say. "Remember the young security guard that was just here?"

"Yeah."

The detective was already smiling as he responded. "His name is Billy. He won't mind taking you to her." Chuck didn't quite understand the reason for the smile but he was sure he'd find out. "You got something else cooking?"

"Nah, I just want to locate her boyfriend and ask him a few questions."

"Alright then, I'll see you in a bit."

The detective loosened his tie as he walked down the hallway and headed for the elevator.

After a brief stop back at the station he was on his way back to the hospital. He thought he'd be able to find an address for a Jeremy Evans back at the station but there was nothing on this guy, not even in the phone book.

Frank, the elderly security guard, greeted him at the door. "Have you seen Chuck Adams around lately?" The detective followed him back to the guard's desk.

"Yeah, Billy's taking him around to a few places."

"Is there anyway you can have him meet me at the third floor nurses station?"

Frank pulled the walkie-talkie from his belt. "No problem." He held it to his mouth and pressed the button. "Billy, come in." A voice came back over the walkie-talkie. "Yello!" Frank couldn't hide his irritation at the comeback. He rubbed his forehead as he spoke. "I need you to take the investigator to the third floor nurses station." Again the voice came back over. "Roger Dodger!"

When the doors opened on the elevator the detective saw Chuck and Billy just arriving at the nurses' station. Billy was already going through his routine with Carol the nurse. Chuck noticed the detective coming down the hall. He already had a big smile on his face. "What

70

are you doing back here?" The detective stepped up to the counter. "I couldn't find a Jeremy Evans in our system or the phone book, so I came back to see if they had one here." The nurse was already looking in the log. "Here it is," she said smiling as she handed the log over the counter.

Chuck noticed out of the corner of his eye as he and Sean were looking at the address that the nurse put her hand up to her head and mouthed the words "Call me." He tried not to smile, but he couldn't help it when he began thinking about what Billy must be doing over his shoulder. As Sean leaned back after copying the address he saw Billy pretending he was scratching his ear. He had obviously been doing something else and just didn't expect the detective to lean back so quickly. He began smiling too. Chuck let out a fake cough and covered his mouth trying not to laugh. The nurse was obviously better at acting as if they hadn't been caught sending little love signals to one another.

The detective took a piece of paper out of his coat pocket. "Carol, I need you to look at this sketch and tell me if this was the guy who was here." He held it up and she was already nodding her head up and down. "Oh yeah, that's the guy." The detective started to fold the piece of paper. "Alright, that's all I needed. Thank you."

They turned and headed down the hallway. Neither of them noticed that Billy was lagging behind. "I want you to put this sketch out. We've got to find this guy fast." Chuck took the sketch from Sean. "I can take care of that. I also got a couple of interesting tidbits for you. The guy left a jar of pickles here. We might have a hard time lifting any clean fingerprints off it though. A couple of nurses and doctors had already started digging into them. No one can say for sure if he went out the front door. They have one emergency exit door on the side of the building that the alarm hasn't been working for a few days. If we can get some good prints off the pickle jar we might be able to match them up with any we get off the emergency exit door."

The detective pushed the Lobby button on the elevator. "Is that it?" Chuck leaned on a handrail in the elevator. "We should have a preliminary report done within a couple of hours." The doors opened on the elevator. "I'm going to pay a visit to Jeremy Evans so depending on where that goes I should be back to the station within a

Michael P. Conlin

couple of hours." The detective headed out to his car while Chuck stayed behind to tie up a few loose ends.

Chapter 11

When the detective arrived at the address he was given, he parked on the street in front of the house because the driveway was actually at the back of the house. The house itself was only about fifteen feet from the street with a short sidewalk that led to another sidewalk that went the length of the block. It had a good-sized lot because it was right on the corner. The detective made his way up the stairs that led to the open-air porch. He rang the doorbell.

Before the ringing of the doorbell had finished the door was already opening. An overweight and elderly woman answered the door. The first thing the detective noticed was her odd hair color. It was gray like a dark overcast day.

"Can I help you?"

"Yes, I'm looking for Jeremy Evans."

She scowled at him. "He's not here."

He smiled trying to see if he could soften her demeanor a bit. "Oh, well can you tell me where I can find him?"

Her expression didn't change. "Maybe, who are you?"

The detective reached into his pocket as he replied. "I'm sorry. Detective Sean Richards." He handed her the business card and she studied it for a moment.

"He's down a couple of blocks at Tommy B's bar."

"Thanks for your help miss…"

Her expression did soften but just a little. "Roberts, Elly Roberts. I'm Jeremy's mother."

The detective was about to turn away but then he realized he had one more question.

"Oh, you don't have the same last name?"

"No, I remarried after his father died. Is there anything else I can answer for you?"

The answer came out so matter of factually, with a hint of annoyance that he decided he just best get on his way. "Thanks for your time." He smiled before turning to walk away.

It was a short drive to the bar. The detective pushed the door open to Tommy B's. There was a stark light contrast from outside. Because it was so bright outside it took about ten seconds for his eyes to adjust to the dimly lit bar. Fortunately he knew his way around the establishment.

In the center of the booths, which ran along the outside wall, was Tommy. He was a round and jolly faced old man. He was sitting there with his wife Daisy and his two best friends, Earl and Ed. Tommy was already getting up and heading his way.

"Sean how the hell are ya?"

"I'm good Tommy." Sean rubbed his right eye trying to get it to focus a little better. Tommy put his hand on the detectives back and began pulling him further into the bar. He let go of Sean as he slid behind the bar. "Can I get you something or are you here on business?" The detective pointed to the end of the bar. "Both," he said with a smile.

At the end of the bar was a young man, maybe in his mid to upper twenties. He was wearing a black turtleneck. Considering he was the only other person in the bar, it had to be Jeremy, but there was only one way to find out. He pulled up a chair along side him. "Jeremy?" The guy seemed to be pulled from a daze, like he wasn't even aware of what was going on around him until he heard someone say his name. "Yeah?" The detective leaned his elbow on the bar and turned so he could see him more directly. "I'm Detective Sean Richards. Do you mind if I ask you a few questions?" Again his thoughts seemed to be elsewhere as his response was kind of slow. "Nope."

Tommy set down the detectives diet coke and then pointed to the beer in front of Jeremy. "Ya need a fresh one kid?" Jeremy didn't say anything he just shook his head no. He still hadn't made eye contact with the detective yet. Tommy seemed a little perturbed by the lack of eye contact too. "C'mon kid you've been nursing that thing for a couple of hours. Maybe if you drink enough you'll forget about all your problems."

The detective had already started waving his hand back and forth across his neck trying to get Tommy's attention but it was too late. Jeremy had already begun to respond, when he finally did get his attention. The detective was surprised by the tone. He expected it to come out furious and vengeful, but instead it was monotone and very quiet.

"What if your wife died giving birth to a son, and then was carved up like an animal? Would you feel like drinking?" Tommy got a puzzled look on his face. "Hell yeah!" He looked over to the detective again. The bar was now dead silent. Earl, Ed and Daisy had overheard some of the conversation and quit talking all together. The detective waved his thumb in the direction of the booth. Tommy took the hint without a word and just headed in that direction.

The detective knew the bar was going to remain too quiet for his liking from here on out. He turned his attention back to Jeremy. "Excuse me a second." He walked over to the jukebox and put in a quarter. He didn't bother to look at the selections. He just pushed the buttons W-2 and turned around. He could see the disappointed look on Earl and Ed's faces. They were hoping to eaves drop on the conversation. Tommy and Daisy didn't know what was going on yet because they were in the booth with their back to the detective but they were soon to find out.

When he pulled his chair out to sit next to Jeremy the selection started to play. He wished now that he had looked at the selections on the play list. It was "Wind Beneath My Wings," by Bette Midler. "Damn I hate this song," he said as he sat down.

Still Jeremy didn't look at him. It was beginning to make the detective a little uncomfortable. He wasn't used to dealing with someone who showed so little emotion. "Hey, I know this has got to be hard for you, so I'm going to be as quick as possible and be on my way." Apparently this is what he must have been waiting to hear because he finally made eye contact. "Fire away."

The detective took a quick sip of his diet coke. "There's a man who came to visit your girlfriend in the hospital. Did you know him?" Jeremy had just finished taking a sip of his beer. It was now just half empty. "No, it was just some guy who gave my girlfriend a ride to the hospital."

"Did you see him?"

"Yeah, he left just shortly after I got there." Jeremy turned his attention away from the detective and just stared straight ahead.

"Did you get his name or anything?" Jeremy thought for a second. "Just a first name. I'm pretty sure it was Michael."

The detective scribbled a note on a mini note pad and then reached into his pocket and unfolded a piece of paper. "Is this the man you saw?" he said holding it out. Jeremy turned to look at it and didn't study it for very long. "Yeah, that's him." The detective didn't bother to fold it as nicely as it was before. He just crammed it back into his pocket. "What time did he leave?" Jeremy faced himself back toward the bar and put both his elbows up on the bar. "To be honest I can't say exactly. I don't wear a watch. After he left things began happening so fast I didn't notice the time."

The detective had already gotten the time frame from the nurses so he didn't pursue the question any further. Jeremy's alibi seemed pretty good. If he had been at the bar for a couple of hours already like Tommy had mentioned, then there was no way he could've committed the crime, got rid of the evidence and made his way here. Not to mention the fact he was in plain sight of the nurses the whole time during the incident at the hospital. He was pretty confident he was on the trail of the right man.

Bette Midler was still wailing away on the juke box, but he had heard the song enough times to know that it was going to be ending shortly. "Is there anything else you can tell me about this guy?"

"Sorry but my mind is somewhere else right now." Jeremy took another sip of his beer and then turned away from the detective and stared straight ahead. Even though Jeremy couldn't see it the detective began nodding his head showing he understood.

"That's understandable Mr. Evans. If you think of anything else, call me."

He extended his business card. Jeremy reached over and took the card but again never made eye contact with the detective. He set the card down in front of him on the bar and just stared blankly straight ahead.

The detective stood there for a few seconds looking at Jeremy's profile.

"Thanks for your time."

Almost on cue the song was coming to an end. Sean was thankful for that. He was so busy with Jeremy that he was actually able to block the song from his mind. "Tommy!" He waved the bartender over. Tommy took his time getting over there. Sean already had a ten-dollar bill on the counter. Tommy gave him a curious look. He never charged the police officers for sodas. "It's for the next round," Sean said as he pointed to the now empty bottle in front of Jeremy.

Jeremy stuck his hand out over the ten-dollar bill and began waving his hand back and forth. "That's not necessary. I get to bring my son home tonight, so I'm staying sober." The detective looked a little shocked. "Wow, so soon?" Jeremy moved the empty beer bottle out of the way. "He's in good health, and besides my mom's a nurse so they agreed it would be alright to take him home."

"That's good," the detective said as he picked up his diet coke and took a final sip. "Would you like some police protection or anything? I mean until we get this guy in custody. It might give you some piece of mind."

"That's not necessary. I don't think this guy is after anyone in particular."

The detective paused a moment. "Do you mind if I ask you one more question?"

Jeremy shrugged tilting his head slightly to the left. "Go ahead."

"How long was it before you contacted Father Reilly to give the last rights?"

Jeremy looked at him. "Who?" It was obvious he hadn't contacted the priest.

"Oh, well maybe your mother took care of it. Well if you change your mind or need anything else, please give me a call." He pointed to his business card sitting on the bar.

The detective nodded at Tommy. "We'll catch you later Tommy." Tommy nodded back without a word. The detective headed for the door. The whole way he was thinking about how odd Jeremy was. He finally decided that he was just different than most of the people he was used to dealing with in this town. As he pushed the door open he had forgotten how bright it was outside. Right now all he was thinking about was getting a pair of sunglasses.

Chapter 12

Michael was glad to be arriving home. It had been a long and tiring drive. Even the thoughts that drifted into his mind about all the amazingly odd things that had happened over the last few days could barely keep him from falling asleep. He was really emotionally and physically drained.

As he turned onto the block where he lived, he felt a little boost of energy as his thoughts turned to how good it was going to be to see Julie again. His headlights lit up the garage door. He waited as the garage door was rising. The house light over the back door came on. He knew Julie was just inside the door and probably saw him pull up. The door finally finished opening after what seemed to be an eternity. He was almost too anxious to get inside and see her. One thing was for sure. There wasn't going to be any unpacking going on tonight. He pushed the button just inside the garage and the door started coming down. He ducked under it and headed for the house.

Julie had opened the main door and he could see her silhouette through the screen door. He pulled the screen door open but couldn't enter. It was as if his jaw was preventing him from entering because it was hanging all the way to the floor. Julie noticed the shocked reaction right away. It wasn't what she expected. "What's the matter? Don't you like it?" Michael was surprised he could even muster a response because it still felt like his jaw was resting on the floor somewhere. "You cut your hair." She got a big grin on her face. "Wow, you're observant. Is it that bad?" He finished closing the door behind him as he entered. "No, I just didn't expect it and I really have to go to the bathroom."

He gave her a quick peck on the cheek and then headed for the bathroom. He was glad his brain was able to come up with something quick and believable. His heart was racing and he felt like he was going to hyperventilate. He closed the bathroom door and immediately reached into his pocket. He unfolded the piece of paper the old woman had given him and Julie now fit the image almost to a tee. She had the exact hairstyle as the young woman he had met earlier that day.

Luckily for him he really didn't have to go to the bathroom. He had stopped to fill up the jeep about 10 miles from home and relieved himself there. He had thought about calling Julie, but he decided it would be nice to surprise her. He didn't anticipate he'd be the one getting the surprise.

His thoughts were racing back and forth between all the events that had happened. He was so tired he couldn't even think straight anymore. His head was just too clouded with information. He really needed a good nights rest.

Julie knocked on the door. "Is everything okay?" He flinched at the knock on the door as his mind was elsewhere. "Yeah, everything's fine. Just aaah, washing up." He turned on the water. It came out so clumsy he thought for sure she'd think he was up to something. He folded the piece of paper and put it back in his pocket. He ran his hands under the water and grabbed a towel. He turned the water off and then spun around heading for the door while still drying his hands. He unlocked the bathroom door and pulled it open.

Julie was waiting right there. He finished drying his hands and threw the towel back toward the sink. Before the towel even landed in the sink she wrapped her arms around him and began giving him a long passionate kiss. Although it felt good he was more concerned about how obvious it seemed that he was holding something back. The longer the kissing was going on the more relaxed he began to feel. Apparently her mind was on something else too. "I missed you," she said with a big smile. She began to unbutton his pants. It didn't take long for him to forget about everything else.

They were still standing in the doorway to the bathroom. He leaned up against the doorway and kicked off his shoes. She finished pulling his pants off as he lifted his feet out of them. She knelt down in front of him and began to pull his underwear down too. He stopped her and pulled her to her feet. He began kissing her with long slow passionate kisses. He wanted it to be an intimate moment for both of them.

He peeled up her sweatshirt and she willingly raised her arms. They paused kissing just long enough for the shirt to rise above her head. He threw it back into the bathroom. He was glad to see she wasn't wearing a bra. It would've just slowed the pace. He now grabbed his own shirt and pulled it off.

Suddenly the pace was at a dead stop. "Michael! What happened?" She was staring at his chest. He looked down to see he had a big bruise across his entire chest, along with several scratches. The bruising didn't look that bad earlier this morning but it was definitely getting darker. "I had an accident, I fell trying to put the boat away myself and landed right on the edge of it." She seemed to buy the story because she got a real sympathetic look on her face. "Does it hurt?" He looked up from his chest. "Not so much now, but it did hurt like hell when it happened." He hated to lie to her but he knew she wasn't even close to being ready for the truth. Besides now wasn't the time to try to explain everything. The more questions she asked the more he was going to have to lie.

He was disappointed that the fiery passion had dwindled to less than a spark.

"Can we get back to that other subject we were on?"

She smiled and reached out and grabbed his penis. "You mean this one?"

They began kissing again. The spark was doused with a little gasoline. They made their way to the bedroom removing what little clothing they had left along the way. Michael even surprised himself at the amount of energy he had during the lovemaking. Julie matched his energy and then some. Michael rolled over onto his back. His fuel tank wasn't even running on fumes anymore.

They just laid there silently for a couple of minutes. Michael began to fall asleep almost immediately. Julie rolled over onto her side and put her right leg and arm across Michael's body. She gave him a light squeeze as she nudged closer. "So are you still having nightmares about your brother?" Fortunately the movement steered him back into consciousness. "Actually, the last few nights I haven't." He was glad to be able to answer truthfully for a change. He knew he had to hold back the real truth. She would never believe reality had become stranger than his dream. He hadn't even realized that he wasn't having the nightmare anymore until she mentioned it.

There was a pause as she squeezed him again. "I have something to tell you."

Michael felt as though he was blasted back into full consciousness with a cannon as only one thought came into his head. "You're pregnant!" He blurted it out almost as quickly as the thought entered his head. Julie leaned up on her elbow and was looking him right in the face. "How did you know that?"

He was wide-awake now. "Just a lucky guess."

She shook her head. "Lucky guess? That's the first thing you thought of?" It wasn't so much the first thing he thought of as it was the first thing he remembered from his conversation with Father Reilly. That was close enough to the truth for him.

"Yeah," he said as he trying to be convincing. "How far along are you?"

"I'm not positive, but at least eight weeks. I have a doctor's appointment on Friday." He reached out and put his hand on her cheek. "Why didn't you tell me?"

She reached up and held his hand while it rested on her cheek. "With everything that was going on for you at the time, I just didn't think you needed one more thing to concern yourself with."

He gently pushed her onto her back and rolled over so the upper half of his body was resting just above hers. "There is nothing that could be going on in my life that would take precedence over you." He could tell she appreciated what he said because she leaned her head forward off the bed and kissed him. He wrapped his arms around her as best he could and squeezed her gently. He kissed her cheek and then let his head come to rest on her shoulder. "I love you," he said as he let his body relax. She turned and kissed the top of his head. "I love you too."

He wished he hadn't gotten involved in the events that led him to this point. This would've been the perfect time to ask her to marry him, but now there was just too much evidence that he was involved in something big. Up until now he had explained everything away to chance or coincidence and he felt like he could just walk away. Now he knew he had no choice. Everything Father Reilly had said was true. There was no way he could've have known Julie was pregnant. He was going to have to go back.

"What are you thinking about?" Julie asked.

"Nothing, it's just nice to be here with you."

He felt her pushing on his shoulder, so he rolled onto his side. "Your sister called." Michael leaned his head on his hand. "Really, what did she want?"

Julie shrugged her shoulder. "Nothing really, she just asked if you were here."

Michael wrinkled his forehead. "Hmmm, what did you say?"

"I just said you left town for a couple of days."

"Well I hate to break this to you now, but I need to go back up there."

Julie got a sad look on her face. "Why?"

"I still have one more place to spread Mark's ashes."

Julie now looked a little confused. "Is that why Margaret called?"

"I don't think so. I just think it's important that I finish it."

She was now going back to the sad look. "When are you going?"

"I'm leaving in the morning."

"What! Oh no you're not. You just got back."

He knew she was serious but he felt like he couldn't afford to put it off.

"Honey, I know, but I have to finish my promise. The last two nights I haven't had the nightmare about my brother and I feel good."

"Why didn't you finish it when you were up there?"

He could tell she wasn't happy just by the tone of her questions. The more questions she asked, the more he was going to have to lie.

"Julie, can you please trust me on this? It's something I have to do. Besides maybe it'll give me a chance to square things with Margaret and get that off my chest too."

She pushed him on to his back and lay on his chest. "This is my last week of vacation and I was hoping we could spend it together."

Michael squeezed her. "Look, two more days and I promise we will go somewhere nice and get away."

She just laid there silently.

He squeezed her again. "C'mon, I promise."

"You promise, only two days?"

He kissed her forehead. "I promise."

She laid her head on his chest and ran her hand up and down his side a couple of times. He was glad she wasn't protesting his plans anymore. That was the last thing he remembered before he drifted off to sleep.

Chapter 13

Father Reilly and Father Davis were sitting in Father Davis' car. It was so dark they could barely see each other sitting there. Father Davis checked his watch. It was ten minutes until midnight. "John I don't think this is a good idea."

"Relax Thomas, all you have to do is sit here. I'm the one doing all the leg work." Father Davis checked his watch again. "Yeah but what if something goes wrong?"

"Listen, if I don't come out of there in ten minutes, you go to the police. Don't even think about coming in after me! One of us needs to survive or it's all over."

Father Davis looked at his watch again. "But why are we even here? I mean why even take the chance?"

Father Reilly leaned over to see the time for himself. "I got the idea from Michael. When he mentioned saving the child, it made me think, maybe we can or maybe we can't, but if they at least think we saved the child it might make a difference."

"I still don't think it's worth the risk."

Father Reilly sighed. "It's worth the risk to stop them from teaching the child to use its power for evil, and to stop the confrontation that evil now has the upper hand in. They know who Michael is, and they probably know who we are. It's only a matter of time before the child is capable of defending itself and they get serious about stopping us. I think it's worth the risk."

Father Davis gently pounded his fist on the steering wheel as he spoke. "I just don't think it's worth risking your life for. There are other ways to fight this battle."

Father Reilly cracked his window just a bit to let in some fresh air. They had been sitting in the car for about an hour. "Thomas don't you see that's what they want? They want us to sit here and have our fate decided by powers beyond our control. We can, and must make a difference, because soon the time for action will be gone and our fate will be sealed for better or worse."

Father Davis understood what he was getting at, but that didn't mean he had to agree with the plan. He looked at his watch again. The glow from the watch had just disappeared as he heard Father Reilly speak. "Look!" Father Davis looked up from his watch. A shadowed figure was stepping out of the house under a dimly lit porch light. Father Davis looked down at his watch again. "It's about time."

They watched as Jeremy hustled down the block sticking mostly to the shadows.

"It won't take long. Give me fifteen minutes, if I'm not out by then, go to the police."

Father Davis noticed the time frame had changed. "You said ten earlier."

Father Reilly pushed his door open slightly and the dome light came on. "I know. I don't want you jumping the gun and leaving as I'm about to walk out. Give me fifteen." He pushed the door completely open and stepped out of the car. Father Davis watched him run in front of the car and disappear into the darkness.

He looked at his watch and let out a long slow breath. He was beginning to tense up even though nothing had happened yet. He saw Father Reilly emerge from the darkness as he neared the back door. He disappeared around the corner of the house. The angle was such that Father Davis couldn't see him attempting to get in the back door.

The light at the back of the house was much brighter than the one at the front. Father Reilly opened the screen door and turned the knob on the main door. He was glad to find it wasn't locked. He hadn't brought anything with him to break in, and climbing through a window was definitely out of the question. He walked over to the edge of the house and gave a final glance over to where the car should be. He couldn't make it out in the darkness but he knew Father Davis was there. He gave him the thumbs up to start the clock. Father Davis looked at his watch. 12:05 a.m. The clock was running.

Jeremy was only a few blocks from home. He was standing underneath a very large tree. He was virtually unnoticeable because it was so dark and he was in-between streetlights on the block. The owners of the home were kind enough to leave their outside light off when they went to bed.

Although his mother told him he couldn't kill anyone else until the child was ready, he still couldn't resist the thrill of imagining killing people. Before he actually killed anyone he used to come here and watch people walk by unaware that he was standing there just off in the darkness.

Most nights no one ever walked by here at this hour, but tonight he was in luck. He noticed a young couple coming up the block. They appeared out of the darkness as they walked into the illuminated area by the streetlight and then disappeared like a ghost into the darkness as they continued down the block. He could hear them giggling and talking as they walked by him unaware he was just off in the darkness. They were obviously drunk as he could hear them slurring their words as they kissed and fondled each other as they went by.

He had never killed two people at once before. He began to feel a rush of excitement as he imagined how he would kill them. He imagined how it would be not to use the stun gun. He hated using that thing but he didn't want his victims screaming out and drawing attention.

The young woman let out a squeal of surprise as the man she was with pinched her ass. Jeremy almost couldn't stand it. He imagined that was quite the same squeal he would get if he plunged a knife into her belly. He was glad they were gone. He was getting way too excited. He could actually feel the sensation of her blood dripping onto his hand as he clenched his fist.

He was beginning to feel disappointment and anger over not being able to do it. His mother had told him not to go out tonight. He had to stay and watch over the child as she worked the night shift at the hospital.

Old habits die hard and he wasn't willing to give it up just like that. Besides the child was asleep, and he only planned to be gone for a little while. "Why should I listen to her now anyway, she's more concerned about the child than me," he thought. He wrinkled his face as he mimicked her words. "Don't do this, don't do that Jeremy."

He had only killed three people so far. He was still angry with her for not letting him be the one to kill the mother of his child. Even though he knew she needed to do it to help establish an alibi for him. He wasn't afraid of being caught. With every murder he was becoming more and more confident. He felt as though he could kill anyone he wanted. He was born to kill.

He could feel the need to kill surging inside him. He decided to turn his thoughts into action. He was going to kill the young couple that had just walked by. They couldn't be that far ahead. He pulled a knife from his pocket. The blade was about six inches long. It was polished to a brilliant shine but in the darkness all he could see was the faint glow of the streetlight in the distance.

He was still standing underneath the big tree. He started to smile as he started thinking about killing them again. He tried to see his reflection in the blade but it was just too dark. The time for thinking about it had passed. It was time to prove what an efficient killer he had become. If he could kill them both and get away with it, then there would be no doubt about his power to kill.

He began to walk toward the sidewalk. He heard an odd moaning sound just behind him. He couldn't identify it just by the sound so he turned around. There in the tree just behind him was a pair of green eyes. He didn't panic, but just continued to listen to the low groan that sounded like someone's stomach that hadn't eaten in days. He saw the eyes rise upward and then start to become larger. It was too late before he realized they were heading straight for him.

It didn't take him long to figure out what it was as he felt the claws digging into his scalp and the deafening hiss it was emitting directly into his left ear. He stumbled backward with the cat attached to his head. He could feel the cats fur on his face. At least before the streetlights gave him some visual sense of where he was but with the cat draped right over his face he couldn't see anything.

The cat may as well have been a lion as it was now growling directly into his ear. He was still stumbling around when he felt the cat bite down on his ear. He could feel the teeth completely pierce through the cartilage. He never even made a sound. He was used to pain.

Just as he reached up and got a hold of the cat he felt something slam into his side. He felt it bend from the force of his weight colliding into it. He had the cat by the scruff of the neck. As he peeled the cat off his head he felt the claws scraping across his scalp. The cat was still growling violently. He had the cat dangling from his right hand. It was just then that he realized he had lost the knife.

A bedroom light came on in the house he had been hiding in front of. The cat was still growling and hissing. He flung it overhand toward the tree. He heard it flying through some of the leaves and branches. Unfortunately it didn't seem to hit anything solid. He couldn't tell if it was dead or alive because as soon as he let it go from his hand it stopped growling. He was pretty sure it had enough and wasn't coming back for more.

He spun around and began looking for his knife. If it did come back, this time it wouldn't have the element of surprise, and if he could just find his knife he would make it pay.

Normally he could see quite well in the dark but he needed to concentrate. "Damn it," he cursed as he got down on his hands and knees and began brushing his hands along the ground. His left hand hit something. It was a pole of some kind. That was obviously what he hit after the cat leapt onto his head. He followed it to the end. The light at the end of it suddenly blinded him, as the owner of the house turned on the outside light.

He jumped to his feet and headed for some shrubs at the end of the yard. He watched as the owner of the home stepped outside to see what the commotion was. "Fucking vandals!" He heard him curse as he noticed his yard light was now parallel with the ground.

Jeremy tried to use the light to help him figure out where his knife was, but he just couldn't see it. The homeowner noticed some movement in the shrubs as Jeremy tried to get a better look at the yard. "Hey!" he shouted as he began running down the stairs. When he arrived at the shrubs there was no one there. They had disappeared in to the darkness.

Jeremy looked over his shoulder and saw the man stop at the shrubs. He decided to avoid the confrontation. Jeremy slowed to a fast walk. It was obvious the man couldn't see him as he was still looking around the shrubs. He wished he could've stayed to confront him but he had wasted enough time. His mother would be very angry if she knew that he had left the child alone. He could feel the blood from his ear running down the side of his neck.

Back at the house Father Reilly was at the side of the crib. Who could imagine that such a sweet and innocent looking child could one day have the power to destroy mankind.

It had taken him a while to find the child. It was sleeping so quietly and he only had a very small and dim flashlight to find his way around. He looked at his watch. Ten minutes had already gone by. He didn't think it took him that long to fumble through the house, but now he had to hurry.

He opened his coat and removed a cross and some holy water. He gently slid the cross underneath the child's back. He opened the bottle of holy water and began to douse the child completely. The child began to stir slightly as his little pajamas were now completely soaked. He began to fuss a little at the discomfort of being wet. "Shhh, hush little one, everything will be alright."

Father Reilly looked at his watch again. Twelve minutes had already gone by. He still had one more thing to do and only three minutes to get it accomplished. He hurried out of the child's bedroom and down the stairs. He knew where to look for the last thing to be done.

He made his way to the kitchen and opened the refrigerator. He glanced around but didn't see what he was looking for. He pulled open the freezer. There sealed in four separate ziplock bags were the hearts of his victims. It wasn't originally in his plan to take them but he figured the more distractions he caused the more time it would buy them.

Father Davis was outside in the car checking his watch about every fifteen seconds. There was only a minute and a half left. "C'mon John," he muttered to himself. He looked up from his watch and back to the house.

He almost jumped through the roof of the car as he saw Jeremy walking up the sidewalk to the front of the house. "Oh my God!" He put his closed fist up to his mouth. He had to think fast. He reached down and started the car. He began revving the engine. He figured a horn honk would alert Jeremy something may be going on.

Jeremy paused for just a moment to glance over toward the revving car. It sounded like the guy was trying to blow his engine out or something.

Inside Father Reilly heard the engine revving. He glanced at his watch. He had a whole minute left. "What the hell is he doing?" he thought. He bundled the zip locked hearts into his arms. He was rather surprised to hear the front door opening. He didn't even bother to look in that direction. He knew who was coming through it.

Jeremy unaware that someone was in the house didn't even notice Father Reilly running out the back door. He did however a second later hear the screen door slam shut as Father Reilly hurried down the stairs not even thinking about anything but getting out of there. Jeremy snapped his head around, as he was about to close the front door. He could see the back door was open.

He ran through the living room and dining room to the back of the kitchen. He saw the refrigerator was left open as he hurried to the back door. He flung the screen door open but could only watch as a car pulled up and an old man jumped into the passenger side and sped off.

Jeremy looked down and saw a ziplock bag at the bottom of the stairs. He went down the stairs and picked it up. It was then he realized this was not just an average burglar. He could tell the old man had something in his arms when he jumped into the car. For the first time in a long time he felt fear.

He ran back into the house. He threw the ziplocked heart toward the sink as he headed up the stairs toward the baby's room. He knew how angry his mother was going to be if they made off with the child too.

Upon reaching the top of the stairs he was greatly relieved to hear the child crying. When he arrived at the side of the crib the child was screaming at the top of his little lungs. Jeremy reached inside the crib and laid his hand on its belly to try to sooth it. He quickly pulled his hand back. The child was soaking wet. He had just changed it before he left.

He noticed an odd looking bottle in the corner of the crib. He picked it up and sniffed it. The child was still screaming and was starting to get on his nerves. Whatever it was had no scent.

He reached down and was about to scoop the child up but felt something hard underneath the child. He turned his hand over and gently pulled it from underneath him. He clenched the cross in his hand so hard his knuckles began to turn white.

Now he realized what had happened. His mother was going to be furious. He could feel the anger and fear surging through his body simultaneously. The child was still screaming. His face turned into an angry scowl. He was thinking about what his mother was going to do to him.

He thought back to his own childhood when his mother used to tie him up and beat him. That's why he had such a tolerance for pain. It

Michael P. Conlin

had been years since the last time. The pain from those beatings came flooding back into his head all at once. He knew he was in for another beating all because of this child.

He didn't even consider it his child because his mother told him he really wasn't the father. He was just an instrument to bring it into the world.

The child's screams only helped remind him of his own, when he was young and first started receiving the beatings. He was clenching his teeth so hard they were about to snap at the roots. He couldn't take any more memories into his head.

He raised the cross high above his head and with one quick plunge into the crib; the child's screaming had ceased.

Chapter 14

Michael woke up and reached over for Julie. She wasn't there. He raised his head off the pillow and looked around. He looked at the clock. He couldn't believe it. It was nine thirty. He never slept that late. He got up and rubbed his face and then headed for the bathroom.

After taking care of some morning business in the bathroom he grabbed his robe and headed down the hall. He could see Julie was outside. She had pulled the jeep out of the garage and cleaned and re-organized everything for his second trip.

He opened the door. "Honey what are you doing?"

She came around the jeep to talk to him. "I want you to get your ass back here a.s.a.p. You still owe me a vacation."

He laughed and motioned for her to come in the house. As she entered he asked, "Did you eat breakfast?"

She shut the door as she entered. "Yeah, now get your ass in the shower and I'll make you breakfast."

He smiled slyly. "You seem to be fixated on my ass." He pulled his robe tight and stuck his butt out and began to head for the bathroom swaying it from side to side. She ran after him and spanked him. He laughed as he finished running to the bathroom and slammed the door shut so she couldn't continue after him.

Michael showered while Julie finished cleaning and organizing the Jeep for his trip. She even made him a couple of sandwiches and put them in a cooler with some snacks and beverages.

Michael entered the kitchen completely dressed and ready. He couldn't help but look disappointed as he saw what he was having for breakfast. On the counter were a bowl, a spoon, and box of Count Chocula cereal.

"You slave away all morning on this?" he said shaking the box.

"I meant it when I said I want you to hurry. Besides I still want you to be hungry for lunch. I made you some sandwiches for the trip."

He put his arm around her neck and began to walk her away from the counter.

"Well then, I'll just skip breakfast and get on the road."

He put his shoes on and stepped outside. Julie was right behind him. Michael walked around to the passenger side of the vehicle. He was glancing inside the windows just to see what she had packed. He was confident she had packed everything he needed without looking too hard. She usually did a good job.

"If you're in such a hurry to get me on the road, why didn't you wake me sooner?" She leaned down slightly to look at him through the window. "Because it's the first time in weeks that you actually slept through the night. I figured that getting that promise to your brother off your chest must have helped. So if you need to finish it, I understand." She watched him finish his walk around the vehicle as she was speaking.

She stepped in front of him before he could make it to the driver's door.

"Two days, you promised!"

He smiled. "I know." He gave her a long kiss.

"Two days!" she said more sternly.

"Two days," he said as he pressed his forehead against hers while maintaining eye contact.

He gave her another good kiss and then jumped in the Jeep. He began backing out of the driveway. He looked for traffic from both sides. He was about to finish backing out of the driveway when he looked back at Julie. She was waving.

He paused for a long time at the end of the driveway and then pulled back into the driveway. Julie stepped to the side as he pulled up. "Did you forget something?"

He pushed the door open to the Jeep and stepped out. "Yeah...will you marry me?"

Julie just stood there in stunned silence. He smiled. "I said..."

She interrupted him. "I heard you." She threw her arms around his head. "Yes," she breathlessly whispered into his ear.

He put his arms around her waist. He could tell she was starting to cry.

"You're supposed to be happy." She began to laugh and cry at the same time. He pulled her back so he could see her face. "Two days," he said as he wiped away a tear on her cheek and then kissed it. She gave him a kiss on the lips and then let him go.

He got into the Jeep and backed down the driveway again. Julie was waving again but it was obvious she was still in a state of shock, as the wave seemed half hearted. He knew it wouldn't be long before she was on cloud nine. He had a feeling of deja vu as he continued driving down the block, just like a couple of days ago.

He began to think about why he asked her now. It seemed so spontaneous, but the more he thought about it, the more he had to admit to himself that he had a terrible feeling he was never going to see her again.

Chapter 15

Jeremy had already cleaned himself up by the time his mother got home from work. The story he gave her was far from the truth. He told her that some priests had stormed into the house and over powered him. They knocked him unconscious, and that they were the ones that had destroyed the child. He was lucky he had received some injuries from his encounter with the cat. It helped make his story a little more believable.

Even so, it did not spare him from the wrath of her anger. He knew what he was in for, but he hoped placing the blame on someone else would lessen the severity of the beating.

"Put your hands in the straps boy!"

As he stepped on the platform and faced the wall he thought back to how his mother used to have to help him reach the straps and put them on. Now he could easily reach them himself. He slipped them around his wrists and knelt down, causing his arms to rise above his head in a Y shape as the straps tightened.

All that was lighting the room were about a dozen or so candles lit in various places.

This part of the basement looked more like a dungeon compared to the rest of it. There was a false door that separated this part of the basement from the rest. It had loosely fitted stones for a foundation and there was a thin layer of dirt that coated every stone in the wall.

He could see her shadow cast across the wall in front of him. He watched it as it paced back and forth. She was yelling at him in a harsh tone but not quite a furious rage. "What am I going to do with you? You're nothing but a failure!"

She might as well have been growling in his ear as the cat had done. He didn't understand a single word she was saying because he had already begun to tune her out.

The shadow began to move back and forth at a quicker pace across the wall in front of him. The dancing flames of the candlelight only added to the menacing action of the shadow. The shadow was building its rage and would soon release it upon him, but for now the growling continued.

The growling suddenly stopped and the shadow disappeared; but it always came back.

A moment later there it was back on the wall, and raised high above its head was the instrument of it's punishment. The lie had worked. He had seen this one before, and out of all them this one was his favorite. It was his favorite because it was easy to block the pain it caused.

The growling began again as he saw the shadow lung forward. The growling was briefly drowned out by the sound of a loud whack. It was as if an M-80 firecracker had exploded upon his back. He barely even flinched, or had the time to as the second whack exploded upon his back.

It had been a couple of years since the last time he was punished. He even surprised himself at how he was handling the beating. He knew this day would come eventually. It was the longest amount of time he had gone without one. He worried the more time that went by without punishment the more he would weaken, and forget how to deal with the pain. He was glad to discover he would never forget.

Even in the soft glow of the candles the old scars were visible, but they paled in comparison to the fresh ones that were being lashed upon his body.

He was surprised at how fast it was over with. It always seemed to last longer when he was younger. In truth, it was indeed shorter. His mother was getting older and no longer had the energy to continue the beatings as she had in the past.

He watched the shadow disappear. He could hear his mother breathing heavily. The shadow never reappeared. He heard the basement door close.

He stood up and released himself from the straps. He was glad he could do that himself now. When he was younger his mother would sometimes leave him hanging there for hours after the beating.

He jumped down from the platform and walked over to a bench. Neatly arranged on the bench were the instruments of punishment. There were various kinds of whips and paddles. Some of the paddles had large spikes that were sure to tear flesh almost to the bone.

He smiled as he rested his hand on the whip that was his punishment for today. It had five two foot long leather straps with silver beads at the ends. It mostly only caused severe swelling and very rarely cut him open. He could've received a far worse punishment as he looked over them on the bench.

He looked up as he heard a creak on the ceiling above. He grabbed his sunglasses and slipped them on as he ran back into the dungeonous room and began blowing the candles out. The room was now almost completely dark except for the light coming from the other part of the basement. He quickly exited the room and shut the lights off in the rest of the basement.

He put his shirt back on and then huddled into the nearest corner. He wrapped his arms around his knees and just stared straight ahead. He loved the dark, at least in the dark you couldn't see the shadows lurking.

Chapter 16

Father Reilly wasn't sleeping well again. This time however it wasn't due to any visions or other phenomena. At first he thought it was just the adrenaline rush from his experience from about eight hours earlier, but now he was questioning if they had done the right thing.

He rolled over and looked at his alarm clock again. 8:15 a.m. He had been doing this about every twenty minutes. He would doze off and then wake up, doze off and then wake up. He let out a long frustrated sigh and sat up. He felt terrible. It had been a long time since he had gotten such little sleep. He was already looking forward to an afternoon nap.

After a brief shower he felt a little more awake but still didn't feel like himself.

The phone rang. "Hello." There was a brief moment of silence.

"John, I don't think we did the right thing." Father Reilly was relieved to hear it was Father Davis. "I know Thomas, but it's too late to change anything now."

"Well what do we do now?"

"I guess we wait."

"For what?" Father Davis demanded.

"I'm sure Michael will come back and when…" Father Davis interrupted him.

"I'm not talking about that. I'm talking about the child. How are we supposed to know if your plan worked or not?"

"What difference does it make if it did or not?"

"At least before we knew what we were up against, now we have no idea what we're dealing with, and let's say for some reason they did fall for it, what's to say they aren't going to concentrate their efforts into stopping us?"

There was nothing but silence so Father Davis continued. "So what do we do?"

Father Reilly already had an idea. "Can you be here in a half an hour?"

Father Davis looked up to the ceiling and sighed. "What are you thinking?"

97

Michael P. Conlin

"See you when you get here."

He hung up the phone. He knew by not answering the question Father Davis was going to be quite irritated when he arrived. He wasn't going to like the plan too much either.

Chapter 17

Although Michael had slept well he was getting tired from driving. He rolled down his window and cranked up the volume on the stereo, but even that wasn't helping. He was still four hours away from his sister's house.

He wasn't looking forward to coming up with a way to get some of his brother's ashes from her. He knew she would just start arguing about everything in the past the minute he brought it up.

He pulled into a gas station. He needed to get out and stretch just to revive himself a little. The gas station was packed full of people. It was the only one for miles just off the highway. Most of them were travelers just on their way through. He decided to fill the Jeep now since he was stopping.

As he began fueling his vehicle the urge to urinate hit him. It was as if his gas tank was a bottomless pit as he watched the price and gallons rise well above what he expected. With every gallon of gas he pumped into the jeep, the urge to urinate increased. It was as if he was filling his own bladder.

Finally the truck was full. He hurriedly replaced the fuel cap on the jeep and then spun around to step between the two gas pump islands when a big Winnebago pulled up to the pump just on the other side of the island. It completely blocked his view of the gas station. He didn't enjoy the detour of an additional twenty feet to the bathroom.

After relieving himself he washed his hands and then rubbed his face with some cold water. He grabbed some paper towels and dried his face. He definitely felt more awake now, but he knew it wouldn't take long for the feeling to wear off. He needed some caffeine or something to finish the road trip. He figured a jumbo cup of coffee would do the trick, but first things first.

He exited the bathroom and walked over to a pay phone. He took out his phone card and called home. Julie answered. "Hey honey, how are you?" he asked.

"I'm doing great," she replied.

He could tell just from the pep in her voice she was still quite happy about this morning. "I'm actually surprised I got through. I thought you'd still be calling everyone you know!" She laughed. "Before I forget to tell you, I made plans with my friend Kathy for tonight. It shouldn't be too late. She wanted to take me out to celebrate."

"Well don't make it short on my account. I'll try to be home sometime tomorrow and I can't guarantee it'll be early either."

She got a very stern tone to her voice. "You just make sure you make it home tomorrow. You owe me a vacation mister."

He leaned his forearm on top of the telephone. "I know. Well, I should get going. I still have four hours left to drive."

She sighed. "I love you."

"I love you too. I'll see you tomorrow."

He hung up the phone and headed in to pay for his gas.

He walked over to the coffee machine and got the largest cup they had. He was glad he got to the register when he did. He only had to wait for one guy ahead of him, but now there was a line of about five or six people behind him.

When he stepped up to the booth to pay, the kid behind the counter was staring at him rather intently. It was as if he thought he knew Michael or something. Michael had never seen the kid before so he just ignored it, assuming the kid just had a case of mistaken identity or something.

"This and pump twelve." The kid turned slowly toward the register but kept eye contact with Michael until the last second. He rang up the gas and coffee and then turned back to Michael. "Twenty seven fifty." Michael reached into his wallet and pulled out thirty dollars. When he looked up the kid was staring at him again. He now felt like asking the kid what the hell his problem was, but he didn't feel like embarrassing himself, or the kid in front of the eight or so people now waiting in line. He just took his change and left.

The kid watched him walk out the door. The next guy in line snapped at the kid. "Hello!" The kid wished his manager hadn't taken his dinner break so early. He looked at the eight people in line. They didn't realize as he did that this was the guy they were looking for on the news. He fit the sketch and description almost perfectly.

He wanted to call the police immediately but he was afraid to even step out of the booth as the impatient mob of customers may decide to lynch him right there. He decided to wait until the manager came back.

As he rang up the next guy in line he tried to get a look at what kind of vehicle he was driving. He disappeared behind a big motor home. "Can I get my change today?" the customer demanded. "Yeah, yeah." The kid was starting to get frustrated. He looked up just to see the back of a dark colored S.U.V. heading toward I-15.

As Michael approached I-15 he decided to drive past and take the back roads. It was going to take him a little longer to get there but he figured the winding back roads might help keep him awake as opposed to a long straight highway.

———

Detective Sean Richards was sitting at his desk going over a report on the most recent murder. Something wasn't making sense on this one, compared to the other three. For one thing he didn't use the stun gun on this victim. Maybe it was the fact she was already dead, but then again that was different too. The coroner said the other three victims were alive when they had their hearts removed. He also did this one in broad daylight, and in a crowded place.

The detective couldn't help but feel a little irritated. He rubbed his temples as he tried to imagine the reason for the change. Something wasn't right. The guy had a proven way to get away with murder. Was he bored? Did he just try to shake things up to make it more exciting? He pulled out a notepad and began writing down key questions on the case that needed answers.

He was about halfway through the list when the phone rang. "Sean Richards," he answered. A very deep toned voice began to speak on the other end. "This is Lee Johnson with the Mariposa County sheriff's office."

Sean leaned back in his chair. "How can I help you sheriff?"

The sheriff reached over to the edge of his desk and grabbed a pen. "I was told you're the lead detective in the Eagle River murder case."

Sean scratched his head. "Yeah, that's right."

"Well boss I got a possible sighting of your man at the edge of my county."

Sean leaned forward and grabbed a map as he began to reply. "What do you mean by possible?" The sheriff started filling out a cover sheet for his fax. "Well there's a gas station at I-15 and Highway 20, and I got a call from them about 40 minutes ago. The clerk there tells me he thinks he saw the guy from the sketch on the news." The detective looked on the map where I-15 and highway 20 intersected. It was about 240 miles away. He looked at his watch. It was 7:30 p.m. "How sure was he that this was the guy?" The Sheriff finished punching in the fax number and hit the send button. "He said he was positive he fit the sketch of the guy he saw on the news."

The detective circled the spot on the map. "How long ago did he see him?" The sheriff looked at his watch. "That'd be almost two hours ago."

The detective rubbed his head. "Two hours!"

The sheriff could tell he wasn't happy about the time frame. "Hold on there boss, the kid didn't call me for over an hour after the guy had already left. He said he had to wait for his damn manager to get back before he could make the call. I showed up about ten minutes after receiving the call, took his statement and drove back to the office. I have two deputies on their way back in. I got a description of his vehicle but it ain't much, just a dark S.U.V. of some kind. They drove around about a five-mile radius but no luck so far. I already faxed the statement and report over. If you need anything else boss, my numbers on there."

The detective couldn't decide which annoyed him more, the fact he was getting the information two hours late and he was four hours away, or that the sheriff kept calling him boss. That probably meant that the sheriff wasn't very good at remembering people's names, and called everybody boss. "Thanks for your help sheriff." The sheriff sat back down at his desk. "Anytime boss."

Sean hung up the phone and walked over to the fax machine. He picked up the couple of pages off the fax. He was surprised to see his actual name on the cover sheet. He thought for sure it was going to be addressed to Boss.

He began reading the fax as he walked back to his desk. He paused on the way to rub his eyes. It was getting late and he had a long day. He sat down at his desk and finished reading the fax. He began rubbing his eyes again. He put the fax in an organizer on his desk, and then stood up and stretched. He decided he would take a trip in the morning to see if he could piece together anything the sheriff might have missed.

Before he got ready to leave he entered what information he had into the database. A dark S.U.V. wasn't much, but it was the best lead so far. He shut off his computer and put on his jacket.

He was ready to walk out of the building when he heard someone yell his name from behind. He turned around. It was Chuck Adams. "You heading out man?"

Sean pointed to his jacket. "Yeah," he said sarcastically.

"I hate to ask you, but can you give me a ride home? My car is in the shop."

"Again! Man when are you going to get a new damn car?"

Chuck got a little defensive. "Hey, I got a new car but I leave it home for my wife in case of an emergency or something."

Sean reached out and put his hand on Chuck's shoulder. "Just so you know, an 82' Buick Skylark is not a classic."

Chuck brushed Sean's hand from his shoulder. "Are you gonna give me a ride or just bust my chops?"

Sean laughed at his irritation. "You better get your coat, I'm tired and hungry. I might forget what I'm waiting for."

"Give me two minutes. I've got to call my wife and let her know she doesn't have to pick me up."

The detective leaned against the wall and waited. Chuck re-appeared after a couple of minutes. "C'mon I'll buy you dinner."

The detective turned to walk with him. "Miss dinner with the wife and kids again?" Chuck got a big grin on his face. "You haven't tasted my wife's cooking…I ain't missing anything."

Sean smiled as he held the door for Chuck to go through. "After you," he said motioning for Chuck to go through.

Chapter 18

Jeremy had stayed in the basement for a couple of hours. After sitting in the dark for a while he went over and flipped a couple of light switches. There were four rows of fluorescent lights all along the ceiling. They flickered momentarily as they came on. The walls in the rest of the basement were painted bright white.

It was now extremely bright in the basement. Jeremy liked it that way. There were only two ways that he didn't notice the shadows, insanely bright, or extremely dark. He put on his sunglasses. Even in the bright lights there were very light shadows but the sunglasses helped to blend them out.

He figured his mother must have been sleeping by now. She still had to go to work tonight. Even though she had gone to working only part time on the night shift, the hospital needed her to stay longer than she liked on most occasions. She even went in during the day shift if they were short handed. "Maybe that's why she's so angry with me?" he thought.

She had been saying that she wouldn't need to work at the hospital for too much longer because once the child learned to use it's power, they would be rewarded with anything they wanted. All that appeared to be gone now. He was beginning to get angry with himself for not thinking about his actions and how they would affect her. If only he could make it up to her in some way.

He heard his name called. It was a gravely whisper. He knew it wasn't his mother because she was upstairs. It had definitely come from within the basement. The voice did sound familiar. He walked over to a full-length mirror that was glued to the wall near the southwest corner of the basement. He expected to see his own reflection, but instead he saw his dead father.

He looked exactly as he did the last time Jeremy saw him. He was very pale with various dark blotches on his skin. The skin around his eyes was dark, and although the eyes were sunk slightly back into the skull, the combination gave the odd visual effect the eyes were actually protruding outward. His hair was all silver and cut into a flat top hairstyle. He was wearing a white dress shirt that had dirt all over it. Half of the shirt was tucked into a pair of black slacks while the other half was hanging out. It was as if he had just crawled out of his grave.

There was a barren tree in the background and it was swaying in a strong wind. There also appeared to be a lot of paper and garbage blowing around. The sky was a very dark gray, as though a storm was about to erupt.

Jeremy was not at all put off by the appearance of his father. He knew he had been dead and rotting in the ground for ten years. He was a tough man. Even though cancer had savaged his body, he hung on a lot longer than anyone had anticipated he would. He probably would have lasted at least another year if his mother hadn't ended her misery.

Jeremy knew his mother had killed him. She didn't do it to end his suffering, but rather her own.

He also imagined revenge was a motive for killing him. He remembered countless nights he would awaken to hear them fighting. Most of the time they had been drinking, and when his father drank, he would become belligerent and violent. He would hear his mother howl in pain at the beatings she would receive. She would continue to tell him what a worthless son of a bitch he was, even after several good blows to the head. That only seemed to egg his father on until she was almost unconscious and was unable to scream anymore.

Jeremy used to fear his father being sober enough to go to work, as he did most days, because then he'd be alone with his mother. Frustrated by the fact she felt powerless to do anything about her own beatings, she often displaced the anger and frustration on Jeremy. At first it started out as severe spankings, but as time went on, it developed more into torture than anything.

His father never laid a hand on him, but that was probably due to the fact he was either working or out drinking most of the time. When his father came home at night Jeremy was usually sleeping, or at least pretending to be. He had no feelings for his father either way. He didn't love him, nor did he hate him. His father was like a stranger that wandered into his life from time to time. It made him wonder why he was back. That question was about to be answered.

The voice that began to speak still sounded like his fathers, but it had a long echoing delay like it was coming from somewhere larger than the basement. "You have a chance to save yourself." Jeremy stepped forward. "From what?" His father raised his hand and pointed to the far wall. "The shadows!" Jeremy turned and looked at the wall. A shadow flashed across it. He instantly stepped back and his heart began to race. There was too much light in the basement for that shadow to have been there.

He turned back to his father trying to hide the panic that was gripping him. "How?"

"There is another child. It too has the power. You must bring it to your mother. She will know what needs to be done."

Jeremy looked over his shoulder. He calmed down just a little when there was no sign of the shadow. "How do I find it?" His father reached out with the reflexes of a cat and snatched a piece of paper that was about to blow by in front of him. "The child lies in the womb of a woman." Jeremy stepped forward to take the piece of paper from his father. On it was a map and address.

As he looked up from the piece of paper he felt something grab him by the shirt at each shoulder. Before he could even react he was being flung forward. His father had a very angry look in his eyes. It was about all Jeremy could see because they were pressed face to face.

As his father spoke his breath smelled as though it came from a man who had been dead and rotting for ten years. "This is the last chance to save yourself from the shadows boy! Don't screw it up!" His father gave him just enough slack in the tension so Jeremy could step back. His father's arms were extended to their fullest length.

He watched in horror as shadows began to close in around his father. He began to desperately try to yank himself away but his father's grip was too strong. The shadows were just about to envelope his father and that was closer than Jeremy could bear.

Just as he was about to scream out his father let go. Jeremy went reeling backwards and fell to the ground. His father had a very evil grin on his face as he disappeared into the shadows. In that same instant the mirror was just a mirror again and Jeremy was looking at his own reflection.

He was holding himself from lying completely on the floor with his left forearm and right hand stretched out behind him. He quickly rose to his feet. The piece of paper his father had given him had fallen out of his hand and was lying between him and the mirror.

He cautiously approached the piece of paper, keeping his eyes on the mirror the whole time. He picked up the piece of paper and moved away from the mirror. He leaned against the wall and studied the map. It looked as though this woman lived some distance away. He was excited about venturing so far from home, not to mention he would have to drive. Those were two things he didn't do very often.

He shut off the lights and headed upstairs. He moved around the house trying not to make too much noise. It wasn't like his mother was a light sleeper; he just didn't want her to find out what he was up to before he had a chance to surprise her.

After gathering some things he figured he might need and loading them into a duffle bag, he paused at the pegboard by the back door. There were several sets of keys hanging there. He grabbed the keys to his dead fathers car. It hadn't been driven since his death because his mother strongly forbade it. He knew she had to go to work tonight and if he took her car instead, she would probably be more upset about having to take his fathers car to work, rather than the fact he had taken it.

Besides when she saw how he had redeemed himself she would probably forgive him for taking the car. He actually felt happy for the first time in a long while. What his father had said about the shadows going away if he made things right must be true. He hadn't had that type of feeling for some time now.

He sat in the car and tried to start it. It took a couple of tries but it finally fired up. White smoke was billowing out of the tail pipe. It was so thick he couldn't even see out the back window. He knew there was nothing behind him so he backed out through the noxious cloud of exhaust.

He stopped in the driveway and then got out and closed the garage door. The car sounded like it was running awful rough. He glanced up at his mother's bedroom window. He felt as though she had been watching him. He was relieved to see she wasn't at the window. He got back in the car and finished backing out of the driveway.

Chapter 19

Father Davis was still arguing with Father Reilly on their way to Jeremy's house.

"I still don't see how going back there is going to tell us anything! I'm not letting you go back inside!"

Father Reilly set his hand on the dash of the car as Father Davis applied the brakes to make a turn. "I'm not planning on going back inside…unless I have to."

Father Davis stopped at a stop sign for a few extra seconds so he could look Father Reilly in the eye as he spoke. "What do you expect to find without entering the house?"

"I don't know, but I do know that you were right when you said we were better off when we knew what we were up against. That's why I can't promise you I won't go inside, but trust me, I'm not going inside the house unless no one's home."

Father Davis continued on from the stop sign. "I just have a really bad feeling about this." Father Reilly was starting to get irritated but tried not to show it. "Look, all you have to do is drive. I promise to be careful, alright?"

They finally arrived at the house. Father Davis parked just far enough away so they could observe the house without looking suspicious. They watched the house for about a half an hour and there seemed to be no activity going on.

Father Reilly decided to he would get out of the car and try to observe a little more closely. Just as he opened his door Father Davis called his name. "John, get back in the car." Father Reilly leaned down to look back in the car. He saw Father Davis pointing toward the house. He looked through the windshield and saw Jeremy leaving the house.

Father Reilly slinked his way back into the car.

They watched as Jeremy pulled the garage door open. They saw white smoke come spewing out of the tail pipe of the car on the left hand side of the garage. They watched as he backed out and then got out of the car to close the garage door. They wondered why he was pausing to stare at the house for so long. He finally got back into the car and backed into the street. The car left a cloud of white smoke lingering in the air like a low-lying fog for several minutes after he had left.

Father Reilly re-opened his car door.

"Well I don't think we'll get a better chance to snoop around than this."

Father Davis leaned down toward Father Reilly as he was stepping out to be sure his objection would be heard. "In case you didn't notice, there were two cars in that garage, which means someone may still be home."

Father Reilly leaned back down so he could see him. "I won't even attempt to go inside the house without coming back to the car first. Okay?"

Father Davis sat back up. "Just be careful. I don't like the way he was looking at the house. The whole place could be booby trapped or something."

"Would you quit worrying! You're starting to make me nervous!"

He slammed the car door and began walking up the block.

The houses were spaced comfortably apart unlike most of the modern homes being built in the new end of town.

As he approached the house he was trying to decide how to look the least suspicious. If he was glancing all around to see if anyone was watching him, that would probably look suspicious. It was harder than he thought. He decided the best thing to do was walk right up to the garage as if it were his own. He glanced at the house on his walk up the driveway. He reached down and pulled up on the garage door. Fortunately it wasn't locked and rose quite easily.

Father Reilly knew Father Davis was probably cursing at him back in the car. He was right. Technically he was sticking to his promise. He promised he wouldn't go in the house, but never mentioned anything about the garage.

He continued on inside the garage, and pulled the door down. There was a house directly across the street from the garage and there didn't appear to be anyone home there, but he didn't want to take the chance someone would see him.

He thought the windows in the garage door would allow enough light for him to see, but it was still quite dark. He thought about what Father Davis had said about the place possibly being booby-trapped. He didn't like the idea of fumbling around in the dark.

He made his way over to the light switch on the wall and flipped it on. One of the two lights that were to have come on flashed intensely bright and then made a popping sound. Father Reilly's heart skipped a couple of beats. All he could think of at that moment was that he had indeed fallen prey to a booby-trap.

After several more seconds he realized what had happened. One of the lights had just blown out. He let out a long slow breath trying to calm himself. "I'll give you a booby-trap," he muttered under his breath. He was irritated at the fact Father Davis even brought that idea into his head.

The other light was working, but not very well. It was covered with thick cobwebs and dust. It did however make a difference; it just took him a few seconds to realize it.

He began snooping around the garage. There was a tool bench at the back of the garage. He could see tools hanging there neatly arranged. They obviously hadn't been used in a long time because they had even more dust and cobwebs on them than the light did.

He walked around to the driver side of the car sitting in the garage. He pulled on the handle. It was locked. He bent down and peered through to the other side. There just wasn't enough light to see if the other side was unlocked or not. The light was giving off just enough glare that it was tough to tell if there was anything in the car.

He walked around the front of the car to the other side. Just as he started down the passenger side he whacked his knee against a pipe of some kind. He knew it was something like a pipe by the metallic clanking sound it made as it bounced off the concrete floor. The shadow of the car made it impossible to see what he had knocked over.

He leaned down and blindly felt his way along the garage floor. He felt the pipe but it was attached to something larger. He ran his hand along it trying to identify it by feel. It didn't take long to figure out it was a floor jack. He left the handle on the floor.

He stood upright and tried the passenger door. It too was locked. He bent forward and tried to see inside the vehicle. The lighting was a little better from this side, but he still couldn't see anything inside the vehicle.

Frustrated he stood up and glanced around the garage for somewhere else to snoop. He noticed a garbage can in the corner of the garage. He wasn't too thrilled about the prospect of digging in garbage, but so far he hadn't found anything.

He made his way more carefully past the passenger side of the car. He thought the initial pain in his knee was all he would suffer, but now that he was moving he could feel it was a little stiff.

He made his way to the garbage can and lifted the lid. He was immediately hit by a foul stench. He put the lid back on without even having a look at what was inside. This time he plugged his nose first, and then removed the lid. Whatever was causing the smell was at the bottom of the garbage can because it didn't appear to be very full. With the bad lighting and shadow cast by the edge of the garbage can he couldn't tell what was sitting at the bottom.

He tipped the garbage can toward the light so he could see all the way down to the bottom. Although he couldn't smell it anymore, just the sight of what lay at the bottom of the garbage can made him want to vomit. He quickly replaced the lid and stepped out the side door to the garage. He let go of his nose and took in some much needed fresh air. He still felt as though he was going to vomit.

He only saw it for a few seconds but the sight of the child with its head crushed and the cross still impaled into its right eye was stuck with him. He didn't even bother to pull the door shut behind him. He began walking very fast down the driveway.

Father Davis watched him coming down the street. He noticed he had a slight limp to his walk. Father Davis started the car and met him half way. Father Reilly quickly got into the car.

Father Davis could tell something was wrong. "What is it? Are you alright?"

Father Reilly just nodded, still afraid to open his mouth for fear he would vomit.

"What about the door?" Father Davis asked.

Father Reilly pointed forward. "Just go!"

Father Davis drove forward looking toward the garage as they drove past. He couldn't see anything that could help him figure anything out for himself.

"What happened?" Father Davis demanded.

Father Reilly spoke very softly. "The child is dead."

Father Davis looked to Father Reilly as he came to a stop sign. "How do you know that?"

As he described it, it was as if he could see and smell the horrific scene all over again.

"The child was at the bottom of a garbage can in the garage, bludgeoned with the cross."

Father Davis took a right turn. "But in a way, isn't that a good thing, I mean for our side?"

Father Reilly still looked a little pale. "How do you figure that?"

"Well without that child around, didn't we just gain an advantage?"

Father Reilly nodded in agreement. "In the long term yes, but right now I think we've made our situation even more perilous. We have to get back to my place and wait for Michael."

Father Davis took another right turn and then glanced over to Father Reilly. "Do you think that this Jeremy is still a danger to us?"

"As long as he's out there, he's a danger to us."

Father Davis took a left turn. "Well can't we go to the police and get him arrested for murdering his own child or something?"

Father Reilly shook his head from side to side. "I wish it were that easy. My fingerprints are all over the cross, and who knows what other evidence they might find to link me there. I can't waste time getting caught up in the investigation right now. I need to get Michael prepared for what he's up against. Once that happens, then I can concentrate on dealing with Jeremy."

Father Davis didn't even want to ask what he meant by "dealing with Jeremy."

Chapter 20

It was starting to get dark out. Michael was only about ten minutes from his sister's house. Even though his headlights were on they didn't seem to illuminate much on the road. It was at that perfect point in the day where there was just enough light left to make them ineffective.

He saw the silhouette of someone standing on a hill against the backdrop of the last few minutes of daylight to the east. They were swinging a pickaxe. Michael remembered the land belonged to Bob Shannon. He had heard he passed away not too long ago. He wondered who would be out there at this time of day digging up the hillside.

Roy Shannon heard the car coming down the gravel road and paused mid swing to watch the car go by. He didn't recognize the vehicle and had no idea if whoever it was even saw him. The vehicle continued on past and Roy began to search in vain for his brother's money.

Michael headed down the dirt road that led to his sister's house. He stopped in the driveway about thirty feet from the house and stepped out of the jeep. He slipped a flashlight into his back right pocket.

Margaret had obviously heard the vehicle coming down the gravel driveway because she was looking out the window trying to identify who was approaching the house. She opened the door before he even got there. "Michael, what are you doing here?"

He smiled politely. "Do you mind if I come in?"

She still seemed a little shocked to see him. "No," she replied stepping aside and opening the door fully so he could enter.

As he stepped inside he heard a voice come from the living room. "Who is it honey?"

But before she could even answer Bill had already turned the corner.

"It's Michael," she said.

He looked even more surprised to see him than Margaret was.

"Hey Michael, what are you doing up here?"

"I came to ask Margaret for a favor."

Margaret turned her attention back to her brother. "A favor?"

Her tone of voice and body language confirmed that it wasn't going to be easy to convince her of doing anything on his behalf. "Yeah, I need to get some of Mark's ashes from you." She was already giving him that patronizing look that usually kick started the arguing. "What happened to yours?"

Michael made a decision on the way up to try to keep things as calm as possible.

"I'll explain, but you have to promise to listen to the whole story before you say anything." There was about five seconds of silence. "Promise?" he asked. She was still giving him that patronizing look. "Okay, I promise," she finally responded.

Bill leaned against the wall. He wished he wasn't standing behind Margaret. He wanted to get her attention, but it was impossible from his vantage point. He was just going to have to wait until they were done.

Michael glanced over his sister's shoulder as he noticed Bill leaning against the wall.

"I promised Mark I would spread his ashes up at the land. Well I was up there a couple of days ago and…"

Margaret angrily interrupted. "What?"

Michael held his hand up to keep her from continuing. "You promised to listen to the whole story first." She pursed her lips together and defiantly crossed her arms, and leaned against the wall.

Michael, at least for now, managed to diffuse his sister's explosive temper, but the clock was obviously still ticking.

"I was up there spreading his ashes. He asked me to spread them in very specific places. One of them was on the lake, so I took the boat out…"

Again she interrupted him but this time it was with a long and slow frustrated sigh. He paused waiting to see if she was going to say anything. She motioned with her hand for him to continue. She was apparently intent on keeping her promise of not saying anything until he had finished. She glanced over her shoulder at Bill. He was giving her a really weird look but she was too angry to even consider what it meant.

"Anyway I slipped in the boat and accidentally dumped the rest of his ashes into the lake." He knew she wouldn't have bought into the truth so he just kept it to a simple explanation. From the look on her face she wasn't buying into the lie either.

"Are you finished?"

He held up his hand again. "Almost; you see I have one more place to spread his ashes but I don't have any left. I promised him I would spread them by the tree house in the big oak tree out in back of the house."

The clock on his sister's emotional time bomb had just expired. "Fuck you Michael!" Michael watched as Bill approached her from behind and set his hand on her shoulder. She threw her elbow back in his direction, narrowly missing his chest. He threw his hands up in a submissive gesture and backed off as she continued to yell at Michael.

"You think you can exclude me from everything, waltz in here, and expect me to do something for you?" Michael watched as tears began to run down her cheeks. He had a brief flash back to when they were small children.

Michael and his brother Mark were up in the tree house. They could hear Margaret down below whining to get into the tree house. "I'm gonna tell mom!" she yelled.

Michael gave his brother a sly grin and then reached into a pail of frogs they had collected from a nearby pond. He looked out the entrance to the tree house. Things couldn't have been more perfect for his plan. Margaret was standing directly below him about fifteen feet. She was looking at the tree trying to figure out how to climb up and didn't notice him watching her.

He dropped the frog with the precision of a guided missile. When the frog was only about five feet away from contact, he called her name. She looked up to see the frog with all four limbs spread wide as it closed in on its target.

She barely had time to close her eyes as the frog bounced off her face. It made a faint slapping sound and then continued its plunge to the ground with a one and a half twist. Margaret's face was now facing the ground too, but the flinching reflex wasn't fast enough to avoid a direct hit. She knew what it was from the brief glimpse of the shape as it plummeted.

The screaming didn't start until she opened her eyes again and saw the frog hopping away into the woods. Her brothers had told her that frogs give you warts. All she could imagine was that the stinging sensation left on her face was the warts beginning to break out. She ran back to the house screaming all the way.

The boys rolled back into the tree house with laughter. They continued laughing until they heard their mother yelling their names as she came marching through the woods. They were already on the ground when she arrived. She made them apologize to Margaret and warned them about the trouble they'd be in when their father got home.

In Michael's mind it was all worth it.

Every time he thought about the incident it would bring a smile to his face, but this time it was different. There were other times he had not been so nice to Margaret, but it was just typical brother and sister stuff.

Besides he wasn't the only one to blame. His mother in large part was the real one to blame. Margaret could've very easily been a tomboy. She always wanted to be doing whatever the boys were doing, but their mother wouldn't have it. She already had two boys, and she wanted Margaret to be a proper young lady.

Michael finally got a little insight into why they had such a strained relationship. Since their mother wasn't around anymore, maybe she just took all her pent up frustrations out on him. He did have a tendency to pick on her a bit too much, but it was all in fun.

"Margaret you don't understand. This is really important to me. I made a promise to Mark and I want to keep it." She put her left hand on her hip and wiped away a tear with the other as she replied. "Well you can leave now then, I'll spread them for you." She was just finishing wiping a tear from her cheek but almost poked herself in the eye when she flinched at Michael's response. "No!" It obviously came out a little louder than he had intended. "I need to do it myself."

He didn't know if it would work for his sister or not, but if there was any information at the tree house, he was the one who needed to hear it.

Before she could even respond Bill appeared from around the corner. Michael hadn't noticed him leaving in the first place. He brushed past Margaret carrying an identical urn to his. "Here, take it and get out of here." Michael stared at Bill somewhat in disbelief.

Margaret couldn't see what he had handed to Michael until her husband backed away. "Bill what the hell are you doing?" Michael glanced back and forth between them.

"I don't need the whole thing." Bill pointed toward the door. "Just take what you want and leave the rest on the stairs." Margaret was furious. "You son of a bitch!" She took a big swing at her husband. He caught her arm mid swing and pulled her close to keep her from trying to swing at him again.

Michael had already turned and headed out the door. He could hear Margaret screaming at Bill to let her go. He opened the urn and poured a handful into his left hand. With his right hand he pulled the flashlight from his back pocket. He could still hear Margaret screaming at Bill as he rounded the corner of the house. He headed through the backyard and into the woods.

Inside the house Bill was trying to calm Margaret down. Tears were streaming down her cheeks. "Will you listen to me goddamn it?" he shouted. She was still trying to pull away even though she knew it was useless. "Remember last night when I woke you up about 10:15?"

He paused for a response. If looks could kill he would have been dead on the spot. "Yes!" she finally replied.

"I told you they had a sketch on the news that I thought looked like your brother."

Her look still hadn't changed. "Yeah, so?"

Bill still kept a firm grip on her arms. "You think it's a coincidence your brother has been in town the last couple of days and the police put out a sketch that looks exactly like him, and he's wanted as a murder suspect?"

She gave him an even sterner look now. "My brothers an asshole. He's not a murderer, you idiot! Now let me go before I knee you in the balls so hard your grandchildren will feel it!"

He quickly released her because he knew she would do it. "I'm going to call the police," he said as he walked into the living room to get the phone. She brushed some hair out of her face. "Good!"

She went into the kitchen and sat down. She finished wiping the remaining tears from her eyes. She could hear Bill on the phone with the police. She took some satisfaction in the fact that even though she didn't think her brother was guilty of murder, that this would certainly cause some disruption in his plans, and maybe he'd even get a little time in jail.

Bill came out of the living room and into the kitchen. "The police are on their way." He put his hand on her shoulder. "Don't you fucking touch me," she snapped. He slowly pulled his hand away. "I'm going to check on the kids." He was worried all the shouting may have woken them. Plus it was an excuse to let Margaret be by herself for a little bit. That always seemed to help. Usually after fifteen or twenty minutes she calmed down enough to at least have a civil conversation, at which point she would usually apologize for her behavior.

Michael was making his way through the woods with the flashlight lighting his way. He finally arrived at the spot. He pointed the flashlight upward into the tree. There were just a few rotted boards left attached to the tree. That's all that was left of his childhood tree house.

He slowly lowered the light from the flashlight down the tree until it came to where the trunk of the tree met the soil. There was a hole dug into the ground right at the base of the tree. It looked as if rain had washed away a lot of the topsoil exposing most of the root system. He was a little apprehensive about spreading the ashes there. He worried about what might come out of the hole.

He decided no matter where he put the ashes, it was just as likely to cause some phenomenon his brain would have trouble accepting.

He opened his left hand and tossed the ashes toward the tree. He took a step back because he was letting his imagination get the best of him. As he did he felt something grab on to the back of his shirt. When he tried to turn to see what it was, he felt something grab his right hand, which was holding the flashlight.

He looked down to see what it was. It was a root from the big oak. It had coiled around his wrist. He was pretty sure the thing that had a hold of his shirt was the same thing. Just as he tried to spin around he was being flung forward. It took him a few seconds to feel the full impact of being flung against the tree. He could feel roots now beginning to wrap around his ankles.

When he opened his eyes, his own flashlight blinded him. His right hand was pinned between him and the tree. He lifted his chin to get his face directly out of the light. When he did he noticed a pair of eyes in the bark of the tree looking directly back at him. There was a knotted piece of bark in the tree just above his head that had morphed into a human face.

He tried to pull himself back as far as he could. He was so close to the tree his eyes were having trouble focusing.

The face in the bark got a stern look to it. "You are wasting time and energy. Every second you waste looking for answers puts more and more people at risk. Especially those close to you." Michael tried to move the flashlight but it was no use. "What is the purpose of all this?" The face in the tree looked more ominous than it really did due to the angle of light coming from below it. "Every day evil will continue to grow stronger until it consumes all that you know."

Michael wasn't sure if it was responding to his question or just making a statement. "Why don't you answer my questions?" The face in the bark still had not lost the stern expression. "Evil can detect the energy and will find a way to stop it. The less energy used, the longer it takes to find the source."

Michael was beginning to feel a little claustrophobic. He got just enough leverage with his left hand to push him back a couple of inches. "Why me?" he asked staring directly into the face. "Why not you? You have a chance to decide your own fate, and with your fate the human race will follow."

Michael was just about to ask another question when the tree released its hold on him. He was pushing himself away from the tree with so much effort, when it released him; he stumbled backward and landed on his back. Fortunately the ground was soft, but not soft enough to keep him from seeing stars when his head snapped against the ground.

When he regained his vision a few seconds later, he could see the flashlight lying by the base of the tree. He walked over and picked it up. He put the beam of light right where the face had appeared in the bark. It still looked like a face to him, but that was only because that's where it had appeared.

He could tell where the eyes and mouth had been, but it was obviously gone now. "Hey goddamn it! I'm not done yet!" he yelled. He was really out of breath. He hadn't realized how hard he was working to free himself from the roots. He watched for a few seconds but the face still had no movement.

Suddenly the area where his flashlight was pointed started becoming brighter. For a split second he thought it might be some other kind of phenomenon, but then he realized the entire area around him was illuminated much better. He turned to find the source. He could only make out two bright dots advancing in his direction. He held up his hand trying to block the light from at least one of them.

A voice echoed into the woods. "This is the police, put the flashlight down and lay on the ground."

Michael stood there in disbelief as he wondered why Margaret would call the police over this. Again the voice echoed into the woods. "Right now!" Michael set the flashlight down and lay on the ground as instructed. He heard a different voice this time. "I heard him talking to somebody else." There was a moment of silence. "Check it out," replied the voice that instructed him to lie on the ground.

He could tell the officer was approaching as the light danced slightly back and forth. He was approaching slowly obviously trying to keep his gun and the flashlight on Michael at all times. "Don't try anything funny now." Michael lay there as motionless as possible. The officer tucked the flashlight under his armpit and holstered his gun. "Are you out here alone?" the policeman asked. "Yes sir," Michael replied.

The police officer pulled Michael's arms back and cuffed him. He looked up and watched his partner come around the tree. "Did you see anything?" The other officer walked over to where Michael was lying. "Nothing, no tracks, no sound, nothing." The officer pulled Michael to his feet. "So who were you yelling at?"

"I was yelling at myself."

The two police officers looked at each other. The officer that had searched the woods just shrugged his shoulders. The other officer motioned for his partner to lead the way out of the woods and the grabbed Michael by the arm. "Okay Cybil, let's head down to the station."

He let Michael continue ahead of him but grabbed the chain between the handcuffs with his left hand while holding the flashlight with the other. Michael followed the first officer as close as he could but with his arms pinned behind him and the officer hanging on to him, he was just far enough back that he could feel the branches the first officer was pushing out of the way come rushing back into place. He bent down and sped up just enough to avoid the major blows.

At first the tailing officer didn't understand what Michael was doing. Just as he was about to yank Michael back to an upright position, he got smacked across the face with a large leafy branch. He stopped, yanking Michael to a stop with him. A couple of leaves had found their way between his lips as it slashed across his face. He spit them out.

"Goddamn it John, slow down. I'm getting the piss beat out of me by these branches!"

Michael couldn't help but smile. He was glad it was dark because he was sure the cop wouldn't see the humor in it.

They moved at a slower pace until they were out of the woods. Margaret was by the house watching as they led him to the police car. She couldn't help but get some satisfaction as she could hear them reading him his rights. She still didn't think he was guilty of murder, but she was glad to see him having his life disrupted, even if it was temporary.

Michael just shook his head as the officer helped him duck into the police car.

Margaret continued to watch them even as they pulled out of the driveway.

Chapter 21

Julie had just gotten home from her date with her friend. She waved as Kathy backed out of the driveway. She was out a little longer than she had planned. Kathy liked to talk. Julie did most of the listening.

She unlocked the back door and entered the house. The house was still warm from the heat of the day. Julie wished Michael would let a professional fix the air conditioner. Since he was home all the time, he was trying to fix a lot of things himself.

She left the back door open but closed the screen door and raised the window on it. She decided to open the front door to try to get a breeze flowing through the house. It had cooled off nicely outside and at ten o'clock she liked to watch the nightly news, so she figured it would cool down the house in the half hour it took to watch the news.

She made a quick pit stop in the kitchen to check the answering machine. It had one message on the display. She pushed the button but the message was blank. She was disappointed it wasn't Michael.

As she went to turn away from the answering machine she felt something brush her arm. She jumped back a little surprised, but the sound of the familiar meow helped decipher what it was before she even saw it. "Buster," she scolded him. "No crawling on the counter!" She scooped him up and kissed him on the forehead. She carried him a couple of feet and then bent down and gently set him on the floor.

She grabbed the television remote and clicked on the news. She stood and watched as they gave headlines on the upcoming stories. When the weatherman came on and started talking about what a hot day it had been she could feel herself begin to perspire almost on cue.

She had forgotten to open the front door. The cool breeze would surely feel good. She unlocked the front door and pulled it open. The screen on the storm door was already open. She could feel the breeze blowing past her and into the house immediately. She paused momentarily just to enjoy the soothing coolness as it chilled her slightly.

As she turned away from the door, she could tell she was about to bump into something. She momentarily closed her eyes as she felt something grab her arm. Her head had not made it completely around yet to look at who it was.

When she opened her eyes she felt herself getting spun around. She saw an arm reach over her shoulder and clamp down across her chest. She knew it wasn't Michael playing games or something. He would have never been so rough with her. Just as the panic was really setting in she saw a white cloth heading for her face. She struggled to keep it away but whoever it was behind her had a good position on her and she was barely able to move her arms.

She tried to scream but it was to late. Just as she started to scream the cloth was placed over her mouth and nose. She tried swinging her head from side to side but it was no use. The cloth had some kind of chemical on it that instantly made her feel lightheaded. She continued to struggle for about thirty seconds but with each passing second she could feel the panic slipping away. She knew that wasn't a good thing. She made one final and feeble attempt to free herself before her body went limp.

Jeremy dragged her back toward the front door and closed it. He removed the cloth from her face and shoved it into his pocket. He was surprised at how far away from the door she had managed to push him. He was glad he managed to strike when he did, because if she had managed to turn completely around it would have made things a lot more difficult for him.

He dragged her into the kitchen. He pulled some rope from his back pocket and proceeded to tie her up. He left her there on the kitchen floor while he ran to get his car, which was parked around the block.

He ran up to the car and got in. A large plume of smoke came out of the car again when he started it, but not as much as before. He noticed a piece of paper stuck under his wiper blade. He rolled down his window and pulled it into the car. It was a ticket for having expired tabs. He crinkled it in his hand and threw it to the floor on the passenger side.

He made his way back to the house and rushed inside. Buster their cat was walking around Julie's head meowing softly and sniffing her head. Jeremy lunged forward and tried to kick the cat out of the way. He made just enough noise for Buster to have a chance to jump out of the way. It hissed as it ran off and disappeared around the corner.

Jeremy bent down and tried to pick Julie up off the floor. It was a lot tougher than he thought it would be. He had to adjust her limp body several times before he could lift her off the floor.

Just as he was about to turn and leave he heard the cat growling at him. He looked down and saw the cat crouched at the edge of the kitchen with its ears pinned back and a look in its eyes that he wished he could match. He bared his teeth, widened his eyes and hissed at the cat as he stomped his foot on the floor. The cat darted off with a hiss of it's own and disappeared around the corner again. Jeremy got a slight grin to his face as he turned to leave.

He pushed the storm door open with his elbow and stepped out into the night. Other than a soft glow of light from the kitchen window, it was pretty dark. He glanced around and then loaded Julie into the trunk.

He got into the car. He had left it running when he went inside but it must have stalled out. He turned the key and started the car again. The engine started sputtering and sounded like it was going to quit again. He pressed the gas pedal to the floor and let the engine rev for a second. When he released his foot from the gas pedal the car hesitated and then backfired. The resulting bang was so loud it even startled Jeremy. He feared it might have awakened some of her neighbors. He quickly backed out of the driveway and was on his way.

Chapter 22

The detective was still very full from the dinner he had just eaten. "I wish I hadn't gotten the salad before the meal." Chuck nodded his head in agreement as he picked his teeth with a toothpick.

They were pretty quiet on the ride to Chuck's house. They had talked quite a bit at dinner. Most of the conversation was about the murder case. It took a long time to get through the dinner because they were doing more talking than eating.

Since Chuck was buying Sean had ordered a big steak. Normally he wouldn't have eaten the whole thing, but the eating was going at such a slow pace, he didn't realize he was consuming everything on his plate.

He pulled up to Chuck's house. "Thanks for the ride man," Chuck said as he stepped out of the car. "Thanks for dinner," Sean replied. "See you tomorrow," Chuck said as he closed the door. Sean looked at his watch. It was 10:45 p.m. He couldn't believe his eyes. It didn't seem like it should be that late already.

He was barely a block away from Chuck's house when the police radio began to crackle. The volume was kind of low. He turned up the volume. All he made out were the words "Suspect in custody." He had no idea what the statement pertained to but he decided to call the dispatcher out of curiosity. "Sally this is Sean, come back." The radio crackled again. "We've been trying to get a hold of you. What's your twenty, over?"

He felt a small surge of adrenaline. "I'm about twenty minutes from the office, over." The radio crackled again. "They're bringing in a suspect on your murder case. Their ETA is about five minutes, over." He took a long slow breath trying to calm himself. "Roger."

He hooked the receiver back up and took another deep breath. "This might not even be the right guy," he thought to himself.

When he arrived at the station the two news stations already had reporters waiting outside the station trying to get information. He was surprised at the fact Pam wasn't one of them waiting to stick a microphone in his face. As he started to approach the entrance he felt a little bit of concern about the fact she wasn't there.

It was good in one sense. When she was around he always tried to be extremely polite because they were involved in a relationship. As a result some of the other news personnel got a little more courtesy than they should have. He didn't want it to seem like he was playing favorites with Pam, even though in the beginning no one knew they were dating. Their relationship was slow in forming, but eventually they started going out more and more together.

Bruce Garvey, one of the most annoying and persistent reporters in town, spotted Sean as he approached. "Detective Richards, Detective Richards," he shouted as he approached. The cameraman was right behind him and flipped on the camera light and began filming.

The detective squinted as the camera pointed directly at his face. He could hardly make out the reporter as he approached but he could certainly hear him. "Is it true you have the murder suspect in custody?" The detective put his hand up to block the light from the camera. "Not now you idiot!"

The reporter had just started to stick the microphone in his face. The detective raised his elbow forcing the microphone back into the face of the reporter. The reporter obviously wasn't expecting that reaction because he let the microphone get forced back far enough that it poked him in the eye.

The detective just continued on his way inside the building, despite the cuss words coming from the reporter. Just inside the door was a police officer.

"How long have they been out there?"

The policeman looked at his watch. "I'd say about fifteen minutes. They were waiting as they brought the suspect in. They must have a police scanner or something."

The detective turned and looked back through the doors. The reporter was still there and gave him the finger. He just ignored it and turned back to the officer. "Where is he now?" The officer saw the reporter give Sean the finger but since he wasn't too upset about it he didn't ask what it was about. "He's in cell number three. We've got him I.D.'d and finger printed already."

"Has he made a statement or anything yet?"

"No, but he did call his attorney. He said he'd be here in the morning."

The detective liked what he heard so far. "Good, why don't we see what information we can get out of this guy before he lets his lawyer do all the talking."

Chuck Adams came walking through the main doors. Sean was really surprised to see him. "Chuck, what the hell are you doing here?"

"They called my house looking for you but by the time I got in the house and got the message, you were already gone."

Sean was still a little confused. "Yeah but that still doesn't explain why you're here."

"Oh, well Jerry's on vacation starting tomorrow, and since we're the only two investigators, I figured I'd check out the vehicle so he wouldn't have to mess around with all that paperwork before he leaves town."

The detective smiled slightly. He wondered what angle Chuck was playing on this one. He never did anything for free, and usually came out on the better end of the bargain. But to be fair, if Chuck was the one who owed the favor he always came through.

"I've got to get whatever info we have rounded up right now. I didn't even know there was a vehicle." Chuck nodded his head in agreement. "Yeah it's a dark SUV, just like the sheriff said." Sean felt his pulse quicken again. He finally seemed to be getting somewhere in the case.

Michael was led to a small room and they handcuffed him to the chair. He couldn't understand why they were being so cautious with him. "A little extreme don't you think?" The officer never said a word. He just turned and left the room.

Michael glanced around the room. He began to feel like something wasn't right. If his sister had him arrested for theft, what was the point of handcuffing him to the chair? There certainly wasn't anything he could steal in this room. It just had the two chairs and a small table.

He had a few minutes to sit there and think about it before the door finally opened. The officer that had handcuffed him to the seat was holding the door open as a man about Michael's age entered the room. He was looking down into a file folder as he entered and glanced briefly over the top at Michael. He continued to look at the folder as he pulled his chair out.

127

He set the folder down as the officer closed the door and waited outside.

"I'm Detective Sean Richards."

Michael raised his left hand so the detective could see the handcuffs. "I'd shake your hand and introduce myself, but I'm sure you already know who I am." He raised his other hand so the detective could see that it too was cuffed to the chair. "A little extreme for a burglary suspect don't you think?" The detective leaned back in his chair. "Burglary? Whoever said you were here on burglary charges?" Michael let out a small chuckle of laughter. "Alright then, how much is my sister paying you to put me through all this?"

The detective was looking him right in the eye. He was trying to get a gauge on whether he really didn't know why he was there or just acting like it. "So you're telling me that you have no idea why you're here?"

Michael turned his palms upward. "If it's not one of the ideas I just gave you then the answer is no." He still had a slight grin on his face waiting for the detective to give in and admit his sister put him up to it.

The detective scribbled a note on a piece of paper. Michael couldn't read it from his vantage point. "Are you going to tell me why I'm here or do I get to keep guessing until I get it right?" The detective raised his head from the note he was writing and looked Michael directly in the eyes again. "You were brought here because you are a suspect in a murder investigation." The little grin had disappeared from Michael face. Now he was trying to read the detective to see if he was serious. "Murder? You're joking right?"

The detective pulled something from the folder and slid it toward Michael. He left his fingertips at the edge of the piece of paper. "Would you say this looks like you?" Michael looked at the paper. It was a sketch, and for the most part it did look like him. "Yes," he replied. The detective pulled it back and slipped it back into the folder.

He pulled something else out and slid it toward Michael. "Do you recognize this woman?" Michael looked at the photograph. It was Jenny. The young girl he had taken to the hospital a few days ago. Now he knew why he was here and it hit him like a ton of bricks.

The detective noticed it right away. "Do you know this woman?" he demanded. Michael looked up from the photo. "Yes, I met her a couple of days ago, but I just took her to the hospital because she was about to give birth." The detective never took his eyes off Michael. "Then you know she's dead?" Michael nodded his head yes but didn't say anything. The detective pulled the picture back and put it into the folder. "If you knew she was dead why didn't you stay at the hospital?" Michael thought a moment. "Our meeting was so coincidental, I really had nothing to offer in the way of help. I knew her all of about an hour."

The detective pulled another photo out and slid it in front of Michael. "What about this woman?" Michael looked down at the photo. It was the old woman that had summoned him into the building where Father Reilly lived. "She's dead too?" The detective didn't even bother to answer the question. "I've got people who can place you at the scene in each location." He stared intently into Michael's eyes. "Seems like bodies keep turning up in places you've been."

Michael realized he was in more trouble than he thought. "I don't think I should answer anymore questions until I talk to my lawyer." The detective leaned forward in his chair. "If you're innocent then why do you need to talk to your lawyer? The truth is the truth, and talking to your lawyer won't change that."

He pulled another photo from the file folder and slid it in front of Michael. "What about this guy?" Michael glanced at it. "No." The detective pulled another photo out and slapped it directly over the previous photo. "Well maybe this is how you remember him!"

It was a photo of the same man only this time it was a wider view. His head was tipped back slightly and his mouth was open. You could almost see every tooth in the roof of his mouth, but that wasn't the worst part. His intestines were hanging out of his torso along with several other organs.

Michael's face was not only blank; it was beginning to look a little pale. "Look you've got the wrong guy. I could never do anything like that to another human being." The detective pulled out another photo and slapped it down. "Are you sure about that?" Michael looked down at the photo. It was someone else he didn't know who had their insides hanging out of their body.

Michael turned his head away from the photo. He had seen the insides of deer that his father and brother had gutted and that never made him queasy, but seeing them sticking out of a human just didn't sit well with him. "You've got the wrong guy! I'm not answering anymore questions or looking at anymore photos until my fucking lawyer gets here!"

The detective pulled the photos back and put them back into the folder. "You better get a good nights sleep because we'll be right back at it as soon as your lawyer gets here." The detective kept his eye contact with Michael all through the twenty seconds of silence that followed. The detective finally stood up and went to the door. "Take him back to his cell," he told the police officer as he left.

Chapter 23

Father Davis watched television while Father Reilly slept next to him on the couch in an upright position. He had dozed off about a half an hour ago. He wondered how Father Reilly could even sleep in that position. He watched as he let out a long slow breath and leaned a little further into the corner of the couch. For a second Father Davis thought he might be waking but he just went right back to sleeping.

He was getting pretty tired himself. They had been waiting all day to see if Michael would show up. He felt his eyelids close for a few seconds longer than he thought they would. He knew he couldn't keep himself awake much longer. He couldn't even remember what he had been watching on the TV for the last half hour.

When he looked back at the television there was a breaking news banner scrolling across the bottom of the screen. A reporter broke into the regular programming. It was just enough to keep Father Davis awake. He rubbed his left eye as he listened to what the reporter had to say. "Police have a suspect in custody in the Eagle River murder case." The scene jumped from the reporter to something filmed earlier, but the reporter kept talking over the footage. "The suspect seen here being led into the police headquarters has not been identified yet."

Father Davis recognized Michael right away. The reporter was still talking but Father Davis was already trying to wake Father Reilly. When he woke he heard Father Davis shouting. "Look, look!" He looked at the television but his eyes hadn't focused yet. They had already cut away from the footage and the reporter was already signing off. The station flipped back to the regular programming. "What was it?" Father Reilly asked.

Father Davis pulled himself to the edge of the couch. "You didn't see him?"

Father Reilly sounded grumpy as he responded. "No!"

"It was Michael! They've arrested him as a suspect in the murders."

Father Reilly scowled at him. "Are you sure?"

Father Davis scowled back. "I'm positive."

They were both exhausted. It was leading to some unnecessary tension, so he just took his word for it. "We have to get down there."

Father Davis looked at him curiously. "What are we going to do about it?"

Father Reilly stood up. "I don't know, but that's the least of our problems. I know where Jeremy was going."

Chapter 24

Chuck Adams came back from checking out the SUV. The first thing he did was stop at Sean's desk. It was dark in the entire area except the light from Sean's lamp in the cubicle. "Sorry buddy, but there's not much to tell from the preliminary. I sent some samples down to the lab, but that'll take a couple days." Sean rubbed his forehead. He had been looking over the info he had on the case for the last hour, and his eyes were starting to get pretty tired.

Chuck leaned down on his desk. "You alright man?"

"Yeah, there are just some things that aren't adding up here. Some things point to this guy and some things don't."

Chuck leaned forward and patted him on the back. "Hey, tomorrow's another day man. It might give your mind a rest and allow you some new perspective in the morning."

"You may be right," Sean said as he rubbed his eyes.

Chuck smiled. "I know I'm right."

Sean stood up and grabbed his coat.

He was just about to walk out of the building with Chuck when he saw a familiar face come in the door. He was tired so it took him a few seconds to remember the name. "Father Reilly, right?" Father Reilly smiled. "Yes it is. Detective Richards, I need to talk to you."

Chuck looked at Sean but he was already responding to the question before he could ask it. "Go ahead," he said as he pointed to the door. Chuck paused before pushing the door open. "Are you sure, I can stay if you need me?" Sean continued to point toward the door. "I'll catch you tomorrow." Chuck had already pushed the door open before he even finished the sentence. "See you tomorrow." It was obvious that the offer wasn't as sincere as it seemed, but he knew if he did need him to stay, he would have.

Sean turned back to Father Reilly. "How can I help you?"

Father Reilly hesitated. "Can we speak privately?"

The detective looked around as he responded. "Sure."

Other than a couple of police officers milling around there really wasn't anyone there. He was curious about what he wanted. He led him back to his cubicle and clicked the lamp on his desk back on. He wasn't always the first one in, but he was usually the last to leave.

"Have a seat," he said motioning his hand toward the chair.

Father Reilly sat down. "You've got the wrong man."

The detective didn't expect that statement. "Excuse me?"

"You've got the wrong man."

"Is this your opinion, or are you making a statement?"

Father Reilly leaned forward with a smile. "It's not only my opinion, it's a fact, and if a statement will help get him released…then yes, I will make an official statement."

The detective couldn't help but smile back. He liked the old man's spunk. He pulled a form out of his desk and handed him a pen. "I don't think your statement will be enough to get him released tonight. I've got a meeting with the D.A. in the morning, and then we will find out if he's staying or going."

"Well I'm sure this can't hurt his cause." Father Reilly pulled out his reading glasses.

Sean watched as he began reading the form. "Let me ask you a question."

Father Reilly never looked up from the form. "Sure." Father Reilly set the form down on the table and began to write.

"Why are you so sure we've got the wrong man?"

Father Reilly quit writing for a moment and looked over his reading glasses as he spoke.

"I know who he is and I know his heart. He's not capable of murder."

The detective leaned back in his chair. "How long have you known him?"

Father Reilly wanted to lie, but he wasn't sure if Michael already told him about their relationship. It would ruin both of their credibility right off the bat. "About three days."

The detective leaned forward as he watched him continue filling out the form.

"Three days; and you're trying to convince me this guy hasn't murdered anybody?"

Father Reilly paused. "Yes, he was with me when the most recent murder happened."

Father Reilly continued filling out the statement.

The detective thought about what he said. He remembered how he had run into Father Reilly and his friend at the apartment complex where Mrs. Kalnacheck had possibly been murdered. There was no evidence to suggest murder yet, but the fact Michael was spotted there seemed to be too much of a coincidence. He also remembered seeing John Reilly's name on the nurse's log at the hospital. That was definitely two places that both Michael and Father Reilly could be connected to, but not necessarily at the same time.

"What's your stake in this guy?"

Father Reilly looked at him a little perplexed. "What do you mean?"

The detective paused a moment. "Well you've known this guy for three days, and the murders have been going on for almost three months. You're willing to put your reputation on the line for a guy you've known for three days?"

Father Reilly signed the statement and slid it over as he responded. "Yes."

The detective shrugged his shoulders. "The only way I'd do it is if I knew who the real killer was."

After he made the statement he noticed a slight change in Father Reilly's expression. His instincts told him Father Reilly might know more than he was telling, but he wasn't positive. The detective took the statement and filed it into a bin on his desk.

Father Reilly put his reading glasses away. "Can I talk to him?"

The detective smiled. "Sure." He was hoping that he would ask that question. He led Father Reilly to the interrogation room. "Have a seat right there and I'll have him brought down in a minute." Father Reilly sat down. "Thank you."

Michael sat up in his cell as he heard someone approaching. It was the detective and a police officer. "You have a visitor." Michael stared blankly for a few seconds as he tried to imagine who it could be. "Who is it?" The police officer started to open the cell. "You'll find out when you get there. Now turn around and face the wall, and put your hands above your head." Michael did as he was instructed.

They handcuffed him again and led him back down to the interrogation room. The whole way down he was trying to imagine who it was. His attorney wasn't going to be up until the morning. There was no way Julie could've gotten up here that fast even if she'd found out. He thought maybe it was Margaret finally owning up to her cruel joke on him.

He was a little surprised to find out it was Father Reilly sitting in the room.

"Father Reilly, what are you doing here?"

Before Father Reilly answered the detective interrupted. "Do you want to talk in private?"

Father Reilly smiled. "No, please stay if you like."

The detective pulled a chair out for Michael to sit down in and then motioned for the police officer to close the door. Michael sat down slowly as his hands were still handcuffed behind his back. The detective leaned his back up against the wall.

"You're not afraid to be alone in the room with your new friend here are you Mr. Reilly?"

Father Reilly smiled at him again. "There's nothing I don't want you to hear." The detective crossed his arms. "Then please proceed."

Father Reilly's demeanor turned a bit more serious as he began speaking to Michael. "How are you?"

Michael glazed right over the question because the answer to that one was obvious.

"They think I've murdered people."

Father Reilly nodded his head. "I know, but tomorrow you will get out and our friend here will eventually discover your innocence."

Michael tipped his head back just slightly and glanced up at the ceiling like he was looking for an answer. "What am I going to tell Julie?"

There was a knock on the door. The detective motioned the officer in the room.

"We have something you should check out."

Sean didn't want to ask for details right in front of the suspect. He knew it had to be something important if they interrupted him. He walked out of the room and closed the door behind him. He didn't mind leaving them alone in the room because there was a microphone on the underside of the table. The extra perception of privacy might open the conversation a little. He knew the tapes could never be used in court but in some cases they provided new information or leads to help convict suspects.

As soon as the detective left the room Father Reilly pulled a piece of chewing gum out of his pocket and stuck it in his mouth. He glanced over to the window in the door. The officer on the other side of the door was watching him. He held the pack of gum up toward the door. The officer shook his head no. He offered a piece to Michael.

The officer pushed the door open and entered the room. "Sir please don't give anything to the prisoner." He held out his hand. "Do you have anything else in your possession?" Father Reilly looked at him. "Just the gum." The officer flapped his fingers toward himself. Father Reilly handed the pack of gum over.

As soon as the officer turned to leave the room Father Reilly knelt down on the floor and quickly placed the gum over the microphone under the table. When the officer closed the door he peered back through the window in the door. He saw Father Reilly just getting up from his knees. He re-entered the room. "Now what are you doing?"

Father Reilly stood up and held up a wrapper from his piece of gum. "I dropped my wrapper on the floor. I don't want to get arrested for littering or something."

The police officer didn't like the sarcasm. He walked over and snapped the wrapper from his hand. "Now sit down or I'll bring in a pair of handcuffs for you too."

Father Reilly sat down and waited for the officer to shut the door. He knew the officer would be watching again. "Listen, I only have a little time, so please save your questions until tomorrow." Michael nodded in agreement. "When the detective gets back here he's going to give you some news you're not going to like." Michael didn't like the sound of that, but he let Father Reilly continue. "There is nothing you can do about it tonight. You will get out tomorrow, but that's only if he believes that there's a possibility you are not connected with this case." Michael nodded again in agreement. "If we get the police involved and they start snooping around they will kill her."

Michael leaned forward slightly. "Kill who?"

Father Reilly paused trying to figure out how to put it to him. He quickly decided there was no easy way and just told him. "Julie."

The officer watched, as whatever Father Reilly said seemed to agitate the prisoner. "You're telling me they have Julie?" Michael snapped.

Father Reilly tried to reassure him. "Yes, but they won't kill her."

Michael shook his head. "How do you know that?"

Father Reilly glanced over to the window. The officer was still watching. "Please calm down. I can assure you she's alright for now, but you must come see me first thing tomorrow when you get out."

Michael did not respond initially. His face was very red. It was obvious he was seething with anger. "If anything happens to her, I swear to God, or whatever you believe in, evil will be the least of your problems!"

Father Reilly was a little startled by his response. "Michael, I'm trying to help you."

Michael's face got even redder. "You're doing a great fucking job so far. I'm a murder suspect! I'm sitting in jail, and now you're telling me they've kidnapped Julie!"

Father Reilly got a little red in the face himself. "If it wasn't for me, you'd both probably be dead by now!"

They turned simultaneously as they heard the door open. The detective re-entered the room. There was nothing but silence for 10 seconds. "Am I interrupting something?" he asked. Father Reilly responded. "No, we're finished." Father Reilly yawned, and then stood up and stretched. "It's way past my bedtime." The detective was pretty tired himself and Father Reilly's yawn didn't help.

He motioned for the officer to enter the room. "Can you please escort Mr. Reilly to the door?" The officer led Father Reilly out of the room.

As soon as they left the detective turned to Michael. "I just got a report from the Langston police department. Do you live alone Mr. Foster?"

Michael replied immediately. "No I live there with my fiancé. I just asked her to marry me yesterday." The detective rubbed his chin. "Well can you tell me why she'd leave the television on and the back door open as of 11:00 p.m.?"

Michael tried to act surprised because he already knew what was coming. "No, why?"

The detective started looking at a piece of paper in front of him. "Neighbors report hearing a gunshot and a car speeding off from your premises. You wouldn't know anything about that either, would you?"

Michael's face appeared to be a little red in color when he entered but now it was a pale white. "No."

"Are you sure?" the detective asked.

All Michael could think about now was Julie being shot. "Was there blood or something?"

The detective thought that was a very odd question. "Why do you ask?"

Michael leaned forward. "She's my fiancé! Are you telling me she's been killed, or missing?" The detective thought the concern was genuine so he decided to give him the facts. "There was no blood." He could see a definite sign of relief on Michael's face.

"It is odd however, that the door was open and the television and a few lights were left on, and no one was home." Michael just sat there quietly. The detective put the piece of paper away. "Do you know of her whereabouts?"

Michael tried to explain it as best he could so the detective wouldn't become suspicious. "She went out with a friend to celebrate our engagement. She probably left the lights and TV on to scare off any potential burglars. As far as leaving the back door open, our air conditioner is broken and she was probably trying to keep the house cool."

The detective pulled out a small notepad. "Do you have this friends name?"

Michael nodded his head. "Yeah it's Kathy."

The detective looked up from the notebook. "Do you know her last name?"

Michael paused. "I think it's Peterson but I'm not really sure. She's a friend of Julie's. I've only met her once." He lied about her last name just to keep the detective busy in case he did go looking for answers there.

The detective scribbled down some information in the notepad and then looked up. "Okay last question. Why are you here instead of celebrating with your fiancé?"

Even though it didn't answer the question directly, he thought it was important to give the detective a good reason. "I was up here to spread my brother's ashes. We grew up just on the outskirts of town. He asked me before he died to spread his ashes in a couple of places. Well I accidentally spilled all I had, and my sister is the only one who had any besides me. My sister and I don't get along too well, so when I tried to get more of the ashes from her we had a fight. Her husband gave me the ashes against her wishes, and so I thought she called the police and had me arrested for stealing them."

The detective had already seen the statement from Michael's sister. It did seem to substantiate his story. "Is there anything else?" Michael asked. The detective was beyond being tired and he knew he was going to have to be in early. "No, that's it." He motioned for the police officer to come back in the room. "You can take him back to his cell."

The detective left the room and started walking back to his cubicle to get his jacket. He almost forgot to go back and check out the tape of the conversation he had missed between Michael and Father Reilly. He was really tired now but his curiosity was winning the battle.

He entered the taping room and shut the tape machine off. Normally there was someone there to operate it, but due to the late hour no one was around, so he just walked in and pushed the record button and let it run.

He rewound the tape a little bit and pushed play. No sound was playing. He thought he had rewound it enough to at least hear something. He pushed the rewind button again and let it run for several minutes. He pushed the play button. Now there were voices on the tape.

He heard the police officer ask Father Reilly not to give anything to the prisoner. "Do you have anything else in your possession?" the officer asked. "Just the gum," Father Reilly replied. There were sounds of movement but no voices. Then there was a squishy and muffling sound and then nothing.

He listened for about 30 seconds before he came storming out of the taping room. He hustled down the hallway and flung the door open to the interrogation room. He knew right where to go. He felt under the table and got a sour look on his face as he pinched the gum off the microphone. He held it up to his face and summed up his anger in one word. "Fuck!"

Chapter 25

Julie slowly came back into consciousness. She couldn't see, even though she knew she had opened her eyes. She then realized something was over her eyes. She went to reach with her right hand to pull it off but it came to an abrupt stop. Something was around her wrist. She tried to reach it with her left hand but it too came to an abrupt stop. She was still a little out of it but slowly she realized she was restrained.

Her brain processed more and more information with every passing second. Wherever she was, it was cool and musty smelling. Now she realized she was in an unfamiliar place. She was lying on her back on what she assumed was the floor.

Like an instant replay, the events of what probably led to her being in this condition, came flooding back into her head. She heard herself begin to breathe heavy. Anxiety was beginning to set in. Wherever she was it was very quiet at the moment.

She attempted to move her arms again but with the same result. She thought for a brief moment about screaming for help, but without knowing where she was she decided it wasn't a good idea. Then another thought entered her head. "What if he's sitting here watching me right now?" She used the tension in the straps on her wrist to help get her to an upright position. "Too late now," she thought to herself.

She leaned forward again using the tension in the straps to keep her from landing on her face. She slowly bent her arms behind her. She used the floor and gently rubbed her head from side to side. The blindfold inched its way up her forehead. She was sure she was making progress but she still couldn't see anything. She finally got it to slide mid way up her forehead but she still couldn't see anything.

There were only two possibilities. Either she was in a very dark place or she was blind. She strained to see anything. There appeared to be a very small and dim strip of light coming from what could've been a doorway. She wondered if her mind was playing tricks on her. She was straining awful hard to make something out.

She heard a creak on the floor overhead. She let out a small gasp and backed against the wall. She still wasn't sure where she was, but the creak from overhead and the musty odor led her to believe she was probably in a basement.

She pulled on her restraints again but it was no use. The more she pulled, the tighter the restraints got. She could feel her circulation being cut off. She relaxed her arms and the restraints loosened just enough to allow the blood flow to resume. She used her fingers to feel what it was that was restraining her. It was some kind of leather strap.

She heard more creaking on the floor. Her brain instantly shut off the feel of the leather straps as she strained to hear anything beyond the creaking floor. Between the darkness and the silence she felt as though it wouldn't be long before she went insane. She had no idea what time or day it was, or even where she was for that matter.

She remembered being attacked from behind and smelling something before she passed out. All kinds of questions started to enter her mind, but unfortunately not many answers. There were only two things she knew for sure. She wasn't at home, because their basement didn't smell like this. The second was at least she was still alive.

Again the floor creaked. She tried to imagine what was going on up there. She never came close to the truth.

Jeremy was pacing back and forth. He had just finished telling his mother about the vision of his father and how he was instructed to go get this woman and bring her to his mother. "He said I had a chance to make things right."

His mother was supposed to be at the hospital, but when Jeremy came home with this woman she was furious. She immediately called in sick because she knew she had to deal with this new dilemma.

She was still very angry, but after Jeremy had mentioned the vision of his father she realized he had a vision like several she had. Jeremy continued pacing and explaining. "He said this woman was carrying a child with the same powers, and if I brought her here, you would know what to do."

Jeremy waited for a reaction but there was none. His mother just sat there with the same stern look on her face the whole time. "Go and check on her." His pacing was driving her nuts. Jeremy nodded and headed straight for the basement.

She had been instructed what to do with the first child, but she wasn't so sure of these new events. She knew Jeremy had to be telling the truth because some of her visions also came from her dead husband.

Julie heard an odd clicking sound. She turned her head in the direction of the sound. The strip of light that she thought was a door suddenly widened. The light on the other side of the door was very dim. She felt more fear at this point then she ever had in her life.

She watched as a hand reached into the room and began sliding up and down the wall like it was trying to find something. She heard another click sound. The room went from pitch black to bright white in a matter of seconds. Her eyes started stinging immediately.

She tried to keep them open as whomever it was entered the room but all she could manage was a very hard squint. She couldn't see any detail, but she could see just enough to tell they were moving toward her. She pressed herself back against the wall but there was nowhere to go.

The room went black again. "No peeking," a male voice whispered as he pulled the blindfold back over her eyes. "What do you want from me?" she pleaded.

Jeremy leaned in very close and when he started speaking it startled her.

"You're going to help me make them go away," he said smiling. She felt like she was going to push herself through the wall. "Make who go away?" she asked nervously.

To her surprise Jeremy's voice came from the left side. Between her breathing and her heartbeat it made it hard to hear the softer sounds in the room. "Don't pretend you don't know why you're here!"

She tried to slide herself away from him. Without the benefit of her sight she felt like she moved a foot away, when in reality it was barely an inch. Julie could tell that whoever this was, they weren't very stable.

She really had no idea what was going on but she decided to try to play along.

"I want to help you. Just tell me what to do. I can help you." There was nothing but silence for about twenty seconds. "All you need to do is be quiet and stay alive. You're going to be here for a while."

Julie felt him grab her arm. Suddenly she got a painful sensation in her bicep. She then felt him rubbing it with something. He had obviously injected a needle into her. She heard him walking away. What little light she could see from under the blindfold was extinguished with a click sound. She heard him close the door.

All she could think about at this point was Michael. She tried to be strong, but she had a terrible feeling she was never going to see him again. She couldn't hold it in anymore. Tears began to flow from under the blindfold. She could feel the effects of the injection taking over. She tried to resist it but there was nothing she could do. Slowly all her thoughts drained away, and she was out again.

Chapter 26

Michael woke from a terrible nightmare. There was no sound in the dream. He saw Julie tied up and blindfolded on some sort of platform. Jeremy was there milling around a table. He walked over to Julie and started removing her clothes. She wasn't showing any emotion or reaction. He spun her legs over the edge of the platform and made her sit upright as he continued removing her clothes. He watched as Jeremy began to caress her breast. Jeremy licked her cheek. She still showed no reaction.

Jeremy began removing his own clothes. Michael could feel the rage building inside him, but he felt powerless to stop it. Jeremy finished removing his clothes and then stepped toward Julie. He gently pushed her onto her back. Jeremy began thrusting his pelvis into Julie's.

With every thrust of Jeremy's pelvis Michael became more and more angry. Jeremy put his hand around the back of Julie's neck and lifted her head off the floor. Her head appeared to tip back in ecstasy. Just as Michael felt like he was going to be able to do something, he saw Jeremy raise a knife and plunge it directly down into Julie's chest.

He was wide-awake now. He was surprised he had fallen asleep at all. He had been tossing and turning all night. He figured it was just a nightmare because he had been thinking about her almost the whole night, but still he couldn't shake the thought that it could've been a vision of an event that already happened, or was going to happen.

He could feel the anger he felt in his dream creeping back into his mind. He rubbed his forehead. He had to let the anger go. He wouldn't allow himself to believe it had already happened. He knew he would go crazy if he allowed himself to believe it. "She's still out there and it's up to you to save her," he thought to himself. He cupped his hands together and then put his head down and rested his forehead on them.

Just as he was wondering what time it was he heard the door open at the end of the hall. He jumped up and waited by the entrance to the cell. It was his attorney being led by a police officer to his cell. "Please tell me you can get me out of here," Michael pleaded as he approached. His attorney smiled. "I haven't had a chance to look at everything yet, but I'm sure I can get it done." Michael stuck his hand through the bars. "Thanks for coming down so early." His attorney took his hand. "Everything will be fine, just be patient my friend."

If only his attorney knew the real circumstances, he wouldn't sound so condescending.

"I at least should be able to get you out of here on bail." Michael never changed his expression. "I don't care how you do it, just get me out of here." There was an odd silence for about five seconds.

His attorney had seen him many times and never saw him look this serious before. He tried to lighten the mood a little. In his best Italian accent he said, "Forget about it. Joey D's on the job." Michael couldn't help but let a small grin appear on his face. Joe Dumbrowski was hardly an Italian name.

He had met Joe through his brother Mark. Along with being an attorney he was one of Mark's best friends. He handled all of his brother's legal affairs before his death. It was the first time in a while since things had started happening that he even thought about his brother. "I'm going to head down to the court house and meet with the D.A. and then we'll know more." Michael nodded in acknowledgement. "Thanks Joe."

He watched as the police officer and his attorney disappeared out of sight. He heard the door close at the end of the hall. He stepped back and sat on the bed. He put his hands on each side of his face and rested his elbows on his knees. Now he was thinking about his brother and Julie. It didn't take long for his thoughts to turn completely to Julie. He was already sick of being in the cell. The only thing that kept him from losing it was the belief he was going to see Julie again.

Father Reilly was hustling up the block to catch up with a man that had come out of the police station. "Excuse me," he said as he caught up to the man. "Are you Michael's attorney?" The man looked him up and down. "Yes I am, and you are?"

Father Reilly held out his hand. "John Reilly," he said with a smile. "I have some statements from people, including myself that can prove Michael's whereabouts during one of the suspected murders." The attorney thumbed through the papers.

Father Reilly pointed to the top one as the attorney got ready to slip them into his brief case. "She works at the convenience store about eight blocks west of here. She checked us out with a jar of pickles about the same time they think one of the murders took place." The attorney nodded. "Good, we can use these." Father Reilly smiled. "Anything I can do to help."

The attorney realized he hadn't introduced himself. "I'm sorry. I'm Joe Dumbrowski." They shook hands. "How do you know Mike?" Father Reilly thought for a moment.

"We met through mutual circumstance."

The attorney didn't expect such an ambiguous statement, but he let it slide. He had other things to deal with right now. "I'm heading down to the courthouse, so I apologize for having to be so brief." Father Reilly smiled. "No problem." The attorney turned slowly away to head toward his car. "Thanks for your help Mr. Reilly."

———————————

Michael sat in his cell for what seemed like an eternity. He had paced and sat down, paced and sat down. Now he was pacing again almost covering every square inch of the cell. He wasn't claustrophobic or anything but every time he walked the length of the cell he seemed to arrive at each corner faster and faster. It did feel as if the cell was closing in on him.

He wished there was some music or something other than the sound of his feet shuffling against the pavement. It was time to sit down again. He started thinking about Julie again and what he was going to do once he got out. He had already gone over it a dozen times but at this point there was nothing else to do.

He heard the door open at the end of the hall. He waited at the door of his cell. It was his attorney and the same police officer that led him there earlier that morning. The police officer unlocked the cell. Michael stood there for a second not sure if his attorney was coming in or if he was being released and could leave. "Come on," his attorney said gesturing with his hand for Michael to step out.

Michael left the cell rather fast, like he couldn't wait any longer to get out. His attorney tried to keep pace as he marched down the hallway to the door. He felt his attorney put his hand on his back as he caught up. "Listen, we need to go somewhere where we can talk in private." Michael just kept marching down the hall to the door. He tried the handle but it was locked. "Excuse me," the officer said as he brushed by Michael to unlock the door. The attorney stepped aside to give him just a little more room.

The officer opened the door and Michael was the first one through. His attorney hustled to keep up. "We have to check you out over here, and then we can go." They approached a small window with an old man sitting behind it. He must have known Michael was coming because he already had a manila envelope on his desk. "Sign here," said the old man.

Michael didn't even look at what he was signing. He just scribbled his name and looked up. They just stood there looking at each other for a few seconds. Michael finally broke the silence. "What?" The old man pointed to the piece of paper. "You owe $110." Michael just stared blankly ahead. "What the hell for?" The old man pointed to the paper again. "For having your vehicle towed here." Michael tried to remain as calm as possible. "You've got to be kidding me?"

"Nope." The old man seemed to be enjoying Michael's frustration a little too much.

Michael knew he wasn't going to stay calm for too much longer and the old man's smirk didn't help him much either. "How the hell do you expect me to pay for it when my wallets in there?" he said pointing to the manila envelope on the other side of the glass.

Before the old man could even respond his attorney slapped a hundred, and a twenty-dollar bill on the counter and slid it under a slot in the window. He could sense Michael's frustration. Before Michael could even thank him he started speaking. "That's nothing, wait till you get my bill." Joey D had a good way of bringing humor into almost any situation.

The old man placed the envelope on the counter and slid it through to the other side. Michael opened it and put this watch on and grabbed his car keys and slid them into his pocket. He then glanced through his wallet to make sure everything was there. The old man handed Joey D his change and a receipt.

As they walked from the police station over to the impound lot Joey D filled him in on a few details. "Just so you know you can't leave town." Michael just kept walking as if he hadn't heard a single word his attorney had said, even though he had. "Are you listening to me?"

"Yeah, I'm just in a hurry." Joey D was beginning to breath heavy trying to keep up. "They don't have enough to charge you with anything yet, but they are damn close."

His attorney was tired of trying to keep up. He pulled Michael to a stop. "There's something you're not telling me. Are you sure everything is okay?"

"I appreciate you getting me out of there. So far you've done everything I've needed, but right now you are going to have to trust me. You're better off not knowing everything."

Michael watched as both a look of confusion and concern came over Joe's face.

"I promise you I didn't murder anybody. I just have a few things to take care of." He said it with a smile, which seemed to put Joe a little more at ease.

"Where are you going to be staying?"

Michael continued to smile. "I'm staying with a friend."

Joe wanted more detail than that. So he started fishing because he knew Michael was being vague for a reason. "John Reilly?" he replied.

The smile slowly drifted off Michael's face. "You know Father Reilly?"

"Well I just met him this morning. He gave me some statements that helped convince the D.A. they didn't have enough to charge you with."

Michael just stared off like he was deep in thought. "That's where I'll be."

Joey D was finally breathing normal again. "Now listen to me carefully. I want you to stay there. They could have held you longer if they wanted to. If they put together enough evidence to charge you, I need to know where to find you." He pulled a business card out of his pocket and began writing on the back. "I'm staying at the Ambassador Motel off Grand. If you need anything, call me."

"Thanks Joe," Michael said as he reached out and took the card. Michael turned to walk away. "This will all be over in a couple of days," his attorney said with a raised voice. Michael raised his hand slightly acknowledging he heard the remark. Michael had a feeling deep down that it was all going to be over tonight.

Chapter 27

Detective Richards pulled up in front of Pam Theisen's house. He walked up and rang the doorbell. It took a little while for her to answer. When she opened the door she was shocked to see him. "Sean, what are you doing here?"

He smiled. "I just came over to see if you were okay."

She smiled back shaking her head from side to side. "Jesus, I look terrible. I don't have my make up on, my hair's not done."

"You look good to me."

She liked the flirtatious way he said it. "Do you want to come in?"

He started stepping inside. "Sure, just for a minute."

Pam turned and headed into the kitchen. "Would you like some coffee?" He pulled out a chair from the kitchen table and sat down. "No thanks, I've had three already." He watched her pour herself a cup of coffee. "I was a little worried when you weren't at the station trying to pry information out of me last night." She turned around with a cup of coffee in her hand and pulled out a chair for herself. "I quit my job yesterday." Sean was caught a little off guard. "What?" She took a sip of her coffee. "I was going to tell you but I didn't think you would notice so quickly." Sean smiled at her. "I'm a detective, it's my job to notice the little things."

Pam took another sip of her coffee. "This could use a little more sugar." He watched as she got up and returned to the counter. "So why did you do it." She glanced over her shoulder. "You're the detective, figure it out." He couldn't help but smile at her sarcasm. "You didn't have to do it for me." She turned back around and sat down. "I did it for us. I was getting tired of chasing people around and getting nowhere anyway. Besides now there's no conflict of interest between us."

Sean didn't know what to say but he figured he better say something. "You didn't have to quit your job. We could've worked it out eventually." Pam gave him a slight grin as she took another sip of coffee. "Oh yeah, it's going real swell so far." Sean reached out and grabbed her hand. "Are you sure you want to do this? I know how much you really loved your job." She squeezed his hand. "Yeah, but a job can't love you back." Again Sean didn't know what to say.

He knew she was making a huge sacrifice. He thought about what she said. He did love being a detective, but he never felt the same at his job as he did when he was with Pam. "Well what are you going to do now then?"

She knew that question was coming but she still hadn't figured out a way to tell him yet. She took a sip of her coffee and continued to hide behind the cup while she thought about how to tell him.

She put the mug down. "I'm going to accept a job hosting a morning show with one of our affiliates." Sean smiled unaware of the landmine in the field of conversation. She smiled back somewhat sheepishly, which he immediately picked up on. It caused him to take that one more fatal step into the conversation. "What is it?" She fidgeted with her coffee. "It's in Santa Fe, New Mexico."

He felt as though a piece of shrapnel tore completely through his heart. He sat there silent and a little confused. Up until this point, everything was looking up. "I don't understand." She was glad to see him so concerned. "I'm flying there next week to sign the contract. I won't start for like a month, so it will give me a little time to find a place and…" Sean interrupted her. "Why?"

She was still fidgeting with her coffee mug as she spoke. "We haven't been doing so well lately. I know it's my fault. I never should've done what I did, but I can't change it. I'm tired of feeling terrible over what happened. I need to change something before I go crazy." Sean let out a sigh. "You said you did it for us. I don't see where I'm going to benefit from this."

She could tell the conversation was about to become a little more heated but she just couldn't help herself from adding to the friction. "I won't be around to interfere with your work." She could tell right away that he was irritated by her comment. "God damn it, you know that's not the only reason." She sat up more erect. "What exactly are the reasons?"

Still irritated he sat there collecting his thoughts but before he could even speak she interrupted. "I'll give you the first one. I made a stupid mistake and got you into trouble at work." She leaned back and continued the count for him. "Two." He still hadn't lost the irritated look. "I've been busy with the case…" She interrupted him. "Work." Now the irritated look turned a little more to confusion. "What?" he said. "Please continue," she replied. Now he was back to the irritated look. "I've been exhausted everyday. I'm putting in overtime trying to catch a break in the case." She leaned forward in her chair. "Work."

This time he caught the drift. "Look, this isn't what I wanted to happen."

She stayed completely calm the whole time, which only added to his irritation.

"A relationship is not just something you can put off to the side and expect it to be the same whenever you decide to get back to it." He suddenly wasn't in the mood to argue anymore. "I get your point. I don't want you to leave." He looked down at his watch. "I have to go. Please promise me that you won't sign anything until we are able to finish this conversation." She watched him stand up but she made no indication of a promise with a look or a word.

She took a quick sip of her coffee and got up to walk him to the door. He took a hold of her arm and pulled her to him. He wrapped his arms around her and pulled her even closer so they were face to face. "I thought about you everyday. It made me realize I love you. I know that sounds weird, but I realized you were filling a void in my life. I can't just let you go now without admitting how I really feel."

Pam's expression didn't change a bit. In all the time they had been together neither of them had told the other that they loved them. She thought that stage would eventually come into the relationship but not now after what they'd been through.

She just stood there staring into his eyes. He didn't quite know how to read her reaction. "I really have to go," he said as he kissed her on the forehead. She followed him to the door. She watched him get in his car and pull away.

Before Pam came into his life all he had was his job. Now he realized he was going to have to learn to manage both. That is if it wasn't already too late. He was hoping deep down that it wasn't, but for now he couldn't help but give his job priority. Even at the expense of his personal life.

Chapter 28

Michael had just arrived at Father Reilly's. Even though he hadn't gotten much sleep, he felt very anxious and alert. "So what do we do?" Father Reilly shook his head. "I'm sorry, but for now we just wait." Michael became a little more irritated than he already was because Father Reilly had already refused to tell him where Julie was. Father Reilly didn't want him rushing over there trying to do everything himself. He could sense Michael's intention just by how zealous he was to do something right away. Father Reilly tried to reassure him. "I promise you Julie is fine and we will do everything in our power to get her back, but now is not the time."

There was a knock at the door. Father Reilly went to the door and answered it. It was Father Davis. Michael could hear them talking softly as they entered but couldn't make out anything that was being said.

Michael watched as Father Davis led Father Reilly to the window. "Right over there." He heard Father Davis say as he pointed through a slit in the curtains. Father Reilly pulled it open just a bit further. He motioned for Michael to come over. "Look through the curtains here. There's a white van about four vehicles down."

Michael peered through the curtains as Father Reilly began speaking again. "The police have us under surveillance."

Michael pulled away. "How do you know that?"

Father Davis took over the explanation. "I saw them bringing a boat load of food into the van, and they were too well dressed to look like they've been living out of there for too long." Father Reilly injected his thoughts. "That would explain why they were so willing to let you go so easily. They just follow you around hoping you will lead them to more concrete evidence."

Father Reilly put his arm around Michael and led him away from the window. "It'll be easier to sneak out once it's dark, and that'll give us time to prepare." Father Davis nodded in agreement as they headed to the couch.

"There are some things I need to explain to you," Father Reilly said as he took his place on the couch. "It's not like we have a lot of experience with this type of thing. A lot of it is learning as you go.

Sometimes I have visions that provide me with answers, and sometimes I have to rely on my instincts."

Michael thought back to his dream he had while he was in jail. Was that a vision of things to come he thought to himself? Father Reilly continued to speak unaware that he had momentarily lost Michael's attention. "I've come to realize that the energy I've been speaking of isn't good or evil. It is just energy. We are actually the ones who will determine if the energy is used for good or evil. That's why they kidnapped Julie, and that's why I know she's all right. They can't kill her because they need the baby, and it's obviously going to be a while before she gives birth."

Michael knew most of what Father Reilly had already told him had turned out to be true. He was hoping he was right in this case too. That would mean there was a chance to save Julie, but he was still a little confused. "Why did they kidnap her, I thought they already had a child with powers?" Michael noticed a change in Father Reilly's demeanor.

"Something happened that changed that." Michael wanted him to elaborate but the look on his face made him think that maybe it was better if he didn't. Besides his main concern was with Julie. Her being pregnant was so new to him he never thought to be concerned about their child she was carrying. "I just want to get Julie back alive. That's all I'm asking."

Father Reilly could see the concern on his face. He reached out and touched Michael's arm. "No matter what happens I want you to know that evil can never win." Michael wasn't sure if he was just trying to change the subject. "How can you be sure of that?" Father Reilly thought a moment. "In a world where there was only good, just imagine how we would flourish. Good people don't do bad things to good people. In a world where there was only evil, evil would eventually turn on evil. It's just in its nature to destroy, and it would continue to do so until there was nothing left. Unfortunately we live in a world where we have to deal with both. Sometimes it can even be hard to tell them apart. It's a constant struggle, and one day we will get too far down one path to turn around. I think we are being trusted to steer it down the right path."

Michael didn't ask any questions. He just sat there quietly. All he was thinking about was what Julie must be going through. She must be terrified trying to figure out what the hell was happening to her. She was probably wondering like he was if they were ever going to see each other again. Just the thought of not seeing her again made him anxious again. He looked at his watch. He wished he could make time go faster.

Father Reilly decided to keep talking even if Michael didn't seem interested. "You have a chance to lead the world down the right path." That seemed to have gotten his attention back. "Yeah, but at what cost?" Father Reilly could not argue that point. It was quite a shock and disruption to the life Michael thought he had. "We all have to make sacrifices in life." Michael looked Father Reilly sternly in the eye. "Well I'm sorry but Julie's not going to be one of them."

Before Father Reilly could even react Father Davis stepped in on his behalf. "That's not what he meant. Even the best-laid plans will go to waste when you have opposing forces working against each other. Believe me this is not how it's supposed to be."

Michael leaned back somewhat despondent. "So how was it supposed to be?"

Father Davis was a little irritated by Michael's tone. "Not like this!"

Father Reilly stepped in to try to settle things down a little. Everyone was a little on edge, and for good reason. He knew Michael was not going to calm down without a better explanation. "The children, when old enough, would begin to slowly divide the world over the course of their lives. One leading down a path of prosperity and unity, and the other to a path of disparity and singularity." Michael looked at each of them. "Wouldn't just about everyone want the path of unity and prosperity?" Father Reilly shook his head no. "You'd be surprised by the number of people who would do something that would benefit them, no matter how many were left behind."

Michael knew what he meant. There were plenty of people he had known in his life that would fit in that description. "What about these special powers?" Father Reilly and Father Davis had talked a lot about this topic so Father Davis felt comfortable handling the question. "To be honest we can't be sure but we think it will be more about influence, rather than power. There may be some capabilities beyond that, but we can't be sure what they are."

Father Reilly reached out and touched Michael's arm to get his attention. "There has been a precedent for this sort of thing." Father Reilly gestured with his hand toward Father Davis. "I know my friend here has his beliefs about the last time an event like this took place, but I believe as I told you before that one of the reasons you were chosen was the fact you are not a religious man. There would be no reason for you to exclude anyone because of their religion, race or creed from the powers your child will yield. I was chosen to help you understand that, and to help guide you through this. I wish I could tell you without doubt that everything was going to be all right, but I can't. Nothing is predestined, but I will do everything I can to make things right."

There was nothing but silence for about twenty seconds. Father Davis had already agreed to keep his beliefs out of the matter whether he agreed with Father Reilly or not.

Michael felt Father Reilly touch his arm again. "We have a long wait until dark. We should get some rest. We're going to need it." Michael nodded acknowledging he was listening. Father Reilly tried to smile reassuringly but it just wasn't going to help put Michael at ease. "The couch is good enough I hope?" Michael shrugged his shoulders. "It really doesn't matter, I don't think I will be sleeping much."

Father Davis got up and walked to the window and spoke as he peered through the curtains. "I think I'll go home until its time." Father Reilly walked to the window to have a look too. "I think you should stay." Father Davis turned to his friend. "You've only got room for two people to sleep here. Besides I'd drive myself nuts waiting around here until…" He stopped mid sentence and grimaced slightly. He turned to Michael. "Sorry."

Michael realized he had no choice but to stay. With the police watching him, it might not work out for the best if they got involved now. Father Davis wasn't even sure if Michael had heard him because he gave no reaction to the comment or the apology. "Besides, I don't think they even know why I'm here," he said pointing his thumb over his shoulder in the direction of the undercover van parked out front.

Father Reilly decided to let his friend do as he wished. The last thing he wanted Michael to see was one of their classic disagreements. They could get quite heated from time to time.

Sometimes they just agreed to disagree and left it at that. He had to give Father Davis a lot of credit up to this point. He had kept his promise not to inject his own beliefs on the Christian aspect of the events that were taking place. He knew Michael needed to see that they were in total agreement, even now, or it would ruin both of their credibility. It also would have made it harder for Michael to know what to believe if the people who were supposed to be on his side couldn't even agree.

"I want you to be back here at eight thirty. If you're going to be late, call."

Father Davis smiled. "I'm not the one who's always late."

Father Reilly walked him to the door. Father Davis turned back as he stepped out the door. "Call me if anything changes."

———

The two undercover police officers watched Father Davis come out of the apartment complex. One of them grabbed a clipboard and documented what time he was leaving.

"We're not supposed to follow this guy right?"

The other officer nodded. "Right, only the suspect."

Father Davis got in his car, and then drove past the van. He tried to glance over at the van as he went by, trying not to look like he was looking.

The officers watched him drive past through the large tinted windows in the van. The officer went to replace the clipboard on the hook in the van. There was a loud bang that sounded like a gunshot. It made the officer flinch and he missed the hook completely. "What the hell was that?" The other officer was already trying to see out the window. "I don't know, I don't see anything." The other officer finished hanging up the clipboard and drew his weapon out of its holster. "Go check it out."

The other officer drew his weapon and opened the doors at the back of the van. He turned to his right and peered around the corner of the van cautiously. He saw a puff of white smoke and a car pulling away from the curb and heading down the street. He shook his head and re-holstered his gun. "What was it?" He heard the other officer ask as he climbed into the van. "Just some bucket of bolts back firing."

———————

Father Reilly and Michael had heard the bang from inside the apartment but it wasn't as loud. "What was that?" Michael asked. Father Reilly went to the window to look. He looked toward the van. He saw the under cover look around the corner of the van. He continued to stare out the window for a few more seconds. He watched the officer disappear and then saw the van wiggle slightly as he was obviously getting back in.

"I can't tell, but they don't seem to be concerned about it."

Chapter 29

Father Davis arrived home. He pulled into the garage and closed the automatic garage door. He was more tired than he initially thought. He was glad he had made the decision to come home. It certainly was going to be more comfortable sleeping in his bed as opposed to the floor at Father Reilly's.

As he entered the house through the front door, he felt the need to urinate come upon him. He pushed the door shut and hung his keys onto a hook just to the left side of the door. He walked through the entryway and took an immediate left into the hallway. He relieved himself of some excess fluid and then turned the water on in the sink.

As usual it was too hot when he stuck his hand underneath it to test the temperature. He quickly pulled his hand back and turned the cold up just a little. He laughed at himself. He did the same thing every time he turned on the water. He imagined that it was some cruel experiment, like shocking a mouse every time it went the wrong way in a maze. "Even the mouse would've learned by now," he thought to himself.

After washing his hands he bent over the sink and splashed his face with water. It felt quite refreshing, so this time he cupped his hands and let the water flow to the top. He then splashed the water onto his face and rubbed gently. He blindly reached up and shut off the water. He grabbed a towel off the rack and threw it over his head.

He still had the towel draped over his head, as he turned right out of the bathroom to head toward the bedrooms. He had lived here long enough to know where he was going without the benefit of sight.

He was still dabbing himself off, when he heard an odd popping sound followed by a stinging sensation on his back. Before he knew it he was writhing on the floor uncontrollably. Although he was barely able to control his actions he did manage to roll over on his back. He watched as a shadowy figure approached him down the darkened hallway.

Although he was incapacitated he was conscious. He didn't recognize who it was until he was right over him. Jeremy leaned down so he was face to face with Father Davis. "I know what you did to me!" He pulled a knife out and held it right in front of Father

Davis' face. "You caused me a lot of pain; and worse yet you made mother angry with me."

Father Davis tried to scream out but it just came out as a soft grunt. He tried to move, but all he could manage was very slight movements.

Jeremy was disappointed with how effective the stun gun was. It just made it too easy. He liked the struggle Julie put up when he kidnapped her. It added a level of excitement he didn't expect. He grew more and more confident with each murder. This one, regardless of what his mother told him, would be the last using the stun gun. "I hope you've said your prayers Father."

He plunged the knife deep into Father Davis' abdomen. He watched as Father Davis' eyes widened at the realization of what had just happened. Jeremy slid the knife farther and farther up his abdomen. He watched as Father Davis' eyes began to flutter. He heard a gurgling sound as Father Davis tried to speak. Blood began to trickle from the corner of his mouth. Jeremy smiled at him. "Oh, there's no need to thank me." Father Davis' eyes rolled back with a final shutter, and he was gone.

Jeremy wondered what his last thoughts were. Unlike the others who had no idea who he was, or why they were being killed, Father Davis had the advantage of knowing both.

Jeremy heard the doorbell ring. At first he wasn't sure if that is what he really heard, but there was no mistaking it the second time. "Ding-dong." He jumped up immediately after hearing it again. Blood was running down his hand and dripping off the end of the knife as he slowly made his way toward the door.

Whoever it was gave up on the doorbell and knocked several times on the door. Jeremy was glad he locked the door just in case things didn't go as he had intended. The house was dark so he was hoping there was no indication that anyone was home. The front door had a small window on it but it distorted the image of whoever was on the other side like a mosaic. He watched as the figure backed away from the door. He heard the outer screen door shut.

Jeremy made his way to the living room window. He used the knife that was still dripping with blood to pry the curtains open just slightly. Now he recognized who it was. It was the detective that had questioned him at the bar several days ago. He watched him walk down the driveway.

The detective did sort of a double take as he reached the end of the driveway. He was looking to his left side, right where Jeremy had parked his car. Jeremy had to shift to his right and force the curtains open just a little more to see what the detective was doing. He saw the detective take out a small note pad and a pen. Jeremy wished he knew what he was doing, but he had a bad feeling he already knew.

The detective went to look down the street as he reached the end of the driveway. Something about the car parked there caught his eye. He walked closer to the vehicle. Sure enough the tabs on the license plate were ten years old. He wondered how even in this town someone managed to drive around with expired tabs for ten years.

He wrote down the license plate number and put a note next to it so he could turn it in when he got back to the station. He wished he could write a ticket and slap it on the windshield but that would have to be left to one of the regular patrol officers at the station. At least they wouldn't be getting away it for another year, besides he had more important things to deal with at the moment.

Jeremy cursed under his breath when he saw the detective head for his vehicle. He imagined in his mind that the detective was already on the radio checking his plates. He ran back to the bathroom and began washing the blood from his hands. He cursed at himself for going out in the broad daylight. He was like a fish out of water during the day. At night he could cloak his actions in the realm of darkness. During the day he had to be a lot more careful. Unfortunately for Jeremy, at this point that lesson may have come too late. He didn't even bother to dry his hands. The water felt much the same as the blood did dripping from his hands.

He went back to the window and again parted the curtains just slightly with the knife. He didn't see the detective's car. He widened the gap in the curtains a little more. He still couldn't see any sign of it. He forced them open as far as he dared. It obviously had moved. He swung to the right. He could see his own car. He swung back to his left and opened the curtains farther than he wanted to. There was no sign of the detective.

Jeremy didn't realize until now that he was holding his breath the whole time he was looking out the window. He decided now would be a good time to try to get away.

His mother had no idea what he was up to, and if he got caught now, it would likely ruin everything. He began racing around the house trying to be sure he was leaving nothing behind. He was breathing quite heavily. Partially due to his holding his breath earlier and partly due to panic. He kept imagining squad cars pulling up and surrounding the house.

Then he started thinking about what kind of beating he was in for if his mother found out. He was so distracted by his own thoughts that when he opened the front door to leave, he instantly spun back around and faced the other way. The sun was still high in the sky and what was out there was far worse than squad cars. He reached into his pocket and pulled out his sunglasses. He cautiously walked out of the house closing the door behind him. He glanced all around. There was no one in sight.

He figured if everything went according to plan, Father Davis' body wouldn't be found for a couple of days at the earliest. He was already thinking of alibis, not only for the police, but his mother too.

Chapter 30

Michael couldn't sleep. His mind just kept going over things. He thought about the dream he had when he was in jail. "What if this has already happened to her?" he thought to himself. Father Reilly was sleeping in his bedroom at the moment. Michael couldn't take lying around anymore. He got up off the couch and walked over to the kitchen. He knew the more he waited, the more likely the dream he had in jail could become reality.

His original intention was to go to the fridge to look for something to drink, but when he got there he saw some pieces of paper on the counter. He picked them up and started glancing through them. Most of them were just advertisements that had come from the newspaper. There were a couple of hand written ones but those were just reminders of things to do and a grocery list.

It got him started on some snooping around. He started pulling drawers open in the kitchen. The first one was obviously a junk drawer. It had all kinds of odds and ends in it. He closed it and opened another. That was a silverware drawer. He looked up and saw a note pad next to the phone in the kitchen. He gave up on looking through the drawers and walked over to the notepad. There was nothing written on the top page. He flipped through a couple of pages, but they were blank too.

As he let the pages fall back into place he noticed some indentations on the top page from the previous note that had been written. He held it close to his face trying to identify any words or letters. Frustrated he set it down.

He noticed Father Reilly's jacket hanging over a chair in the small dining area. He walked over and reached into the left pocket. There was a set of keys there. They jingled slightly as he rolled his hand around trying to discover anything else. He then reached into the right pocket. He felt a piece of paper. He pulled it out and unfolded it. He couldn't believe it. Right there on the paper was Jeremy's name and address. It was on a notepad piece of paper with the county hospital logo on it.

He was instantly debating with himself on what to do with this newly found information. He thought about the dream again. What if he waited and he was too late. He knew he wouldn't be able to live with the fact he let that happen to her.

He also knew that if he was going to save Julie he was going to have to be prepared to kill Jeremy. He had never thought of killing anyone before but with the image of his dream still fresh in his mind, it left no doubt he would have the capacity to do it. He could feel himself tensing up just at the thought of Jeremy laying a hand on her.

His mind was made up. He started pulling more drawers open until he found a phone book. He picked up the phone and called a cab company. He instructed them to meet him at a gas station several blocks away. He knew the police were out front watching his vehicle, so he couldn't just stroll out and drive off.

He grabbed the note pad next to the phone and started writing a note for Father Reilly.

"I am sorry for not trusting you, but we both have our agendas. Yours is to save the world at a price I may not be willing to pay. Mine is to save Julie, and for that I am willing to pay the price."

Michael put the phone book back in the drawer and then stood there looking at Father Reilly's bedroom door. He slowly turned and opened the door to the apartment. He stepped out into the hallway and quietly closed the door.

He made his way down to the main floor. He figured if the police were watching the front of the apartment they probably were watching the back too. He was going to have to find another way out. He walked down the hallway to the other end of the apartment. There was a door that had a sign on it. He walked closer and saw it said "Laundry Room".

He could hear a dryer running as he opened the door. He was glad to see two things. First, there was no one in the laundry room, and second, there was a small push out window about six feet off the ground. It was already open due to the temperature in the room. With the dryer running it was still like a sauna even with the window open. There was no wonder as to why no one was there waiting for their laundry to get done.

It looked like the window was just large enough for him to squeeze through. The first thing he had to do was get the screen off. He popped it off pretty easily. He set it on the floor just below the window. He noticed a restraining rod on the window that only allowed it to open about twelve inches. He knew he couldn't fit through the current opening. He grabbed a hold of the restraining rod and snapped it off. He was surprised at how easily it had come off.

The window now swung freely. He set the rod next to the screen on the floor. He jumped up and got his armpits wedged onto the windowsill. With his elbows now hooked on the outside he tried to pull himself up, but with the window swinging freely all he really was accomplishing was rubbing his forehead on the glass. He swung his foot over to the nearest washing machine. He got just enough leverage to force the upper half of his body out the window. He glanced around quickly. There was no one around so he pushed with his arms to force more of his body out the window.

It didn't go quite as graceful as he had envisioned. Before he knew it he was heading face first toward the ground. His feet had flipped over his head, thrusting the window upward as he poured out.

The resulting bang of the window coming back down didn't sound as loud to him as it actually was. He was too busy trying not to get hurt as he rolled onto the grass. He did manage to get his arms out in time to keep from landing on his head. He was fortunate there wasn't pavement just outside the window.

He stood up and rolled his right shoulder around. It was a little sore as it took the brunt of the fall. He winced slightly at the pain, but after a few more rotations it loosened up.

He walked to the rear of the building and peeked around the corner. The police were apparently not so concerned with secrecy at the back entrance. There was a squad car sitting in the far corner of the parking lot. The officer appeared to be facing the other way at the moment. Michael tried to walk over to the sidewalk without looking suspicious. Every step he took made him feel more confident, but he didn't relax until the police car was out of sight. He walked as fast as he could without trying to look like he was in a hurry.

He barely beat the cab to the gas station. He glanced down at his watch as the cab pulled up. It was ten to seven. Michael opened the door and sat in the cab. He pulled the notepad sheet with Jeremy's address out of his pocket. "Seventeenth and Johnson," he said. The cabbie nodded and headed out of the gas station parking lot. "It's a beautiful day isn't it?" the cabbie said trying to make small talk. Michael noticed the cabbie watching him in the mirror. He tried to sound convincing but the half-hearted smile that accompanied the words wasn't very convincing at all. "Yes it is."

The cabbie put his attention back to the road, as he was about to make a right turn.

"I'd be walking on a day like today. You wouldn't catch me wasting my time sitting in a cab on a day like today. No sir."

Most days Michael would have caught the irony in the statement the cabbie just made, but today he had other things on his mind.

The rest of the ride was quiet. It was obvious to the cabbie that Michael was not in the mood for conversation. It was only a couple of miles away, but the silence made it seem a lot longer.

The cab finally pulled over. "Here we are," the cabbie said with a smile. Michael saw the meter read six dollars and seventy-five cents. He took a ten out of his wallet. "Keep the change." He opened the door and stepped out of the cab. The cabbie rolled down his window. "God bless you sir," he said still smiling as he drove off.

Michael had the cab drop him off a couple of blocks away from Jeremy's address. He figured it wouldn't be wise to pull up and just march in.

He started walking toward Jeremy's. As he did, what the cabbie had said as he drove off made him think about Father Reilly. He knew Father Reilly wouldn't be far behind him, even if he waited until dark to come.

Michael thought for a brief moment about just waiting for Father Reilly and Father Davis to show up. But then he started thinking about the dream again. His blood felt as though it was going to boil when he thought about Jeremy laying a hand on her. He realized he needed to calm down. He needed to be rational and not let his emotions get the best of him. He had to focus and be thinking of every scenario.

As he neared Jeremy's house he stopped a few houses away. He decided it was best to do some surveillance first. He had no idea at this point if Jeremy was even home, or if he was alone. He could be standing there waiting for Michael to show up right now. He found a nice spot in some shrubs where he could lay on the ground virtually unnoticed. He had a good view of both the front and rear exit from here. He looked at his watch. He decided if there was no activity around the house for about a half an hour he would try to get in. It wasn't very comfortable lying on the ground in the middle of these shrubs but it was the smart thing to do.

Chapter 31

Detective Richards was sitting at his desk going over some of the documentation in the case again. He had convinced himself he was missing something important in the case. There just weren't enough pieces to the puzzle yet to complete the big picture. He looked at his watch and couldn't believe his eyes. It was 7:30 p.m. already.

He started tidying up his desk to go home when a police officer stepped into his cubicle. "Thanks for the hot tip on that delinquent tax payer who hasn't purchased his tabs in the last ten years." The detective noticed the sarcasm in his voice. "What do you mean?" The policeman laid a sheet of paper on his desk. "Well when we went to the address you gave us, the car was gone. So I ran the plates. Turns out the cars registered to a guy who died ten years ago." The detective smiled as he picked up the sheet of paper. "I guess that would explain why he hasn't purchased his tabs. Well somebody's driving it around." The policeman pointed to the paper in the detective's hand. "Yeah, I'm going to go by the address tomorrow and see if I spot it over there."

The detective looked a little more closely at the information on paper. It was registered to a Larry Evans. The name and address looked familiar. He started to make a mess of his desk again as he began to pull files out and spread them onto his desk. He forgot about the police officer until he spoke. "I'm heading out. We'll see you tomorrow." The detective looked up briefly but the officer had already turned out of his cubicle and was walking away. "See you tomorrow."

He began pulling more files out until he found the one he was looking for. It was a piece of paper he had written some notes on. It had Jeremy Evans address. It matched with Larry Evans. He had scribbled a note down. "Father deceased." He stapled the note and the paper the officer gave him together.

He wrote down a couple of questions about the new information. He wondered if it was just a coincidence that a car either Jeremy or his mother had been driving was parked outside Father Davis' house. He remembered asking Jeremy about Father Reilly but not Father Davis. Maybe Father Davis was playing a larger roll than he expected.

He decided to head home. He had a long day ahead of him tomorrow. He was going to try to get a hold of Father Davis again tomorrow and stop by the Evans' place. He hadn't heard anything from the surveillance team in a while so he decided he would stop by there and get an update before he headed home.

Chapter 32

Michael laid in the bushes for only a few minutes when he noticed some activity at the rear of the house. An older looking woman came out of the back door. He wondered for a moment whether he had the right house. He was about to reach into his pocket for the piece of paper when he saw Jeremy come out a few seconds later. Michael wondered who the old woman was. Possibilities started running through his mind, but when Jeremy kissed her on the cheek as she got in the car; it erased several possibilities. The only one that made sense now was that it must be his mother.

That brought up even more questions. Did she know what was going on? Did she live there, or was she just visiting? He decided at this point none of that mattered. The only thing he cared about was the fact Julie was in there somewhere and hopefully he wasn't too late.

He watched the car drive off and Jeremy re-enter the house. He waited about five more minutes and then made his way toward the house. The sun was approaching the horizon behind him. There was no need for him to turn and look to tell it would be setting soon. His shadow stretched far out in front of him as he headed for the house. Another clue was the soft yellow glow everything had to it.

He began walking around the house trying to get a look into each window as he approached them. There was no way to hide the suspicious prowling around. He had to take the chance no neighbors would spot him snooping around.

All the shades were pulled down on the windows in the house. There was nothing he could do about getting a look into the second story windows. The fact that the woman had just left, meant Jeremy was probably alone in the house with Julie.

He made his way around to the west side of the house again. He could see the sun was just above the horizon now. He knew the sun wasn't going to be providing light for too much longer. He didn't notice any lights on in the house and he didn't want to go in having to turn on every light in the place.

He made his way back to the front door. As he approached it, he doubted now more then ever if he was doing the right thing. The only part of his dream that came back to him was right when Jeremy plunged the knife into Julie's chest. He couldn't stand the thought of thinking he was already too late. He was willing to die trying to save her, rather than living with himself if he was too late.

He tried the door handle. It was unlocked. He slowly pushed the door open. It was hard for him to proceed so cautiously with his heart practically pounding out of his chest. The house was very dark. He stood in the doorway listening for even the slightest sound. His eyes began to adjust to the darkness. There was just enough light coming through the front door so he could make out the layout of the room.

He stepped inside closing the door almost completely behind him. He was worried if he tried to shut it completely that it would make too much noise. He turned and put his back against the wall. He stared straight into the next room trying to detect any movement. Jeremy was in here somewhere so he had to be cautious with every move he made.

He made his way over to the nearest window. He kept his back to the wall and faced the center of the room the entire time. He reached out to the window. He could feel the window shade that was pulled down over the window. He pulled down gently on the shade and let it rise up several inches. It let in just enough light to improve his vision slightly but he still couldn't see to every corner. At this point even the light coming from under the shade would've gotten Jeremy's attention. He pulled down on the shade again and let it slide halfway up the window. He was relieved to discover Jeremy wasn't there.

He still wasn't happy with the amount of light coming in. The next room, which appeared to be a dining room, was still very dark even though the opening between the two rooms appeared quite large. He made his way past a rocking chair and a lamp in the corner of the room, all the while keeping an eye on the next room.

There was a window that faced to the west on the other side of the rocking chair. There was sure to be more daylight allowed in the room by raising this shade. He pulled down on the shade and let it up slowly. It squeaked slightly with every rotation of the roller. He let it all the way up while keeping his eye on the next room. His heart raced as he expected Jeremy to come flying out of the next room at him, but he did not.

He took a split second to look out the window. The sun was halfway over the horizon. He took one more survey of the room to make sure he didn't miss anything obvious. Next to the rocking chair he had just slinked by was a knitting basket. It had a couple of knitting needles and rolls of yarn in it. He glanced around the room some more. The way it was decorated definitely led him to believe it had a woman's touch to it. Besides that Jeremy didn't seem like the knitting type.

He didn't want to bring a weapon with him when he left Father Reilly's apartment just in case the police did manage to apprehend him as he was leaving. He reached down and grabbed one of the knitting needles. It wasn't exactly his weapon of choice, but with many rooms left to search it was going to have to do for now.

He made his way to the edge of the other room. He tightened his grip on the knitting needle as he entered the dining room. There was still no sign of Jeremy. The shades were pulled down in this room too. With the sun going down he opted to turn the lights on. It wasn't going to be providing light for too much longer and he may need to come back this way.

There was at least one more room on this floor to go through. He was sure Jeremy wasn't in this room but he prepared himself just in case the light got Jeremy's attention and he came rushing in from the next room. He reached out and flipped the switch, and then leaned back against the wall with the knitting needle in a ready position.

He waited for about ten seconds. There was a doorway on the east side of the dining room. Michael assumed it was a closet of some kind just due to the minimal space that appeared to be left in the design of the house. He decided to check the main rooms first before he started looking in every nook and cranny the house might contain.

The entryway from the dining room into the kitchen was a little smaller than the previous one. He stepped in front of the entryway and looked into the kitchen. He paused, trying to checkout as much as possible before entering the kitchen. He was gripping the knitting needle so hard it felt as if it were melting in his hand. He realized his right hand was sweating. He was afraid if he ended up using it would slip right through his hand. He switched it to his left hand.

While he stood there wiping the sweat from his right hand he could feel how hot the knitting needle had gotten while gripping it in his other hand. It was almost too hot to hold. He switched it back to his right hand since he had removed the sweat, and it was already use to the temperature.

He entered the kitchen keeping his back against the nearest cabinet while keeping his eye on the room. He noticed a kitchen knife set in the corner of the counter. He set the knitting needle on the counter and grabbed what appeared to be the biggest knife in the set. Satisfied he had a more suitable weapon he continued to prowl along the edge of the counter keeping his back against it. He passed the sink and finally came to the refrigerator.

He saw the door where Jeremy had re-entered the house. It was closed completely. He approached the door and pulled the small window curtain to the side. It was getting dark but there was just enough light for him to be able to tell Jeremy wasn't out there.

He continued past the back door. There was a stairway that led to the second floor of the house. He was about to head up the stairs when he felt the urge to double check where he had been in the house. The last thing he wanted was for Jeremy to sneak up behind him. At least if he saw him coming he had a chance.

He made his way back through the kitchen. He carefully looked around trying to be sure he didn't miss anything. He then re-entered the dining room. He saw the door he assumed was a closet. He hadn't bothered to look in there.

He made his way to the door. He twisted the handle slowly and then yanked the door open. He was surprised to see a stairwell. There was just enough light from the dining room so that he could see all the way to the bottom. There was another door at the end of the stairs. He could see a strip of light coming from the edge of the door. It wasn't closed completely.

He gripped the knife tightly as he descended the stairs. He stayed off to the right trying to avoid the middle of the stairs, where they were most likely to creek. He was moving so slowly it seemed like an eternity before he reached the bottom of the stairs.

He tried to peer through the crack in the door but the light from the room was so bright compared to the darkness in the stairway. He couldn't make out a thing. He gently nudged the door open another inch. He had to squint to keep his eyes from burning. He concentrated on the strip of light trying to detect any movement in the room.

Sensing none he nudged the door open another inch. Now that there was more light coming through on his side of the door his eyes began to adjust. The door was open about two and a half inches. He could see a fair amount of the room now but still not enough to feel comfortable to enter.

He pushed it open another inch. He could see a pair of tennis shoes lying on their side. It took him a second to realize there were feet in them. He pushed the door open a little more. Now he could see the blue jeans that went down to the feet. He was pretty sure it was Julie but with the limited view there was only one way to find out for sure. He pushed the door open another couple of inches. That was all the farther he needed. He could see it was indeed Julie. She was lying on her side facing him. He couldn't tell if she was alive or not. She was blind folded but not gagged. She was wearing her favorite white sweater. It was the exact outfit she had on in his dream.

He slowly pushed the door open just enough for him to squeeze in. He was still squinting quite a bit. He wondered why the room was so damn bright. He also wondered where Jeremy was. He continued to keep a good grip on the knife as he looked around.

He didn't see Jeremy anywhere, but what he did see disturbed him almost as much. There was a bench with many medieval looking torture devices on it. He hoped that Julie was not on the receiving end of any of these. He walked over to a platform that Julie was strapped to. "Julie," he whispered as he approached.

She heard it the first time but thought that her mind had begun to play tricks on her. She heard it a second time and then felt someone touch her arm. She flinched because she didn't expect it to be real. Her reaction caused Michael to flinch himself.

When she heard Michael ask her if she was all right, she instantly began to cry and tried to sit up. She still had some lingering effect from the last injection Jeremy had given her. Michael put his hand behind her head and tried to help her sit up. He could tell she was weak but he wasn't sure from what. Julie tried to reach for him. "Michael," she sobbed.

He was just about to lift her blindfold off her face when the room went black. He heard the door shut behind him. He instantly leapt to his feet. "Michael, what's going on?" Julie cried out. She didn't have the benefit with the blindfold still on of being able to see what was going on, and now neither did he. His only reply to her was "Shhh." She heard him shuffle away. "Michael," she cried softly.

He hadn't moved far from her at all. He was listening as hard as he could. It was the only sense he had left.

Jeremy was so used to sitting in complete darkness he could actually make out Michael's form against the blackness of the room. He could tell Michael was standing still trying to get a bearing on where he was. Jeremy pulled his sunglasses from his pocket and tossed them to the opposite corner of the room. He watched Michael swivel in the direction of the tumbling sunglasses. Michael raised the knife in a defensive position. He still couldn't make out a damn thing.

Jeremy circled slowly like a spider sneaking up on an unsuspecting insect. Michael never saw it coming. Jeremy raised a black leather club high above his head and then swung with all his might. It struck Michael right in the back of the neck. It didn't knock him out but it did stun the hell out of him.

Without the benefit of his vision he quickly became disorientated. He stumbled sideways trying to keep his balance. What the club didn't accomplish the floor did as his head made contact with it. The floor slowly absorbed his consciousness as he struggled to hang on.

Julie started shouting his name again and again, until she felt someone grab her face. "You'll be quiet if you know what's good for you," Jeremy angrily whispered to her.

Julie pulled her face out of his hand. She had no idea what just happened but she was sure it wasn't good for Michael. "Please don't hurt him," she begged. She felt a terrible sting on her face as her head snapped to the side. "Don't tell me what to do!" Jeremy shouted. It took her a second to realize he had slapped her.

She heard him stand up and begin to walk away. Jeremy turned the lights back on. "I don't need anyone else telling me what to do." She assumed Michael was still alive. From what she heard there was no way he could've killed Michael so easily. Had he been stabbed or something there would've been a lot more commotion. Her kidnapper must have surprised him somehow. She decided it would be best to remain quiet rather than risk something worse than a slap in the face.

Chapter 33

Father Reilly awoke a little bewildered. He felt as though he had been sleeping a lot longer than he had intended. He rolled over and glanced at the alarm clock on his nightstand. 8:45 p.m. His intuition was correct. Father Davis should've called by now.

He got up and walked out of the bedroom. He looked around the living room. There was no sign of Michael. He turned and went into the kitchen. When he saw the sheet of paper on the dining room table he instantly felt uneasy. He walked over and picked it up. Almost as quickly as he picked it up, he slapped it back down.

He raced to the phone and tried Father Davis. After the fourth ring he began to mutter to himself. "Damn it Thomas, pick up." After the eighth ring he knew something was wrong. It was not like Father Davis to be late.

It was already dark outside. Michael must have somehow found out where she was. He knew he had to get over there before all was lost. He was in a very panicked state. He had to get over to Jeremy's as fast as possible.

Although he was concerned about what had happened to his friend, he couldn't afford to wait to see if he showed up or not. "Maybe he forgot to call before he headed over," he thought to himself. Deep down he felt as though he was fooling himself, but right now he had enough to deal with, let alone trying to figure out what happened to Father Davis.

He wrote a quick note just in case he did show up. "Gone to the root of evil to save some souls." He set it down next to Michael's note. He left it very vague just in case he didn't come back alive. He figured between the two notes Father Davis would figure out what happened.

Michael had left his keys behind. Father Reilly didn't know whether it was intentional or just coincidence. Either way it was good fortune. He picked them up off the table and slipped into his coat. He headed out the door leaving it unlocked.

As he headed down the stairs he stuck his hands into his coat pocket. He fished around in his pockets as he reached the bottom of the stairs. The note with Jeremy's address was gone. He cursed himself for being so careless. Now he knew how Michael had found out. He couldn't remember the exact address but he did remember how to get there.

He walked out of the apartment complex and walked right up to Michael's Jeep and got in. He was disappointed to find out it was a manual transmission. He had only driven a manual a couple of times in his life. "Just like riding a bike," he said to himself.

He had so much on his mind he had completely forgotten about the surveillance van parked down the street behind him. He put the Jeep in first and lurched ahead as he released the clutch a little soon. Fortunately the vehicle kept moving without stalling. He shifted a little more smoothly into second but still surged slightly as he continued on down the block.

———

Detective Richards was standing outside the driver's side door of the surveillance van. He had been there a lot longer than he had planned. He tried to politely end the conversation several times but the officer kept bringing up new subjects to talk about. It was obvious the officer wasn't looking forward to sitting there for the next six hours by himself.

They only had two officers available until sometime in the early morning, so they split them up. They needed one to cover the front entrance, and one to cover the rear. He had planned to talk to the officer covering the rear, but his time had been so monopolized, he decided to just leave.

Just as he was about to excuse himself, for sure this time, the officer interrupted him. "Hey!" he said pointing toward the apartment complex. The detective watched as Father Reilly got into Michael's Jeep. "Do you want me to follow him?" the officer asked. The detective glanced back to the officer. "No, this might be some kind of diversion. I want you to stay here. If you see the suspect come out, follow him, and call me on the radio. I'll take care of tailing this one."

The detective raced back to his car. As he pulled away from the curb he saw Father Reilly take a right a few blocks ahead. The officer in the van watched him speed by in pursuit.

Chapter 34

Michael finally came to. He had a terrible headache. The room was intensely bright again. The wider he opened his eyes the more his head would throb. He hadn't even tried to move yet. All he could see was white. Frustrated by the inability to open his eyes beyond a thin gap in his eyelids, he tried to raise his left hand. It was a lot harder than he thought. He came to realize his hand wasn't moving at all. He could feel himself tugging on his right hand every time he tried to move his left. They were tied together behind his back. Although that wasn't a good sign, at least he was still alive.

His eyes were slowly becoming more accustomed to the amount of light in the room, and the throbbing in his head was beginning to subside. He couldn't make sense of what he was looking at. His brain finally registered the fact that he was laying on his right side. That's why he was having such a hard time deciphering what he was looking at.

Every second that passed he became more acclimated to the light and position of his body. He could see Julie across the room. She was tied up and lying on her side too. She still had a blindfold on. Michael tried to call her name, but it hardly came out at all. He tried it again, but with the same result. It was then he realized he had been gagged.

He saw motion from the left side of the room. Jeremy grabbed him by the shoulder and sat him upright. He pushed him against the wall and then let go. "I'm glad you're awake. I wanted you to see this." He smiled as he stood up and walked over to a table. Michael saw a flash of light as Jeremy picked something up off the table. He wasn't sure what it was because Jeremy had turned away from him, but he had a good idea.

He watched as Jeremy walked over to Julie and pulled her upright too. She had her hands tied behind her back. She was sitting facing Michael in almost the exact same position he was. Julie was having trouble sitting up by herself. She seemed kind of out of it as her head was rolling around.

Jeremy turned to the side and looked at Michael. He pulled Julie to the edge of a platform she was on and let her legs hang over the edge. Michael could now clearly see the knife in Jeremy's hand.

This is where the dream he had in jail had started. This seemed more like a dream than the actual dream. In the dream all the colors seemed so vivid and sharp, but with all the bright lights everything seemed pale and appeared to have a slight glow to it.

Michael tried not to show it but he was working feverishly trying to get untied. He wasn't having any success and Jeremy didn't seem too concerned.

Jeremy reached down with the knife still in his hand and deliberately began to slowly unbutton Julie's sweater. His grin grew ever wider with each button he unsnapped. He watched Michael squirming to get free.

Just like in the dream Jeremy placed the knife underneath Julie's bra. He then pulled the knife outward cutting the bra in half. Jeremy took his eyes off Michael for a brief moment to set the knife down. He then reached out and slipped his hand under the open sweater and cupped Julie's breast in his hand. He looked back at Michael. Michael was still struggling and getting nowhere. Jeremy could see a mixed look of panic and anger in his eyes. That only added to Jeremy's pleasure as he was massaging her breast.

Michael looked away from Jeremy to look at Julie. Her head was now hanging back and her mouth was slightly open. Her head came forward. He heard her begin to cry. Without the benefit of sound in his dream he could see how his mind could misperceive it as ecstasy. Tears were beginning to run down her cheeks. Jeremy too looked at Julie. He stuck out his tongue and licked a tear from her cheek. She leaned away from him but he yanked her right back into position.

Michael was trying as hard as he could but still wasn't making any progress. He was more determined than ever to get loose. This wasn't happening exactly like the dream, but he was sure the end result was going to be the same. It wasn't going to be long before Jeremy picked the knife up and plunged it into Julie's chest. Jeremy reached down and unsnapped Julie's blue jeans. Michael kept his eye's on what Jeremy was doing the whole time he was struggling to get free.

Suddenly there was a flash of movement to Michael's left followed by a loud bang. He turned as far as he could to the side. Father Reilly had kicked the door in and was standing right there shielding his eyes.

Michael glanced over toward Jeremy. Apparently he had been startled too. He had jumped up and was looking in their direction. Michael began kicking his feet up and down. Father Reilly reached down and un-gagged Michael. Jeremy had already reached down and grabbed the knife.

As soon as he could Michael yelled, "Watch out!" Father Reilly jumped back. Jeremy had only made it about halfway toward them. Michael yelled out more instructions.

"Keep him away from the light switch. The son of a bitch can see in the dark!"

It was as if Father Reilly didn't even hear what he said because he instantly shuffled around Michael and positioned a table to his right between him and Jeremy.

Jeremy slowly circled the table following Father Reilly around it. Jeremy began waving the knife at Father Reilly. "You started this whole mess, but I'm going to finish it."

Father Reilly continued to circle the table trying to stay ahead of Jeremy. "You're not even part of the equation!" Father Reilly snapped. He was beginning to breath heavily as he really had to keep moving to stay ahead of Jeremy. "No matter what happens tonight you will always be answering to someone else."

Michael continued struggling to get loose. He took his eyes off of the action at the table for a brief moment to check on Julie. She was struggling to get loose too. Unfortunately she was having the same amount of success that Michael was. "Hang on Julie!" he shouted. That seemed to inspire her to try harder as she wiggled more noticeably on the platform.

Michael finally felt like he made a little progress. He felt the rope loosen slightly but there was still too much tension to keep him from getting a hand loose.

Jeremy felt as though he was beginning to lose control of the situation, and he was tired of chasing Father Reilly around the table. He waited until Father Reilly got around to the shortest side of the rectangular table. He reached down and grabbed the edge of the table and flipped it toward Father Reilly. Initially Father Reilly stepped forward to try to keep it from happening, but he was too slow to react. He jumped back trying to keep it from landing on his feet.

Jeremy was already coming over it before it had completely landed upside down. Father Reilly raised his arms to impede Jeremy's progress but it was too late. Jeremy shoved his forearm against Father Reilly's throat and forced him backward with his momentum. Father Reilly only felt the pain of his head slamming against the wall for a brief moment. A static haze replaced his vision for a few seconds. All that became secondary as he realized he wasn't getting any oxygen. Jeremy kept the pressure on Father Reilly's throat until he succumbed to the lack of oxygen.

Michael thought for sure Jeremy was going to kill Father Reilly right there, but he didn't. It was as if Jeremy was reading Michael's mind because he started explaining as he dragged Father Reilly's limp body over toward Michael. "I was going to kill you first, but your friend here just won that honor." Michael was still trying to get loose, but he was trying not to be so obvious with Jeremy right next to him. Jeremy started tying Father Reilly's hands behind his back.

Michael was glad Father Reilly at least got the gag out of his mouth because he definitely had something to say. "If you lay a fucking hand on her again, I don't care if it's this life, or the next one, or even the one after that, I will fucking kill you!"

Jeremy stood up as Michael was still talking to him. Michael saw it coming but there was nothing he could do about it. Just as he finished his sentence Jeremy wound up and punch him across the jaw. "You're in no position to tell me what to do!" Jeremy shouted angrily at him.

Michael's head was still turned to the side. He spit out a little blood and saliva. It felt like a lot more should have came out. His teeth had cut into his lip and part of his cheek.

Michael looked forward to see Jeremy walking away.

Jeremy reached down and turned the table back upright. He began picking the various torture devices off the floor and placing them on the table.

Michael decided it was best to remain quiet. He said what he had to say, and he was in no position to defend himself, or Julie. He realized Jeremy was quickly moved to violence when he became angry. At least for now Jeremy was preoccupied.

Michael looked over toward Julie. She was just lying there motionless. She must have learned this was the best way to deal with Jeremy. He decided for now to follow her lead.

Chapter 35

Detective Richards watched Father Reilly enter the house. Once Father Reilly stepped inside, he pulled up to within a few houses and parked in a good spot to observe from. He recognized the house right away.

He remembered a few things from earlier in the case that had stuck in his head. Jeremy Evans said he didn't know Father Reilly. Yet Father Reilly had marched right in like he owned the place. He also knew this was the address where the delinquent and dead taxpayer had lived; who also happened to be Jeremy's father.

He waited a half an hour to see what activity would go on inside the house, but not even a light was turned on inside the house in that half hour. He knew something didn't seem right, and his curiosity got the best of him. He was about to open his car door when he noticed a car coming down the street at the far end of the block. He decided he would wait to approach the house until it passed. To his surprise the vehicle stopped right in front of the house.

There was just enough light from the street light on the other side of the road, that he could tell it was someone in a nurses uniform that hurried into the house. For the first time he saw a light come on inside the house. He saw the nurse rush past a window silhouetted by the surrounding light. "A priest and a nurse?" he thought to himself, trying to make a connection. The only thing he could think of was that someone was dying. At least that would seem like a good reason for him to be stopping by to see if everything was all right. He decided to give it a few more minutes to see what other activity would go on.

———————

Michael was glad Father Reilly arrived when he did. He at least seemed to have managed to distract Jeremy away from Julie. Jeremy had gone upstairs for a couple of minutes but Michael still hadn't managed to loosen the ropes that restrained him. His wrists were starting to get sore from the slight rubbing while he wiggled them back and forth.

Jeremy came back into the room and immediately walked over to Julie. Michael saw him kneel down in front of her. He was worried Jeremy was going to pick up where he left off.

Father Reilly stirred for the first time. Michael saw his leg move slightly from the corner of his eye. He looked at Father Reilly. He was lying face down on the floor. He wasn't conscious yet but he was definitely starting to come around.

Fortunately Jeremy didn't see the movement. He was just starting to stand up. He turned around and headed toward Michael. He was surprised to see that Jeremy had buttoned Julie's sweater back up. Jeremy reached out and grabbed Michael by the shoulder and pulled him forward. He felt Jeremy checking the ropes. Michael was glad he didn't get anywhere now. There's no telling what Jeremy would've done if he had managed to loosen them.

Michael had tried to get Julie's attention while Jeremy was gone but she wasn't responding. He felt bad for her. She was still blindfolded and was probably afraid to answer him, afraid it was Jeremy playing some kind of trick on her.

As Jeremy walked away, Michael heard the basement door open to his left. He thought for a moment as he turned that it might be Father Davis. He was surprised to see it was an elderly woman in a nurse's outfit coming through the doorway. She looked familiar but he couldn't remember where he had seen her.

Jeremy rushed toward her. Michael expected her to be stabbed or wrestled to the ground. The embrace Jeremy gave her confused him.

"I promised you I wouldn't kill them until you said it was okay," Jeremy said as he pointed in Michael's direction. The old nurse turned around. She didn't look too happy.

It wasn't until Michael saw her face completely that he realized where he had seen her. It was the old woman that had left the house just hours ago. He also remembered when he was at the hospital and almost ran into her as he rounded the nurse's station a couple of days ago.

Jeremy continued trying to impress his mother. "I told you I could make everything right." She still looked unimpressed as she finally looked away from Michael and began raising her voice to Jeremy. "What the hell are they doing here?"

Jeremy stood silent, trying to figure out how to explain. The moment of silence cost him a chance to explain himself. His mother was obviously furious. "Do you listen to anything I tell you?" she snapped as she turned to walk away. Jeremy got a panicked look on his face. "Mother!" he shouted as he grabbed her shoulder to stop her.

With the grace of a ballerina she did a pirouette, while simultaneously grabbing a knife from the table. Michael saw the angered look on her face the split second before she had spun around.

She pulled the knife upward ramming it into Jeremy's abdomen. Michael couldn't believe what he just saw. Jeremy stumbled back a step. His mother removed the knife as he retreated. Jeremy looked down at the wound in disbelief. "Mother what are you doing?"

Jeremy stuck his hand over the open wound. It didn't stop the flow of blood that continued to pour out of the wound. Even against the black turtle neck he was wearing you could see the dark stain of blood expanding and running down his clothes.

As his mother responded Jeremy fell to a sitting position on the floor. "You have been screwing this up from day one. You don't make things better, you make them worse."

Jeremy took his hand off the wound and held it out in front of his face. Normally the sight of blood on his hands would excite him, but it was a much different feeling that came over him now. "Why?" he asked as he put his hand back over the wound. His mother shook her head as if she couldn't believe he didn't know why.

"Because all you've ever done is fail me!"

Jeremy tried to get up, but he stumbled backward before he was even halfway up. He fell back to the floor and then rolled onto his side. Michael could see an enormous amount of blood beginning to pool on the floor next to him. Although he was glad to see Jeremy taken out of the picture, he was even more worried about the kind of woman who would kill her own son.

Jeremy rolled onto his back and attempted to sit up again. He began to cry as he could see his vision narrowing. It was as if the shadows were closing in on him. His breathing became erratic. This was in part due to three things, a punctured lung, panic, and the fact he was crying. He took a deep breath and suddenly began to cough. Blood exploded out of his mouth.

Michael could see him trying to speak. It sounded like the same word over and over. Blood was still being projected from his mouth as he tried to speak. It wasn't until he said it for the last time that Michael understood what he was saying. "Mommy." Jeremy's body went limp. Even though his mother had betrayed him, his last thoughts were of her. Michael watched as she just stood over Jeremy's body. She never moved or showed any emotion as he struggled to hang on. Michael saw another drop of blood fall from the tip of the knife. He wondered if things just got better, or worse.

Detective Richards knocked on the door several times before entering. He drew his weapon and cautiously proceeded into the house. As he walked through the living room he could hear yelling. He stepped cautiously until he located the area the sound was coming from. He could see the door at the bottom of the stairs was open just a crack. He heard more yelling as he started descending the stairs.

As he reached the bottom of the stairs the yelling ceased. He waited on the other side of the door listening for more activity. After hearing nothing for about twenty seconds he quickly, but quietly pushed the door fully open.

He didn't know what to expect but he certainly didn't expect the brightness. He held his left hand up shielding his eyes while pointing the gun forward with the right. He could see the nurse standing there. She was unaware he had entered the room. He saw the body on the floor in front of her and the knife she was holding. It was still dripping with blood.

Just as he was about to say something to her he heard someone yell off to his right. "Shoot her!"

The detective turned in the direction of the voice. He saw his main suspect Michael Foster tied up and leaning against the wall. Right next to him was Father Reilly. He was also tied up and lying on the floor. Sensing no danger from that direction he turned his attention back to the nurse with the knife.

She had already spun around and was facing his direction. "Drop the knife!" the detective shouted. When she didn't comply right away, he heard Michael yelling at him again. "Shoot her goddamn it!"

Detective Richards recognized the nurse. It was Jeremy's mother, and that was definitely Jeremy behind her lying in a pool of blood. It didn't make any sense to him that she would kill her own son, but she still hadn't dropped the knife. He pointed the gun more sternly at her. "Drop the knife right now!" Michael had seen too much go wrong already so he pleaded one more time. "Fucking shoot her!"

The detective ignored the request. He hadn't had enough time to assess the situation.

The nurse got a very angry look on her face. "Nobody wins!" She immediately spun around and headed for Julie. Michael screamed at the top of his lungs, "No!" But like the detective it did nothing to prevent what was about to happen.

Before the detective even got a grasp on what was happening Jeremy's mother plunged the knife into Julie's pelvis. As she pulled the knife out and raised it a second time, the detective fired his gun. The shot was right on target. The nurse's head blew open like a pumpkin being dropped from a ten-story building.

Fortunately the knife missed its intended target the second time but it did cut her thigh as it only entered a couple of inches.

The nurse's body initially had slumped over Julie's but when she started screaming and writhing in pain it had slid off of her for the most part. Nobody could hear what was going on as a result of the gun going off in such a confined area.

The detective moved in Julie's direction. Michael could not tell if she had been stabbed or if the detective had fired in time. He was yelling in a panic for the detective to come over and untie him. He didn't know if the detective could even hear him as his own ears were ringing so badly he could hardly hear himself.

The detective could hear Michael yelling but he couldn't tell what he was saying. He spun around wanting to be sure Michael wasn't trying to warn him about someone else approaching from behind. He looked at Michael. He could see he was still shouting but he was unconcerned about what he wanted at the moment. Satisfied there was no danger from behind, he turned his attention back to Julie.

There was blood everywhere. How much of it was Julie's he couldn't tell. She was curled up in a fetal position. He could hear her screaming over and over. "Oh my God!" He reached down and touched her. Now she was just screaming. He pulled her blindfold off.

"I'm a police officer!" he yelled as he took out his badge and showed it to her. She could barely make it out in the bright lights but along with his words it was enough for her to quit screaming. He gently rolled her onto her back so he could see the wound. It looked worse than he expected. "I've got to get you some help. I'll be right back."

The detective jumped off the little platform to leave. The gunshot apparently had stirred Father Reilly awake because he was struggling to get himself upright. Michael tried to get the detectives attention as he passed but it did no good. The detective continued on up the stairs and out to his car where he radioed for an ambulance and a couple of squad cars at the scene. He then rushed back to the house. He was just as cautious entering the second time, as he was the first.

Father Reilly had managed to get himself upright just after the detective had left. Michael explained what had happened as they tried to get each other untied. Michael noticed Julie had stopped crying. He called her name several times but she wasn't responding. Michael was working so feverishly to get untied he was counter-productive. Just as Father Reilly was about to explain that fact to him, the detective re-entered the room.

He pointed his gun at Michael while glancing around the room for other danger. "What the fuck is going on here?" he said firmly as he looked back at Michael.

Michael didn't even know how to explain; besides he had other concerns. "That's my fiancé over there. She's stopped crying. Is she all right?" Michael couldn't see her very well from his vantage point as the table almost completely blocked his view of Julie.

The detective made his way in Julie's direction. He stepped over the pool of blood that was still expanding on the floor from Jeremy's body. He could see she wasn't moving and appeared to be unconscious. He reached down and checked her pulse. It was weak, but there was one. The detective began to untie her.

The whole time Michael was asking how she was. The detective didn't respond to his questions. Every time he asked his tone grew more irritated at the lack of response.

There seemed to be a lot of blood coming from Julie's wound too. "There's an ambulance on its way," the detective said as he turned his attention back to Michael and Father Reilly. He saw Michael had finally managed to get a hand free with Father Reilly's help.

The detective made his way back over to them. "You still haven't explained what's going on?" Michael looked up from untying his legs to see the detective pointing the gun right at him. Michael was about to tell him where he could put his gun. Fortunately Father Reilly started speaking before Michael said something he would regret later. "They kidnapped her, and told us if we went to the police, they would kill her."

Michael had finished untying himself and stood up. The detective took a step back, while still pointing the gun at Michael. "Stay where you are," he ordered. Michael looked him right in the eye. "I'm going to check on Julie. If you want to shoot me for it, go ahead."

He walked right by the detective. The detective took another step back keeping his gun aimed at Michael the whole journey across the room. He watched Michael squat down next to Julie. His aim followed the motion. "Jesus Christ," Michael said as he covered his mouth with his hand. The detective lowered his gun just a little.

Michael put his right hand on Julie's shoulder. "Just hang on," he said as he took his hand off his mouth. The detective could see Michael fighting his emotions as he heard him whisper he was sorry to her. "There's nothing you can do for her. The ambulance will be here any minute."

Father Reilly was not having any success getting himself untied. Frustrated he snapped at the detective, "Will you give me a hand?" The detective didn't move anything but his head in his direction. Father Reilly went from frustrated to irritated in a split second. "Damn it, we're the good guys," he snapped. Still the detective didn't move.

Michael left Julie's side to help Father Reilly. He realized what the detective said was true. There was nothing he could do for her. "Where's the fucking ambulance?" he said as he reached down to start untying Father Reilly. Almost on cue a police officer entered the room with his gun drawn, but upon seeing the detective with his gun drawn, he holstered his gun and shouted up the stairs. "Down here!"

Another police officer and paramedic entered the room. "Jesus!" the paramedic said as he entered the room. There was blood everywhere, and against the white background of the room, every drop stood out. He wasn't even sure if any of them were alive.

The detective pointed to Julie. "Take the woman over there. I don't think there's much you can do for the other two." The paramedic grabbed a walkie-talkie off his chest.

"Jerry, get a stretcher down here ASAP!"

Michael finished untying Father Reilly and then turned around to see the detective still pointing his gun at him. Just as he was about to tell the detective where to put his gun, the other paramedic stepped in-between them. Michael was instantly distracted as he watched him bring the stretcher over next to Julie's body.

As they loaded her limp body onto the stretcher he heard the police officer ask the detective. "What are we doing with these two?" The detective reached behind him and pulled his handcuffs out. "Cuff them, we'll take them to the station for questioning."

As the officer began moving toward them Michael was already objecting. "Hey!" he shouted in the detective's direction. "I'm going to the hospital with my fiancé." He took a step back as the officer continued to approach. He bumped into Father Reilly but kept his attention on the approaching officer. Father Reilly put his hand on Michael's shoulder.

"Everything will be fine. Trust me."

The officer had stopped his approach due to Michael's defensive posture. The police officer glanced over his shoulder. The detective still had his gun drawn. He saw the detective flick the gun up and down for him to continue.

Michael knew it was in his best interest just to submit. The police officer told them both to face the wall. As the police officer was cuffing him, Michael could hear the paramedics talking about Julie's condition.

"She's lost a lot of blood."

"Her vitals are low."

It certainly didn't sound like everything was going to be fine.

He looked at Father Reilly, as it was his turn to get handcuffed. Father Reilly smiled reassuringly at him. Michael turned away and watched as they began carrying Julie out of the basement. Images of her flashed through his mind in rapid succession. He fought back his emotions; even though his face couldn't hide the fact he was thinking he would never see her again.

The detective stepped forward and took Michael by the arm. The detective allowed Michael to go up the stairs first. He could see another police officer waiting at the top of the stairs. As they waited for Father Reilly and the other police officer to get to the top of the stairs, the police officer at the top of the stairs began speaking with the detective.

"The rest of the house is secure."

The detective nodded. "Don't let anybody touch anything until Chuck gets here."

"You got it."

As they exited the house they passed a few more police officers. There were blue and red beams of light dancing off everything, as there were four police cars and an ambulance parked in front of the house with their lights flashing.

The detective pulled Michael to a stop halfway down the sidewalk. He waited for the police officer and Father Reilly to catch up. "Take him right to the station. I'll bring this one in myself." As the police officer led Father Reilly by Michael he caught a look from Father Reilly. He could tell that he was telling him without words not to say too much.

The detective led Michael to his car and helped him into the back. Once the detective got in the car and shut the door, he spun around to face Michael. "Look, I don't know what the hell is going on, but if that is your fiancé…It might help your cause to give me the truth right now."

Michael nodded in agreement even though he knew he couldn't tell the detective the whole truth. "Part of it is I just happened to be in the wrong place at the wrong time. I just happened to help that psycho's girlfriend because she went into labor. I didn't even know her. I just happened to be the only one around when it happened. Some how I screwed up this guys plans, so he decides to kidnap my fiancé. Then I run into Father Reilly. He tells me he knows who kidnapped my fiancé. He tells me we can't go to the police because if they show up on his doorstep he will kill her. So I had to put my trust in him. I had no choice."

The detective studied Michael the whole time looking for the slightest hint he was lying. "So how do you explain what happened in there?"

Michael took a deep breath to give him a chance to collect his thoughts. "Father Reilly was trying to convince me to be patient, but I just couldn't do it. Once I found out where she was, all I could imagine was what kind of terrible things could be happening to her. So I took it upon myself to try and stop him, but now I think that may have been a mistake, because I'm here, and I have no idea whether she's dead or alive." Michael swallowed hard after finishing that sentence.

The detective saw him fighting his emotions again as Michael turned away from him and looked out the window. He saw the ambulance had already left.

"You still haven't explained what was going on in there."

Michael turned his attention back to the detective. "All I know is he kidnapped my fiancé. I tried to do something about it, and it didn't work out. He managed to get the best of me. Father Reilly came after me, but he ended up in the same predicament I was in. The guys mother comes home, they start arguing and she stabs him. Then you come in, and you know the rest from there. As far as who or why, you are asking the wrong guy. I don't care about who or why. All I care about right now is how my fiancé is doing."

The detective spun back around in his seat and started the car. He looked up into the mirror so he could see Michael. "I'm going to take you to the hospital before I turn you in, but I swear if you try anything funny…" Michael interrupted him before he could finish the threat. "Thank you." It wasn't that the detective was so convinced by Michael's story as it was that if he was telling the truth, the detective would've felt awful guilty if his fiancé did die.

———

Julie had stopped breathing about two minutes from the hospital. The paramedics had managed to stop the bleeding, but they were still working feverishly to revive her as the ambulance pulled up to the hospital. She started breathing again as the doors opened at the rear of the ambulance. The paramedics handed her off at the entrance to the hospital. There was a flurry of activity as the paramedics were shouting information at the nurses as they made the exchange. There was a doctor that approached and shouted out instructions as he heard the information from the paramedics. "She's still breathing." One of the nurses said as they wheeled her down the hallway.

Once they were convinced she had stabilized they rushed her in for x-rays. The doctors were stunned to learn she was pregnant. It complicated things more than they already were. There appeared to be a lot of internal damage done by the first knife wound. They decided they needed to get her into surgery right away.

The first thing they tried to determine was if the baby was even still alive. They detected a strong heartbeat, which they took as a good sign. They began to prepare to address Julie's internal injuries.

One of the nurses tapped the surgeon on the shoulder. "Doctor," she said. He turned to see the nurse pointing and beginning to back away. He looked to where the nurse was pointing and there on the table, Julie's abdomen was beginning to glow a soft orange.

"What the hell is that?" he asked.

No one in the room answered him. He noticed every one of them step back as it was glowing even brighter now. The doctor was the only one who stood his ground. He pulled the sheet further back looking for a surgery light or anything that could explain the glow coming from inside her. The glow was now beginning to fade. As it did the doctor watched the entry wound seal itself. "Did you see that?" he asked the nurse across from him. She was just staring in disbelief but did manage to nod indicating she did.

The doctor glanced around as the glow had completely disappeared. Everyone was still keeping their distance. "I need readings people! What do we got?" One of the nurses checked her vitals. "Everything is normal." The doctor took his stethoscope and placed it on Julie's abdomen. "I don't hear the babies heartbeat. I want you to get her back into x-ray right now."

The doctor exited the operating room and took off his mask and gloves. He walked over to the sink and began to wash his hands. As he did a nurse came in from the hallway. "Doctor Ford, there's a man in the lobby who says he is this woman's fiancé." The doctor grabbed some paper towels to dry his hands. "Good, I'll be right there."

Michael and the detective were handcuffed to each other. The doctor didn't notice as he approached. "I'm Doctor Ford," he said as he extended his right hand. "I'm Michael Foster." The detective's left hand followed Michael's right as he greeted the doctor. The doctor's attention was drawn to the synchronized movement. Before he could even ask about the handcuffs the detective introduced himself. "Detective Sean Richards," he said extending his other hand. The doctor was obviously distracted by the handcuffs because he talked slowly with a confused look on his face. "Perhaps we should talk in private?" The detective nodded.

The doctor led them to a private waiting room. After getting a satisfactory reason for the handcuffs, the doctor began explaining the situation to both Michael and the detective. "By all rights, we literally probably had minutes to save your fiancé's life. I don't even know how to explain what happened." The doctor realized that Julie was early in her pregnancy and Michael might not even be aware that she was. "Are you aware that your fiancé is pregnant Mr. Foster?"

Michael nodded as he responded. "Yes."

The doctor could hear the anxiousness in his answer. So he figured he'd better get to the point. "We weren't sure if we could save your fiancé, let alone the child, in her weakened state. We were just getting ready to operate when…" The doctor paused as he thought over how to put what he saw into words. The momentary pause caused Michael to get a very concerned look on his face. He was expecting bad news. The doctor continued. "Well there's just no other way to put it. It was a miracle. I still don't believe what I saw." He noticed Michael relax a bit. "I watched her wound heal itself. Now I don't want to mislead you. We're not sure if everything is all right. We took her back in for x-rays just a little bit ago. I won't know anything until I see the x-rays and examine her." There was a knock at the door. "Come in," the doctor shouted. A nurse entered the room. "Doctor, the x-rays are ready." The doctor stood up. "If you'll excuse me gentlemen."

The doctor entered the x-ray lab and a nurse immediately handed him the x-rays. He clipped them up next to the other ones. He couldn't believe the difference. He looked at the nurse. She just shrugged her shoulders. He pointed to the x-ray. "I'm still concerned about this area right here." He turned his head to look at the nurse. "How is she doing?"

"Good," the nurse replied. The doctor turned the switch off to the light that was illuminating the x-rays. "Okay, the first thing I want to do is see if the child managed to make it through, and then check to see what damage, if any, is left."

It seemed like an eternity with the complete silence in the private waiting room. Michael and the detective never said a word to each other during the whole time the doctor was gone.

Finally the doctor entered the room. Both Michael and the detective rose to their feet when he entered. "Please, sit down," the doctor said as he was already taking a seat. "I have some good news and some bad news." The doctor could sense Michael needed the good news first. "Your fiancé should be fine. She's still unconscious, but I don't see any reason she shouldn't make a full recovery." Michael let out a long drawn out breath. He subconsciously held it until the doctor gave him the news.

He felt so relieved he almost hated to ask. "What's the bad news?" The doctor leaned forward resting his elbows on his knees. "The baby didn't make it." Michael wasn't sure how to react to that news. He did feel a sense of loss, but the good news far out weighed the bad news. That was, until the doctor continued. "I don't think she will be able to have children again." That news had a little more effect on Michael. He was thinking of Julie more than himself.

Although they had never talked about having children, he knew just from how much she enjoyed being around them that it was something she was looking forward to. "Can I see her?" Michael asked. The doctor looked to the detective for approval. The detective nodded raising his hand that was still attached to Michael's by the handcuffs. The doctor stood up. "I want to caution you. She is still unconscious and there's no way of telling if and when she is going to come out of it." Michael nodded understandingly as he pulled the detective along behind him as the doctor led them out of the room.

Once they were in the hallway the doctor slowed a little and turned his head to talk to Michael. "If it's all right with you we would like to run a few tests on your fiancé." Michael didn't respond right away so the doctor figured he had better explain further.

"By all rights your fiancé should be dead, but somehow her wounds healed themselves. If we could figure out even one tenth of a reason how that happened, it could help save others." Michael still didn't respond. "I promise you we are not going to dissect her. Just some blood work and analysis." The doctor stopped in front of the room obviously waiting for a response from Michael before he would be allowed to enter.

"Okay," Michael finally responded. That appeared to be the magic word because with his response the doctor pushed the door open and let him in.

As Michael approached the bed he could hardly stand to look at her. She just didn't look like the Julie he knew. Her hair was slicked back. Her face was slack and without expression. Michael pulled a chair out next to the bed and sat down. He unknowingly pulled the detective along side him. His mind was completely on Julie as he took her hand in his. This was not the last memory he wanted to have of her. "I'm sorry," he whispered as he reached down and kissed her hand. The doctor tried to give him some reassurance. "I don't see any reason she shouldn't make a full recovery. I just don't want to make any promises at this point."

The detective tugged on his end of the handcuffs to get Michael's attention. "I'm sorry, but we have to go to the station. The sooner I get this mess cleaned up the sooner you can get back to your fiancé." Michael knew there was still nothing he could do for her, so he gripped her hand and kissed it one more time.

Chapter 36

The detective was leading Michael into the station when an officer approached them. "Hey Sean, you know that old guy you had brought in?"

The detective directed Michael to the counter. "Yeah."

The policeman saddled up next to the detective at the counter. "Well, he asked us to go check up on a friend of his. He thought he might be in some kind of trouble. So we sent over a squad to check it out. Turns out we got another body on our hands."

Both Michael and the detective knew who it was. "Who's on it?" the detective asked. "Chuck's on his way over there now."

The detective quickly scribbled down some information on the form. "Can you finish processing this guy? I want to head over there." The policeman pulled the form over in front of him as he spoke. "Sure, no problem." The detective patted him on the back. "Thanks Paul." He handed him the pen and then turned around and headed out the door.

Father Reilly had been sleeping in his cell until he heard the main door to the holding area open. Just by a stroke of luck the policeman put them together. Father Reilly never said a word until the guard had left. "What took you so long?" Michael sat down on the cot across from Father Reilly. "He took me to see Julie." Father Reilly leaned forward.

"How is she?"

"The doctor said she should be fine but he wasn't making any promises."

There was a few seconds of silence before Michael continued. "The baby didn't make it."

Father Reilly nodded. "I know. I had a vision again. I was told it would be the last one. It said one life would be taken and one would be spared. I knew how to read between the lines. The child wasn't going to make it, so what energy was left was used to save Julie's life."

Michael still hadn't had time to sort out how he felt about the situation. He didn't even know if he wanted anything to do with Father Reilly after all was said and done. He still had a mix of emotions going on. He was angry at the fact Julie had been put in so much danger without him even realizing it. He also felt some pity for Father Reilly. He had paid a price too.

Michael didn't want to be the one to tell him about Father Davis, but he couldn't stand knowing and not telling him. "Jeremy got to Father Davis." Michael watched Father Reilly try to fight his tears but he just couldn't do it. "I know," he said as he raised his hand to wipe away a tear. "I was just hoping it was something else." Michael felt a little guilty for only thinking of himself during the whole situation. "I'm sorry." It was the only thing he could think to say. He knew from the moment he had met them that they had been friends for sometime.

Father Reilly wiped away another tear. "It's not your fault in any way. I'm the one who dragged him into it; and like a true friend he stuck by me, even when he thought I was nuts." Michael reached out and set his hand on Father Reilly's shoulder. "So what now?" Father Reilly took a deep breath. "We're back to square one. The human race will decide its own fate for generations. Someday in the future maybe the balance between good and evil won't be so even. We and our children and their grandchildren will help decide our fate until then."

The detective had just arrived back from Father Davis' place. He had so much information coming at him from the two recent crime scenes he felt a little overwhelmed.

Slowly he was going over the new and old evidence. The puzzle was slowly coming together but there were still many pieces missing. It would be a few days, and in some cases weeks, before any of the lab results came back on lots of key evidence. What he did have mostly pointed to Jeremy, but there wasn't enough to let either Father Reilly or Michael go at this point.

He decided to talk to Father Reilly. They had found the baby along with the cross and bottle of holy water in the garbage at the

Evans' residence. He figured Father Reilly would know something about this.

The detective was already in the interrogation room when Father Reilly was led in. He was glad that he and Michael had a chance to talk before he talked to the detective. Michael had been vague enough with the detective for Father Reilly to come up with a believable story. He hated to lie, but the truth sounded more like a lie. He had to come up with something the detective would accept.

The detective pointed for him to sit down. "Do you have any gum?" he asked. It took a second but Father Reilly picked up on the sarcasm. "No they took it from me when they took me into custody," he said smiling sheepishly.

Father Reilly pulled his chair forward moving it closer to the table. "Before you ask me any questions, do you mind if I give you the whole story from the beginning and then you can ask me any questions the story doesn't answer." The detective leaned back in his chair assuming it wasn't going to be a short story. "All right." Father Reilly knew he only had pieces of the story and was going to have to put it together in a way that made sense. Much of the real information had no way of being proven anyway, and the only people who could dispute what he said were already dead.

"It started several months ago. Jeremy had gone to Father Davis. He claimed his child, yet to be born, was the child of Satan. Father Davis could tell he was dealing with a disturbed individual, but had no idea of the crimes he had been committing. They met several times until the baby was born. On the day the baby was born Father Davis came to me and told me about his meeting with Jeremy the night before. Jeremy had confessed to the murders that were going on in the area. Father Davis was extremely shaken by the news. That's why he came to me. He wanted to know what I would do. I told him we should go to the police with the information the next day. Unfortunately we didn't do it right away. Jeremy called him and asked him to be at the hospital when the baby was born. Father Davis didn't want to go, but he feared for the child and what Jeremy might do if he didn't show. We debated outside the hospital in the car whether we were doing the right thing or not. I finally convinced Father Davis that I should be the one to go inside since Jeremy didn't even know who I was. He finally agreed that it would be safer for him to wait in the car while I checked things out. Unfortunately we were too late. Things had already started happening. I figured with Jeremy right in the hospital at the time the police would put two and two together. I figured I should get Father Davis somewhere safe until you took Jeremy into custody. Then the plan was to come down to the station with what we knew. The only problem was you didn't arrest him. We didn't even know about Michael until the next day. Jeremy contacted Father Davis and told him he was angry with him for not showing up to save his child. He said the devil himself had showed up to make sure his child was delivered and he was using the name Michael to disguise himself. Father Davis was both confused and concerned. He called me and asked me to accompany him to Jeremy's to make sure the child was all right. I was reluctant at first, but he insisted we had to do it. Jeremy was actually happy to see Father Davis. He ignored me as if I wasn't even there. He never even asked who I was, or why I was there. Father Davis baptized and blessed the child right in its crib. He was in such hurry to get out of there he had left the cross and the bottle behind. He was practically pulling my arm off as we continued through the house and out the door. Jeremy seemed to be quite pleased about it. I admit we should have gone to the police right then and there. We were both concerned for the safety of the child, but we couldn't figure out why the police had not taken him into custody yet. We feared that if you couldn't pin anything on him yet, he would figure out who went to the police and come after Father Davis. Later that day Jeremy called Father Davis. He was furious. He accused Father Davis of purposely being too late to save his child. He said he was going to make the devil pay for taking his child. At the time we had no idea what he meant. We knew he considered a man named Michael the devil. We had no idea we already knew who Michael was. Michael Foster had come back to the area where he grew up to spread his brother's ashes. I ran into him completely by coincidence. I went to Barry's supermarket to pick up a few things. I bumped into Michael there. He was there buying a jar of pickles for a woman he had just dropped off at the hospital. You can ask a young woman named Lisa…I can't remember her last name, but she was working the register that day, and she checked us out."

The detective wrote down the information but continued to listen as Father Reilly continued.

"He told me what he was doing in town, and that he used to live in the community. I introduced him to Father Davis. They did some talking about this and that, like how much things have changed since Michael had lived there and stuff like that. It was a very brief encounter because Michael wanted to get back to the hospital. It wasn't until you took him into custody as a suspect that we made the connection. Father Davis saw Michael on the news being led into the station as a suspect. We now realized whom Jeremy was talking about when he said the devil was using the name Michael. Father Davis called Jeremy to find out how he was going to make the devil pay. Jeremy told Father Davis that he took something from the devil. Father Davis asked him what it was. Jeremy told him he only took what the devil took from him. He could hear a woman crying out for help in background. He knew he must have Michael's fiancé. Father Davis pleaded with Jeremy to let the woman go and turn himself in. Jeremy became quite angry and told Father Davis he was done listening to him. Father Davis asked him what he planned to do with the woman. Jeremy said he was going to keep her until the devil came looking for her. Again Father Davis begged him to let her go. I heard Jeremy myself shout. "Why are you on his side?" Father Davis hung up the phone about ten seconds later. He told me the last thing he said was if anyone other than the devil came after her, he would kill her. That's when I decided I'd better get down to the station and let Michael know what was going on. That's why I put the gum over the microphone. I couldn't have the police finding out and trying to do something about it. I urged Michael not to give any of the information I told him to the police. He wanted to tell you in order to clear himself, but I told him that would lead to Julie's death. I truly believe it would have. He put his trust in me. I don't know whether that was right or wrong. A lot of things may have worked out differently if he hadn't lost it at the end. Anyway, once he got out of jail he came to my apartment. We filled him in on what was going on. We had planned to go over to Jeremy's and try to prove to him Michael was not the devil. We had to wait until late at night. Jeremy wasn't much of a day person. Unfortunately Michael apparently didn't believe that we would succeed in convincing Jeremy. The plan was for the three of us to go over there together. Father Davis went home to freshen up and I decided to get some sleep. I hadn't been sleeping well with everything going on. Father Davis was supposed to come pick us up around 8:30 p.m. I awoke to find Michael gone and Father Davis had not shown up. It was very unlike him to be late. I feared that something had happened to him, but I was more concerned about where Michael was. It didn't take me long to figure out where he had headed. I knew it was too dangerous for him to try something on his own so I headed right over there. I left Father Davis a note just in case he showed up late, but the fact that he's not here right now..." He paused to swallow a lump in his throat. "I know that means Jeremy must have gotten to him."

The detective could detect the sense of loss in the way he said it. "I'm sorry about that. He seemed like a good man."

Father Reilly took a couple of deep breaths to compose himself. "He was a good friend too." He could feel tears beginning to well up in his eyes so he quickly changed the subject. "Anyway when I got to Jeremy's he had already incapacitated Michael. I'm afraid I didn't fair much better. Twenty years ago I may have had a chance, but at least I bought enough time for you to arrive." There was about ten seconds of silence. "That's about it."

The detective leaned forward and leaned his face on his left hand. "What about the mother? How was she involved?" Father Reilly took his time in responding, trying not to get forced into a corner on the question. "Most of this is speculation, because the truth is I'm not really sure." The detective nodded as he prepared to write. Father Reilly continued. "I don't know if she knew about all the murders Jeremy committed or when she found out, but I think she took the heart from Jeremy's girlfriend to give him an alibi and lead your investigation in a different direction. It obviously worked. I know Jeremy committed those murders, and so did his mother, because when she came home and saw us tied up in the basement she was furious. She was yelling at him about how she had worked so hard to create an alibi for him and now he had ruined it. They scuffled and then she stabbed him. You came in just after that."

The detective began to collect his stuff from the table. "So why did she stab..." He paused trying to remember her name. "Julie?" The pause gave Father Reilly just enough time to decide that not having the answer was better than continuing the conversation.

"I wish I knew. She is probably the only one who could've answered that."

Fortunately the detective didn't push for any more answers. He waved for the police officer to enter the room. "Unfortunately I won't be able to release you until sometime tomorrow. That's if your story and the evidence checks out."

Father Reilly smiled. "I understand completely detective."

That night was the longest Michael had ever experienced in his life. Even though the doctor was encouraging when he left the hospital, he kept imagining his life without Julie. It made it very hard for him to sleep. They allowed Father Reilly and Michael to stay in the same cell. Father Reilly had again apologized to Michael and tried to assure him that everything was going to be all right. After that not much was said. Father Reilly could tell Michael's mind was elsewhere, besides he was dead tired and was looking forward to some sleep.

Michael slipped in and out of sleep the whole night. Every time he woke up Father Reilly was lying in the exact same position. He finally wondered what time it was. He wished they hadn't taken his watch, but if he had been able to check his watch it would've made time seem to go much slower. He heard the door open at the end of the hall. He stood up and pressed his face against the bars trying to get a look at who was coming. It was just a guard coming to check on them. Michael rubbed his right eye.

"What time is it?"

The guard looked at his watch. "7:30"

Michael yawned and stretched. "Thank you."

Michael turned and walked back to his bunk. He sat down and looked over at Father Reilly. He still hadn't appeared to move all night. Michael thought back to all the times he woke up and looked at Father Reilly. He still was lying there with his back to Michael, as he had been the whole night. He started to feel a little uneasy. The blanket Father Reilly had draped over himself made it hard to tell if he was even breathing or not.

Michael couldn't stand it any longer. He knelt down next to Father Reilly's bunk and gave him a nudge. "Father Reilly," he said waiting for a response. When nothing happened he began to feel a terrible pit in his stomach. He gave him more of a shove this time. "Father Reilly," he said just a bit louder.

Before his eyes even opened he was starting to sit up. "What? What is it?" he said blinking his eyes rather confused. Michael now felt embarrassed for letting his imagination get the best of him. "I just wanted to be sure you were okay." Father Reilly still a little confused looked around as he spoke. "What time is it?" Michael sat down on his bunk again. "About 7:30 in the morning."

Father Reilly rubbed his face with both hands. "I haven't slept that hard in a while." He moaned slightly as he started to stand up. "Not the most comfortable thing I've ever slept on." He raised his arms above his head as he stretched. "Oh do I need to shower." Father Reilly moved toward the bars of the cell. "It won't be long now," he said as he peered through the bars down the hall.

Chapter 37

Detective Richards had been in the office since 5:30 a.m. going over some of the new evidence and matching it up with some of the old evidence. He had constructed a time line and pasted pieces of evidence along it in the order in which they had presumably happened.

There were three previous murders without much evidence other than the fact a stun gun had been used to immobilize the victims. He pinned up a note next to those dates.

"Stun gun found at Evans' residence matching description of type used."

He moved on. "Mrs. Kalnacheck, suspicious death, but not linked to others." He pinned up another note next to that information on the timeline. "Also residence of Father Reilly." He turned and grabbed another note. "Enter Michael Foster."

He moved on. "Jenny Larson died giving birth at County Hospital." He turned and pinned up a note. "Girlfriend of suspect Jeremy Evans." He reached behind him and grabbed another note. "Heart removed like previous three victims with the exception victim was already dead." He turned and grabbed another note and pinned it up. "Michael Foster brought victim to the hospital."

The detective grabbed a pen and a piece of paper and started writing down some questions at this point. "Why if he was with the victim earlier, would he wait to kill her here?" He pinned it up and then grabbed another piece of paper. He remembered some of Father Reilly's story. He started writing. "Mother of suspect Jeremy trying to provide alibi could have had access to body." He pinned that one up and then moved down the time line. "Michael Foster taken into custody."

He turned and grabbed another note. "Michael Foster's fiancé kidnapped." He turned and grabbed another note. He read it before pinning it up. "Ticket found for expired plates on passenger side floor of vehicle belonging to John Evans, who's been deceased for ten years, and also father of Jeremy Evans. Vehicle ticketed one block from Foster residence."

He moved down the timeline. "Michael Foster released." He pinned up a note. "Suspect under surveillance." He pinned another right next to it. "Suspect exits premises undetected."

He moved on. "Father Davis murdered." He grabbed another note. "Visited Davis residence, vehicle registered to John Evans parked outside." The detective had already assumed sometime ago that Jeremy was the one driving his father's car around.

He moved down the time line. "Scene at Evans' residence." He pinned up another note here. "Arrived on scene to see Elly Roberts holding a knife apparently used to stab her own son." He pinned up another note. "Roberts is maiden name of Elly Evans. Never remarried." He remembered she had told him she had remarried after her husband died, but in fact she had given him her maiden name, and there was no record of her getting married again.

He had found some older files on the Evans' residence. The police had been called to the residence on several occasions for a domestic disturbance but no charges were ever filed. He remembered seeing all the whips and clubs laid out on a table in the basement. The coroner had not finished his report yet but he had called Sean to tell him that Jeremy's back was like a road map of whip marks and God knows what else. He wondered what went on inside that house, but he never came close to the reality.

Then there was Father Reilly's statement, which seemed to corroborate with everything on the time line and even fill in a few spaces. There was a still lot of evidence sure to turn up in the case, but he was fairly confident things were pointing in the right direction.

The detective looked down at his watch. It was 8:00 a.m. He knew it wouldn't be long before Michael's attorney showed up, so he decided to start the process of getting them released. He knew Michael was probably dying to find out the condition of his fiancé so he decided to call the hospital and find out her condition before he went down there to talk to Michael and Father Reilly.

He finally reached Doctor Ford who had been running tests all night. "The only way I can explain it is it's a miracle. She's conscious. She's alert. It's as if it never happened." There was nothing but silence on the detective's end of the phone so the doctor continued. "I ran every test I could but nothing's coming up abnormal or anything."

The doctor wasn't even sure if the detective was on the line anymore. "Hello?"

The detective finally spoke up. "Sorry, I was just thinking. How long until she can be released?" The doctor shrugged his shoulders as he spoke. "Other than being confused about what's going on, she seems fine. Maybe this afternoon."

"Does she remember anything?"

"It certainly doesn't seem like it. It could be from the trauma, mentally or physically, who knows." The doctor leaned back in his chair.

Again there was nothing but silence from the detectives end. "She's been asking about her fiancé but we've been avoiding telling her too much." The detective tapped a pencil against his forehead. "You can tell her he'll be there soon." The doctor was a little surprised. "Really?" The detective tossed the pencil down on his desk and stood up.

"Yeah, I think I have enough evidence to support letting him go."

The doctor smiled. "Well that's good news. She'll be glad to hear it."

"I don't think she'll be the only one. Thanks for your help doctor."

The detective hung up the phone.

———

Michael heard the door open at the end of the hall. He was already standing and waiting at the bars when the detective and a police officer arrived at the cell door. The police officer opened the door and let the detective enter. "There's still a lot of evidence to go through in the next few days, but I think I have enough to release you."

The news brought an instant smile to Michael's face. He looked over at Father Reilly. He was smiling back at him in an I told you so fashion. The detective continued. "Your fiancé is conscious and they should release her this afternoon but I'd appreciate if you stay in town one more day in case I have any questions." Michael looked at Father Reilly again. He was still giving him that I told you so smile. "Not a problem," he responded. Michael extended his hand to the detective. "Thank you."

He was glad to be getting out of there and he couldn't wait to see Julie. The smile still hadn't left his face. The detective shook his hand and then stepped aside so Michael could exit. Michael's mind was only on one thing and that was getting to the hospital to see Julie.

He stopped at the discharge desk to pick up his things. While the officer stepped in back to retrieve them Father Reilly had managed to catch up to him. The smile that looked so permanent just a minute ago wasn't on Michael face anymore but it quickly returned as Father Reilly approached. "Would you mind if I came with you?" Father Reilly asked. Michael didn't respond right away and the look on his face told Father Reilly he needed a reason.

"I just need a distraction right now. I don't think I can deal with Father Davis' death right now." Michael nodded understandingly as Father Reilly continued. "Besides I'd love to meet this woman of yours. Judging by the risk you took to save her, she must be something special."

Michael couldn't have said no, even if he wanted to. He felt as though Father Reilly's loss was definitely greater than his own, and his life unlike Father Reilly's had a chance of returning to normal. Michael put his hand on Father Reilly's shoulder. "I think she'd like to meet you too."

The police officer returned with Michael's belongings in a manila pouch and slid a piece of paper out to Michael. He remembered the last time he went through this and looked at the sheet of paper. Sure enough they were charging him sixty dollars for towing his vehicle. "I'm not paying this!" Michael said angrily. The police officer shook his head from side to side. "I can't release your possessions until you sign the form agreeing to pay for the tow charge." Because Father Reilly was there Michael toned his anger down just slightly. "Are you guys getting a commission or something?"

Just as he finished the sentence the detective turned the corner. From the look on Michael's face he could tell he was upset. "Is everything all right?" Michael let out a sigh. "Not really! You guys towed my vehicle for the second time and are expecting me to foot the bill again." He put some emphasis on the word again to make the point he wasn't too happy about paying the first time. The detective just smiled politely and took the sheet off the counter. "Don't worry about this one Phil."

The police officer slid the envelope out to Michael. He felt a little embarrassed for being so undiplomatic about the charges. He still didn't feel like himself. "Thank you," he said to the detective as he began to collect his things. The detective understood Michael had been through a lot. "I'll see what I can do about re-imbursement on the other tow too." Michael smiled at the detective. "That would be great. Thanks again." Michael turned as Father Reilly received his belongings. Father Reilly didn't even bother to open his envelope. He just turned with Michael and they headed out the door.

Chapter 38

The drive to the hospital was pretty quiet. They both were pretty much involved with their own thoughts. Even as they were entering the hospital Michael was rehearsing what he was going to say. They checked in at the nurse's station. One of the nurses led them to Julie's room.

There had been so much traffic going by her room she didn't even notice Michael until he had entered the room. As they approached Michael could see she was watching television. She slowly turned her head as she noticed someone approaching out of the corner of her eye. As soon as she saw him she switched the television off. "Michael," she said as she held her arms out.

With every step toward her, everything he had rehearsed left him. He bent over the bed and embraced her. It wasn't until she opened her eyes that she noticed someone had come in the room with Michael. The old man just smiled at her. She smiled back. Michael still hadn't let her go. She was briefly distracted from the old man when she noticed Michael was crying. She rubbed her hand up and down his back. "Honey, are you okay?" Michael finally let her go and pulled back a bit. He kissed her on the forehead. "Yeah. I just thought I might never get to do that again." She smiled and touched her hand to his face. "Who's your friend?" Michael stood up and wiped his face. "I'm sorry, this is Father Reilly." Father Reilly stepped forward. "It's quite all right." He extended his hand. She shook his hand and then looked to Michael. "I'm really confused." Michael nodded. "I know."

Father Reilly stepped back to allow Michael to get closer if he wanted. Michael took advantage and moved closer to her. "What do you remember?" Julie looked back and forth between them as she thought about it. "The last thing I remember is coming home after being out to dinner with Kathy." She watched as they looked at each other. Michael sat down on the edge of the bed. "It's a long story. I don't think this is the right time to go through everything." She saw Father Reilly nodding in agreement. Michael put his hand on hers. "The important thing is that you're all right." She was a little disappointed. She didn't like not knowing what was going on but she trusted that Michael would tell her eventually.

His hand felt good. She rubbed her thumb over the back of his hand. "They said I could leave in a couple of hours." Michael raised her hand and kissed it. "Good that'll give me a chance to clean myself up a bit." Julie pulled his hand toward her. "Don't leave! You just got here." Suddenly Michael didn't feel like leaving, but he really wanted to take a shower and clean up. Father Reilly stepped a little to his right so they both could see him. "I can stay and keep her company if you want to shower at my place?" He held up his keys. Michael looked at Julie. She gave him the okay but still looked disappointed. He smiled at her. "I'll be back in an hour." They kissed and then hugged for about thirty seconds. Michael whispered into her ear as they hugged. "I love you." She whispered it back.

Michael turned to Father Reilly. He was still holding his keys out. "Thank you." Father Reilly just smiled as he took the keys. Michael turned back to Julie. "One hour, I swear." She smiled at him as he turned to leave. He hesitantly left the room.

As he was passing the nurse's station one of the nurses stopped him. "Mr. Foster." Michael stepped back a step or two. "Do you have a change of clothes for your fiancé?" Michael shook his head no. The nurse stepped closer to the counter. "I don't think she'll want to put the ones back on that she came in here with," the nurse said with a smile.

"Good idea. Thanks." The nurse let Michael continue on his way.

The whole time Michael was gone Father Reilly talked to Julie about what happened. He gave her the same story he had given the detective with just a few more details. He noticed every time he mentioned Michael's name that she would check the time. He was becoming a little concerned himself. It was already over an hour and a half since Michael had left. Just after that thought entered his mind Michael stepped in the room. He had a pair of jeans, a sweater and shoes stacked in that order in his hands. All of them still had the price tags on them. "Sorry I'm late. They told me you needed new clothes on the way out so I stopped and bought you some." He laid them at the end of the bed. "They said you could check out whenever you're ready."

That was all Julie needed to hear. She was already getting out of the bed as Michael finished the sentence. She was making her way around the bed when she felt a draft on her backside. She could tell one of the ties on her hospital gown had come undone. She reached around and pinched the two halves back together with her fist. Even though nobody could've seen anything she still felt embarrassed. She scooped the clothes off the edge of the bed with her left hand and proceeded to shuffle toward Michael. "Thanks honey," she said as she kissed him. She turned continuing to shuffle and headed for the bathroom.

At first neither Michael nor Father Reilly could understand the reason for the shuffling, but once she had turned and headed for the bathroom the reason became apparent. All the ties but the one around her neck had come undone on the hospital gown. She had her right hand clenched in a fist holding the gown together over her butt. Between trying to hold the gown together and carry her new clothes she couldn't help but walk in the shuffling manner. The sight brought a smile to both their faces. She quickly shut the door.

Michael turned to Father Reilly who was still smiling. "So what did you tell her?" Father Reilly continued to smile as he spoke. "I gave her the tame version, it's up to you if you want to tell her the whole truth." Michael nodded. "I don't think she'd believe it if I told her the truth. Besides we best keep the story consistent just in case the detective asks her any questions."

Julie could hear them talking outside the door but it was very muffled and she couldn't make out anything being said. She was concentrating on getting dressed. She already had her jeans on and was pulling the sweater over her head. She went to slide her right foot into her new tennis shoe. She got her foot in just over halfway and it wouldn't go any further. She lifted the shoe from the floor. Michael had left the paper inside the shoe. She pulled it out and threw it in the garbage. She slipped her foot inside the shoe and tied the shoelace. She figured if he hadn't bothered to pull the paper out of the right one he certainly didn't do the left.

Michael and Father Reilly waited quietly for her to come out. For as much of a hurry as she appeared to be in she certainly was taking longer than they expected. When the door finally opened Julie went rushing toward Michael and threw her arms around him. Father Reilly was a little confused but Michael knew why she did it. "I forgive you for being late. It's beautiful," she said with a huge smile on her face.

She held up her hand and now Father Reilly understood what was going on.

Michael had gotten her an engagement ring along with the clothes. Michael turned to explain to Father Reilly. "I went to the strip mall to get her some clothes and the first thing I saw when I entered the mall was this ring at a jewelry store. I hid it in one of her shoes. I knew it was perfect."

Julie was still beaming. Michael turned back to Julie. "Ready to go?" She took his hand. "I'm more than ready." Father Reilly followed them out the door to the nurse's station.

As they were signing out at the nurse's station Detective Richards showed up. "I was hoping you were still here." Michael was a little worried about why he was there. The detective could tell just by the look on his face. The detective smiled. "It's good news, I promise." Michael felt a sense of relief. "I know I asked you to stay one more day but I think some of the evidence I've received in the last few hours will allow me to let you go now."

Michael was finally beginning to feel like himself again. He had Julie back and everything seemed to be getting better. "This is my fiancé, Julie." The detective extended his hand. "Detective Sean Richards." Julie took his hand and smiled. "Nice to meet you." The detective glanced over to Father Reilly and Michael. "That's it folks. Have a nice day." The detective turned and headed back down the hall.

Father Reilly broke the ensuing silence. "Well I guess this means you don't need a place to stay. I would appreciate a ride home if you have the time?" Michael smiled as he responded. "No problem."

The ride to Father Reilly's was fairly quiet with the exception of Julie and Michael discussing whether they were going to attempt to drive all the way home. Julie brought up the point that no one had probably fed their cat Buster in the last few days, so they decided it would be best just to go all the way home.

They came to a stop in front of Father Reilly's apartment complex. Michael turned to face him as he was sitting directly behind Julie in the passenger's seat. "Are you sure you'll be all right?" Father Reilly nodded. "I'm as ready as I'm going to be." He extended his hand to Michael. They shook hands and then Father Reilly set his hand on Julie's shoulder. "It was very nice to meet you my dear."

Julie pulled her right hand across her body and laid her hand on top of Father Reilly's. "It was nice to meet you too," she said turning her head to the side.

Father Reilly slipped his hand out from under Julie's and exited the jeep. "Take care now," he said as he closed the door. Michael watched Father Reilly waving in the rearview mirror as they drove off. He looked over at Julie and she was doing the same thing in the side mirror. They both waved before they had gotten so far away he wouldn't see it.

Julie turned and looked at Michael. He had already turned his attention back to the road. He could feel her looking at him. "What is it?" he said as he glanced at her. Julie let out a sigh. "I just feel sorry for him." Michael took his right hand and placed it on her knee. "I know." She took her left hand and placed it on his shoulder.

The ride home didn't seem to take long at all. Julie had lots of questions for him. Michael tried to answer as many of the questions as truthfully as possible. She noticed that Father Reilly's version of the events made Michael sound much more heroic. She thought Michael was just being modest. When she finally stopped asking questions about what had happened they started talking about future plans. Michael was just happy to be able to discuss the future with her.

Chapter 39

For the first time Father Reilly really began to feel alone. It had been a week since Father Davis' funeral. He was glad that Michael and Julie had returned for the funeral. He was so busy taking care of Father Davis' personal affairs leading up to the funeral that he didn't have time to think about himself. For a couple of days afterward there were plenty of people giving their condolences and well wishes, but now there was just nothing.

He was sitting on the edge of his bed. He was thinking about taking a nap. Even though it never bothered him before, he hated the thought of taking naps now. It was just wasted time. If he decided to take a nap every time he got bored he might as well be dead he thought to himself. He got up off the bed. It was a nice day so he decided he would take a walk instead.

Just as he was putting on his coat the phone rang. He thought for a moment about not answering it and just heading out for his walk. After he answered it, he was glad he did. It was Michael. He told Father Reilly that he and Julie were in town and wanted to see him. Michael could tell he was excited just by how his tone had changed from when he answered the phone. Michael said they'd be there in five minutes to pick him up.

He already had his coat on and was ready to go so he went outside and sat on the front steps. When they pulled up, Father Reilly was sitting there enjoying the warmth of the sunshine. He jumped up immediately when he noticed them.

He got into the backseat of the Jeep. Michael smiled as he entered. "How are you Father Reilly?"

Father Reilly smiled back. "Fine, but please call me John."

Michael gave him a quizzical look.

"I just feel uncomfortable using that name without Father Davis around."

Without missing a beat, Julie turned around. "Hello John, nice to see you again." Father Reilly was smiling again. "Nice to see you!"

Michael got Father Reilly's attention back. "We'd like to take you out to lunch if you wouldn't mind." Father Reilly shook his head no. "Who would? I've never been known to pass up a free lunch. So what are you doing up here?" Michael started pulling out into the street and was looking for traffic. Julie turned to talk to Father Reilly. "Well, we'd like to try to convince you to move down by us." Michael looked in the rearview mirror to see Father Reilly's reaction. He apparently was a little stunned because he didn't say anything at first. He noticed Michael looking at him in the mirror. "I, I don't know." Michael smiled. "We can talk more over lunch." He pulled into the parking lot.

They just sat in the restaurant and talked for hours. At first they discussed the pros and cons of having him move. They offered to let him stay at their place while he searched for somewhere to live. Michael already had a few places in mind that might be ideal for him. Father Reilly told them that he would have to think about their offer.

Slowly the conversation changed to more genuine topics. They traded stories and shared some laughs. The time just flew by. It was a nice distraction for Father Reilly. Michael paid for lunch and then apologized to Father Reilly for having to leave.

He and Julie were taking a small vacation. They were busy too and needed some time alone. They dropped Father Reilly off and continued on their way.

It didn't take Father Reilly long to make up his mind. Although he had lived here for 15 years now, without Father Davis around, it just didn't feel the same. His life just wasn't the same anymore. Michael and Julie had been gone for two days. It seemed a lot longer. There was nothing here for him now, so it made his decision easy. He was actually kind of excited about the change. Unfortunately, it was going to be another two days before they made their way home and he could inform them of his decision.

The time away from everything but each other had made their bond even stronger. Michael thought about everything that had happened. He was surprised how many positive things had actually come out of it. They had already been home for an entire day and had not heard from Father Reilly. He worried a little. "Maybe I should call him." Julie knew who he was talking about. She wasn't as concerned as Michael, but she did find it curious that they had not heard from him. She could tell from the way he said it that he was just thinking out loud and not really looking for a response.

He picked up the phone and called Father Reilly. Michael thought for a moment he might not be home. After several rings he finally answered. "Hi John, Michael Foster here." It brought an instant smile to Father Reilly's face. "Michael, how are you?"

"I'm good." Michael decided to get right to the point. "So, have you made a decision?" There was hesitation on the other end. The pause made Michael expect that he wasn't going to move. Father Reilly almost reconsidered in that instant, but decided to just go with it. "When can you pick me up?"

Michael smiled. "As soon as you're ready." Father Reilly looked around his apartment. "Would this weekend be too soon?" Michael laughed. "No, that will be fine." There was about 5 seconds of silence. "So why didn't you call me to let me know what you had decided?" Michael asked. Father Reilly had two reasons, one of which he was willing to share with Michael. "I just didn't want to interrupt you right after your vacation." Michael laughed again. "All right. Call me when you're ready." Father Reilly smiled. "I will." He hung up the phone.

The other reason Father Reilly wasn't sharing is that he didn't want to seem too anxious. It wasn't going to take him that long to pack, but again he didn't want to seem too anxious even to himself so he took his time. Father Reilly gave what furniture he did have to some of the residents of his apartment complex. Many of them were sad to hear of his plans to depart, but he never let that affect his decision because it had already been made.

Michael was surprised at how little Father Reilly had to move. Not that he wanted to move a lot of stuff, but Father Reilly reassured him he had everything he needed.

Father Reilly only stayed with them for a month. He wasn't pressured to move out or anything, and even though they went out of their way to keep him from feeling like a third wheel, he still felt out of place.

He felt much more comfortable in his own place. He saw Michael and Julie almost every day, especially Michael. Father Reilly was teaching him how to play chess. Over time, Michael became fairly good, but not good enough to defeat Father Reilly. Michael vowed to find a way to beat him if it was the last thing he did. Father Reilly liked his competitive spirit; it made him think of Father Davis. Over the next two years, Michael had come close to defeating him, but the old man always seemed to have a trick or two left that he wasn't passing on to Michael.

Chapter 40

It was a cool fall day. There was a light breeze and the sky was overcast with light gray clouds. Most of the trees had lost their leaves. Everyone around was wearing warm jackets along with gloves and hats. Michael never thought he'd go back to his hometown again, but standing along side Father Reilly's grave, he knew he had made the right decision. Father Reilly had never mentioned where he wanted to be buried, but Michael knew this is where he should be.

Just before they started lowering the casket into the ground, Michael pulled a white pawn out of his pocket and set it on the casket. As he stepped back, he felt Julie put her right arm around him. He turned and looked at her. She had tears running down her cheeks and was unable to wipe them away because she was holding their one-year-old daughter Emily in her left arm. He reached up and wiped them away for her. They smiled at each other.

Michael then reached over and pinched Emily's cheek. She gave him a quick smile and then proceeded to drool on her chin. Michael wiped it away. Michael was glad that Father Reilly was around to witness the little miracle that ensured his life was going to get back to normal.

Everyone was starting to leave. Michael looked over to Julie. "I'll catch up to you in a minute." Julie just smiled and gave him a quick kiss and then started for the car. Michael turned directly to his left and knelt down beside the grave next to Father Reilly's. He pulled another white pawn out of his pocket and set it on the headstone of Father Davis. He remembered something Father Reilly had told him during a chess match they had. "In the grand scheme of things, we're all just pawns."

He smiled as he tapped Father Davis' headstone. "Beat the old man once for me."

Michael stood up and headed for the car. Halfway there he came to a stop, as he was about to descend some stairs that led to the cemetery parking lot, he realized he was leaving an important part of his life in the past. He looked back toward the cemetery. He was probably never going to return home again. Even though he only knew Father Reilly for a very short time, he was one of the most influential people in his life. He seemed to have a saying for everything. He heard Father Reilly's voice in his head as he was reaching the last stair. "Without the past, the future isn't possible." He looked up and saw his future waiting for him in the car.

Michael P. Conlin